DEATH IS MY LIFE

BY
SUSAN AYRES WIMBROW

ISBN 978-162806-190-1 (print | paperback)
ISBN 978-162806-191-8 (print | hardback)
ISBN 978-162806-192-5 (print | ebook)
ISBN 978-162806-193-2 (print | ebook)

Library of Congress Control Number 2018955207

Published by Salt Water Media
29 Broad Street, Suite 104
Berlin, MD 21811
www.saltwatermedia.com

Cover design by Salt Water Media;
cover photograph used courtesy of unsplash.com user Josh Applegate
and back cover photograph courtesy of Maurice Wimbrow III.

For it is in giving that we receive...

Saint Francis of Assisi

IN MEMORY OF

Ann Ayres Bannon
sleep tight, my angel,
you did not die in vain.
1935-1961

and

Eleanor Ayres Bruehl,
the epitome of a Steel Magnolia
1913 - 2009

DEDICATION

In honor of
Maurice Oliver Wimbrow III
an exemplary husband
and
Barbara Lockhart,
In my doubt, I go on believing

ACKNOWLEDGMENTS

I would like to thank the following people:

Charles Hastings - the quintessential of a professional funeral director and
owner, for introducing me to a rewarding career at only nineteen.

Dear friends, Jacqueline Rafferty and Jonathan Fedora,
for refreshing my memory on life as a morgue rat.

Donna Hicks - the angel who walked beside me every morning
in the park and listened to characters, plots, and scenes.

Christine Selzer for her monthly cards of endorsement
to live the life you love.

Tim Rayne, Jr. - my big brother who listens in a positive manner.

Deborah Dashiell Everett and her cabana boy Michael for promoting the
novel and supporting a struggling writer with a glass of wine or two.

The Worcester Country School Golden Girls - Hannah Todd Wilgus,
Barbara Warren Carmean, and Elizabeth Quillen Fisher,
for believing in me and this project. Yes, it is finally finished!

Stephanie Fowler of Salt Water Media - we bonded from day one.
Love you, kid.

My greatest debt is to Maury, who encouraged me to pursue my dream of
the written word. Thanks for the co-editing, laughter, and tears.
Good job, Cabana Boy.

Most of all, to you, dear reader.
May you derive courage, endurance, and a deep faith when heartache knocks.

PROLOGUE

My mother's murderer and rapist, respectively, died today of natural causes—Elizabeth kept ruminating, feeling nothing at all. *Respectively is the keyword in this crime,* Elizabeth thought, wishing she could finally let her emotions erupt and put it all behind her. It was a heavy burden to carry all these years once she discovered her mother was raped *after* being killed by the stalker that she vaguely remembered as a five-year-old child. The maintenance man had given her Clark candy bars and stuffed animals that he had won on the boardwalk in a honky-tonk arcade. When she visited her grandparents that summer at the hotel they owned, these gifts were presented to her by the odd-looking man only to be discarded in the trash a few months later. He was never seen again. In the years that followed, loss, anger, and grief had to be tucked away because she came from an intensely private family.

The telephone rang around three o'clock in the afternoon as Elizabeth was coming in from weeding and thinning the antique boxwood garden. The greyhounds were sleeping peacefully in their overstuffed beds in the library and raised their heads to the jarring ring, glancing at her with irritation for the disruption.

"Good afternoon," Elizabeth said, as she slipped off the other gardening glove while cradling the receiver between her chin and shoulder.

"Hello, is this Elizabeth Eyre Barclay?"

"Yes, it is."

"This is Mrs. Culver from the Department of Corrections Victims Services Unit."

"What's happened?" Elizabeth asked, feeling her knees weaken.

"I'm calling to inform you that Stephen Dennis was pronounced dead at twelve-seventeen this morning in his cell at the Hagley Correctional Center. He was found by a correction's officer in his bed. The death is under investigation."

"Is there suspicion of foul play?" Elizabeth wanted to know, although she was aware it would be illegal for Mrs. Culver to say.

"I'm sorry I cannot divulge that information due to privacy concerns," Mrs. Culver stated.

"Natural causes?" Elizabeth challenged, not letting the matter drop. There was silence on the other end of the line. That was enough to answer her question.

"Thank you, Mrs. Culver, your organization has been so kind and understanding to me every step of the way all these years. I will always be grateful."

"You're so welcome. I'll send you the paperwork confirming what we have discussed. I wish you all the best Ms. Barclay. May you now have closure."

"Thanks again," Elizabeth eked out hanging up the house line.

The victim's family has no rights, Elizabeth thought. It had been decades ago that the Commonwealth of Virginia was ordered to keep Stephen Dennis in custody and control in the Hagley Correctional Center. Would it be too much to ask the cause of death? It all seemed insidious.

Elizabeth glanced at the grandfather's clock on the stair landing. The course of the conversation had only lasted a few minutes but would conjure up a plethora of mixed emotions to work through. She went into the kitchen and pulled out a bottle of Pinot Noir and a corkscrew from the cabinet, slowly pouring a glass of wine into a Waterford goblet.

"It is done," she said out loud to no one, toasting the air.

The boxwood courtyard behind the back porch was filled with hummingbird feeders. David, her husband, had a sanctuary for them; they kept returning year after year, coming back to where they were born, staying from the middle of April until the first day of autumn. As the days of breathless humidity went by, David would spend the height of the summer boiling simple syrup on the stove and filling the feeders three times a day. There were up to twenty hummers and counting. Elizabeth knew watching these tiny bejeweled birds would calm her mind as she tried to gather her thoughts.

Sipping her wine and staring into space, she remembered the court transcripts and yellowed newspaper articles found in her grandmother's attic so many years ago. She continued to remember the dark day, discovering by accident the unbelievable truth. Reviewing it again and again in her mind, the shock never wavered. How could this have happened to her family?

"If I couldn't fuck her alive—I'd fuck her dead. I dreamed last night I done it," Stephen Dennis stated to the police detective at the scene of the crime. Elizabeth had read those words which had haunted her for years to come when she laid her head on the pillow at night before closing her eyes, only to awaken in the morning with the same anxiety of the morbid scene.

Elizabeth sat lost in her memories then suddenly realized that she needed to call the other family members to inform them that Stephen Dennis was dead. In her fog, it dawned on her there was no one left—they were all deceased as well.

David came from around the corner of the courtyard checking on the hummingbird feeders to see if they needed refilling for the third time during the sultry August afternoon. "What's wrong honey? You look as if you've seen a ghost."

"A ghost of the past is finally dead," she whispered. She sat quietly for a moment and then thought, *I'm glad I took the time to finally write that letter.*

PART 1

CHAPTER ONE

Alfred and Margaret Eyre were in the process of closing their hotel, The Virginia Tide, in Virginia Beach for the season. Once Labor Day was over, the weather turned slightly cooler in the evenings as guests and their children had returned to work and school. The only red light in town had been turned off, allowing a lonely car to meander Pacific Avenue.

"This is the seventeenth year we've done this, Alfred," Margaret sighed.

"I wish I had a nickel for every time I rode that ferry across the Chesapeake," Alfred chuckled, glancing at his wife. "The Buick is full. Let's pick up Elizabeth and head back to Sycamore Creek before it gets too late. Boy, it's going to be great to see our little town. I wish we could keep our granddaughter a few more days, but I promised Suzanne we would have her back by Sunday evening."

"Four days with our little girl will be fun, but I agree I want to make sure she doesn't miss kindergarten on Monday morning. Suzanne says she loves it. I think Edward is in Richmond opening another branch for his company. Let's see if he'll be home Sunday evening. We can all go to dinner at the Whispering Pines Inn and catch up," Margaret said.

It was by the grace of God Alfred and Margaret had picked up their granddaughter late morning–the day of the crime. They would travel to their home on Virginia's Eastern Shore for a long weekend, returning late Sunday to continue closing the hotel.

"I'll call Suzanne, and let her know we are on our way," Margaret said.

"Elizabeth, Nana and Poppy are on their way to pick you up, let's get the rest of your clothes packed. They need to catch the early afternoon ferry," Suzanne called out hanging up the phone.

"I want to take Chatty Cathy to Sycamore Creek, please Mommy please," Elizabeth called back from her room.

"All your Barbie Dolls are there, honey. Leave Chatty Cathy home. Remember you went on a scissors spree the other day and decided to give all your dolls a haircut. I want you to take good care of your Barbie Dolls; they'll be valuable someday. Your grandmother is protecting them from your little hands."

Suzanne was percolating Maxwell House coffee, strong and black, the way her father liked it. Setting out the china coffee cups, cream, and sugar as her parents pulled into the driveway, she met them at the door with a hug and a kiss.

"Nana! Poppy!" Elizabeth squealed running into their arms.

"Come in for a cup of coffee. I just perked a fresh pot," Suzanne said to her parents.

"We don't want to miss the ferry, honey." Margaret sounded anxious in fear of being late.

"Just one at least," Suzanne countered.

They all made plans for Sunday evening, dining at the Whispering Pines Inn. "That's my favorite restaurant. The service is impeccable and all the waiters wear white dinner jackets," Margaret said. "I'll look forward all weekend to dining on lobster tail with drawn butter, the best in town. Let's celebrate the end of the season with a bottle of champagne as well."

"That sounds delightful, Mother. I'll make reservations. Edward will be elated to see you both before you close the hotel for the winter."

With that, Alfred and Margaret hugged and kissed their daughter goodbye, not realizing they would never see her again—alive. Suzanne knelt to Elizabeth and hugged her tightly. Feeling her mother's soft blonde hair on her cheek and breathing in the floral scent of her perfume, she nuzzled her face into her neck for a deeper whiff of the heavenly fragrance. Elizabeth loved the way her mother regularly had makeup, jewelry, and high heels on without fail. She spent hours playing dress up in her mother's closet mimicking her with strands of pearls wrapped around her neck as she clunked around the rancher in oversized heels and a Kentucky Derby picture hat.

"You're so pretty, Mommy," she said gazing into her blue eyes.

"Be good for Nana and Poppy. Remember, I love you with all my heart," Suzanne whispered in her daughter's ear.

Elizabeth, in her innocence, thought she would hear her soft words forever. "I love you, Thor. See you Sunday," Elizabeth said as she patted the family's boxer on his head and wrapped her tiny arms around his neck.

"The day is so beautiful I'm going to take Thor for a long walk, then let him soak up the sunshine this afternoon in the backyard. A tired dog is a happy dog, I always say. By the way, Eleanor and I are going to try the new Greek restaurant in the city, and do a little pre-Christmas shopping this evening after she gets off from the bank. I expect her around five-thirty," Suzanne said not being able to hold back a smile in anticipation of seeing her special Greek gentleman.

With goodbyes being said, Elizabeth cuddled between her grandparents as all three of them rode on the front seat of the Buick on what she thought was the longest ride in the world back to Sycamore Creek. After boarding the ferry, her grandfather took her hand as they walked to the stern of the vessel to feed the seagulls with newly purchased Cracker Jacks. Throwing up the kernels of popped corn for the aggressive birds was the highlight of the trip. The seagulls accompanied them across the bay in the wake of the ferry, never tiring of the flight. Poppy started the ignition once the boat docked, and they were off again for the tedious drive through the southern Eastern Shore of Virginia. It was all worth the journey; even as a child Elizabeth had felt safe and secure when she visited their small hamlet. Her grandparents respected each other, allowing a calm atmosphere to flow throughout their Victorian home of tranquility.

Suzanne and Edward Barclay were one of the "beautiful couples" of Norfolk, spending many evenings wining and dining at the infamous Cavalier Club in Virginia Beach—where everyone wanted to be seen. Yearly dues were astronomical, but if you were successful with a beautiful wife on your arm and climbing your way up the corporate ladder, it was guaranteed that your company would insist that you be a member of the prestigious club. The dining room had crystal chandeliers, tables for parties of four or more draped with white linen tablecloths and napkins. Aubusson rugs covered the floor except where the entertainment and dance floor were. Windows overlooking the sea were festooned with heavy silk jabots and swag treatments. Valets, maitre d', and bathroom attendants were all dressed in tuxes or white uniforms and were instructed to speak to each guest cordially.

Champagne cocktails, jazz, and dangerous flirting with the opposite sex were the norm. All patrons were dressed to the nines and had a voracious hunger for the lush life. A supper club was a must during the late fifties in the executive world of social climbers.

Edward was tall, dark, and handsome—always in the latest Brooks Brothers suit—his French cuffs and collar starched to a crisp. Being a stickler on detail, his cufflinks were purchased from one of the finest jewelers in the Norfolk area who happened to be a prominent client of his. He drove the latest sports car, washing and waxing it to perfection every Saturday morning. He was the consumate playboy, juggling a martini in one hand and cigarette in the other, as he admired his gleaming car.

Suzanne was a Grace Kelly look-a-like with exquisite taste in couture. She read all the fashion magazines, emulating Grace's appearance and mannerisms. Style, grace, and elegance, soignée personified in public and private life. The latest diet would ensure a tiny waist for the form-fitting attire her husband insisted on.

Elizabeth remembered her parents being so jealous of one another; they were a prime example of *can't live with, can't live without*. This made life for an only child very insecure, wondering when the next screaming match would erupt.

One evening, after her father had taken the babysitter home, they began a barrage of accusations in their inebriated states.

"Why do you always want me to face the wall when we go out to dinner?" Suzanne cried.

"The Naval Officers were staring at you all night. I saw them flirting when I went to the men's room. One jerk got up to light your cigarette!" Edward hollered. "The nerve of him!"

"He was just being a gentleman, that's all," Elizabeth heard her mother say.

"You were talking to them as soon as I left the table," Edward's voice growing louder.

There was a loud crashing noise as though something had been thrown against the wall. Elizabeth held her breath as to what would happen next, pulling the blanket over her head. She heard the front door open and slam, then the sound of her father's car squealing out of the driveway. Her mother would fall into bed crying in the next room.

Edward would return by morning with red lipstick on his collar, and the nightlife would begin again the following day after dark. There were yacht clubs, country clubs, and business cocktail parties to attend as they climbed the social ladder rung by rung.

As the car turned off Highway 13 onto Market Street, young Elizabeth felt excited to be approaching the town of Sycamore Creek, Virginia. The picturesque street was lined with Victorian houses and Sycamore trees on both sides of the main drag. In the center of Market Street was the bank, post office, and hardware store. Continuing past the commercial buildings leading to the creek were the painted ladies, as her grandparents called this Victorian style of architecture.

The Sycamore trees were Asian maples. The dark bark would break off their trunks leaving a pristine, creamy-white wood. The leaves of these magnificent trees formed an umbrella effect as if you were lost in a tunnel. At the very end of the street, when the leaves had succumbed to frost, you could see the sun's rays hit the creek as it sparkled like diamonds in the midwinter, late morning light.

During the warmer months of spring and fall, Alfred and a small gathering of locals would hang out around the wharf. Hours were spent watching the boats come and go, generally shooting the breeze. A bench was erected for some of the town's old-timers to gather next to the harbormaster's house. It was labeled "the liars bench" and became a favorite spot to gossip the afternoon away.

One of the oldest general stores on the east coast next to the harbormaster's residence had become a restaurant and bar for the aging sailors and watermen in the winter, when the chilling wind blew off the creek. On any given afternoon, these old salts lamented how many wars, hurricanes, and women—not necessarily in that order—they had been through.

An old steamboat ticket office was located next to the restaurant and bar, as Sycamore Creek offered daily steamboat passage to Baltimore in the late 1800s.

Between the hub of Market Street and the wharf were the immense grand dames of Victorian houses that were painted a variety of colors in accordance to the period, making one structure more elegant than its neighbor with their vibrant hues. In mint condition and magical, they reminded Elizabeth of the gingerbread house displays she used to stand and gaze at with awe in the department stores during the Christmas season in Norfolk. This slice of small town Americana was a special place for her even at a young age. Her Uncle Harvey's funeral parlor, which was the predominant structure on the street, was across from the Episcopal Church. Two houses down toward the water was her grand-parents' Victorian where her mother was raised.

The Buick turned onto the oyster shell driveway as Elizabeth glanced up toward the turret on the second floor. The turret was in the corner of her mother's bedroom overlooking the aged, manicured English box-woods that formed a maze in the side garden. The room was occupied by an antique tester bed, Persian rug, and hand crocheted dollies on every table. The room had not been touched since her mother had left for business school in Baltimore, Maryland shortly after graduating from high school. She soon settled into her haven of tranquility for the long weekend with her favorite people.

That Thursday evening was normal as usual with Margaret cooking dinner. The dining room was set with an antique lace tablecloth that Margaret's mother had tatted with cotton thread using a shuttle. There were linen napkins, Wedgewood china, and Fostoria stemware. The Waterford chandelier over the table sparkled as a brilliant gem, casting light downward on the place settings.

"Help Nana place the flatware, Elizabeth."

"Nana, why is it so shiny?"

"Blanche polishes it once a month. It's sterling silver and was my mother's. Someday it will be passed down to you. You must always make your meals civilized; it's part of our southern upbringing, handed down through the generations. Our table is set with some of my family's equipage and your grandfather's as well. Our attic is full of serving pieces and you will inherit all of these treasures to pass down to your children," Margaret lectured.

Elizabeth loved it when Nana made her feel grown up. It was if they had a secret code all their own when they discussed the beautiful artifacts that sparkled and glittered.

Alfred's ice clinked in his glass as he poured a stiff Virginia Gentleman in his tumbler. He plopped down in his chair taking a sip. "Ah, the bourbon of Virginia." he grinned.

A fist full of Virginia peanuts in one hand, a cocktail in the other, he had to negotiate what hand he would use to pick up the telephone on the table next to his wing chair ... the one that was interrupting his happy hour with a most offensive ring.

"Oh, for God's sake." he complained. "Hello," he said trying to balance everything.

"My goodness, Benjamin, we've not heard from you in ages! How's the Coast Guard treating you?"

"Uncle Ben!" Elizabeth squealed.

Benjamin Johnson was stationed in Elizabeth City, North Carolina, serving in the Coast Guard. He had just settled down for dinner when the local news announced that a crime had occurred in the Norfolk area. His ears percked up as he listened intently to the two names the commentator reported.

"Uncle Alfred, have you received any telephone calls regarding Suzanne or my sister?" Ben asked trying to catch his breath.

"What's wrong, Ben? Where's Suzanne and Eleanor?" Alfred asked.

Elizabeth's grandfather grew ashen as he listened to his nephew give him details he had heard about his sister and cousin on the television. Margaret had just placed the salad fork in the appropriate spot and turned toward her husband with a puzzled expression.

"There has to be a mistake. They never report a victim's name without notifying their family. There's been a mistake. It must be a mistake." Alfred's voice quivered. "I need to hang up and call the police."

"What's wrong, Alfred? What's going on?" Margaret asked.

Alfred's throat constricted, and he told his wife to go turn off the television. "Something terrible has happened. Take Elizabeth to her room and meet me in the kitchen."

Before Elizabeth reached the top of the stairs with Margaret, Harvey, Alfred's brother and the local undertaker, rushed in wearing a black suit. "I've just received a call from the Virginia State Police. There's been a terrible accident regarding Suzanne and Eleanor," Harvey stated fighting down a sense of panic.

"I'm so confused. Why haven't the police called us?" Alfred said in a state of shock. "Ben just called. What happened? He says Suzanne's dead?! Please tell me what has happened!"

Harvey nodded and embraced his brother. "They will be calling you soon. Please don't worry about a thing. I'll take care of all the details on your behalf and bring her home, God bless her heart. I've checked in with the Norfolk City morgue and an autopsy is going to be performed later this evening. This sickens me. Sickens me. Where's Margaret?"

Alfred looked up to the top of the stairs unable to speak, he pointed his trembling finger at his wife and granddaughter. Incapable of absorbing the information pertaining to the crime, his eyes pleaded for Margaret to join him.

Elizabeth sat on the top step and watched her grandparents and Uncle Harvey move quickly into the kitchen, closing the door behind them. Uncontrollable sobs sounded from the other side of the door in a matter of minutes and incomprehensible words were uttered in low tones.

"It just can't be—it can't be. My God, why, why?" Margaret wailed. "I never trusted that man. The way he stared at her ..."

Suddenly the family grew quiet behind the kitchen door. Elizabeth sat on the staircase landing in a state of confusion. She had never heard or seen her grandparents cry before or erupt with such a display of emotion.

The Grandfather clock chimed seven o'clock behind her.

The Eyre family was old High Church Episcopal, one steeped in tradition. Sex, death, and money were swept under the oriental rug. Speaking of these subjects was not only in the worst of taste, but downright vulgar. Manners in the South are more important than a sprig of mint in your julep—well almost. It was drilled in Elizabeth's little cortex that finances, romances, let alone death were *confidential. Period. The end.* Therefore, Elizabeth would never be aware of the details regarding her mother's death until the day she discovered the box of newspaper clippings in her grandparents' attic.

Havoc erupted in Sycamore Creek that evening as news broke of Suzanne's death. The Eyre home became Grand Central Station with mourners paying their respects, always with a dish of Southern food in their hands. Blanche, the housekeeper that the Eyres shared with Harvey, was called to assist during the days before, during, and after the funeral.

"Lordy, Lordy Miss Margaret, I never seen such flowers in all my life. My peoples don't send poesys like this," Blanche stated as the florists delivered enormous arrangements of bouquets.

"They're beautiful," Margaret cried as she read the cards of each new delivery with emotion. The vases filled the rooms with a heavy sweet scent, color, and life amongst the mourners with expressions as dark as their attire.

Elizabeth was lavished upon as guests walked by patting her head, blessing her little heart with each passing. She had never received so much attention by absolute strangers. No one knew how to express themselves due to the murder of the town's twenty-five-year-old beauty queen, which made for long pauses of awkward conversation. Elizabeth wondered, *what is the big mystery? What are they keeping from me? Am I going back to Norfolk?*

"Elizabeth, Father Henderson is coming over for lunch this afternoon. We'll meet him in the library. He needs to discuss something with you before we eat." Margaret was drained.

Elizabeth was dressed everyday throughout this mysterious ordeal as if she were attending Sunday School: pink dress, shiny black Mary Janes, and little white anklets with lace ruffles around the tops.

The priest entered the Eyre home and was offered a Virginia Gentleman bourbon whiskey which he downed with one tilt of the hand. Father Henderson, Elizabeth, and her grandparents proceeded to the library.

"Come sit with me," Margaret said, patting her lap.

"Elizabeth, God bless your little heart, I have some bad news to tell you in regards to your mommy," Father Henderson softly whispered.

Elizabeth went from her Nana's lap to his, as he began to inform her that her mother had been in an accident and was not coming back.

"A car accident?" Elizabeth questioned.

There was silence.

Father Henderson explained, "She is with the angels now, and you will see her again someday in heaven."

"Does she have wings?"

"She does," the priest choked on his words.

She started to cry, but stopped abruptly. "Does this mean I'll always live here with you?" directing her question to Margaret.

Margaret was still in a state of shock, her eyes red and swollen due to the lack of sleep and constant weeping. She could only manage a nod at the child who had dramatically been placed in her care. Life had changed in an instant, and there was no doubt inside her that she would not be up for the task.

"I'm going to go watch the goldfish in my room," Elizabeth stated, kissing Father Henderson on the cheek. "Was Thor in an accident too?" she asked before leaving the room.

The three of them could only nod.

Blanche knocked softly, opening the library door and asked Margaret, "Mista Edward just arrive. Which room he gonna stay in?"

"Daddy, Daddy," his daughter squealed running and jumping into his grasp. Edward picked her up and wrapped his arms around her as he began to sob.

"It's okay, Daddy. Mommy is in heaven with wings. Father Henderson said she's with the other angels. I'm sure they're all friends by now,"

Elizabeth assured him.

Margaret and Alfred greeted Edward with an embrace as Father Henderson began to pray the Lord's Prayer.

Through the years, Elizabeth would play this scene in her mind frequently, realizing that it was her first experience comforting the grief-stricken—her father who had lost his wife to murder.

CHAPTER TWO

Stephen Dennis was born in 1937 to a young woman in Sycamore Creek who had been raped by her constantly raging, intoxicated stepfather at fourteen years of age. Her mother accused her of flirting and teasing her husband, thereby bringing on the set of circumstances that had befallen young Lillian Dennis. Once her flat belly began to bulge, she was promptly kicked out of their one-bedroom apartment on the bad side of town with nothing to claim of her own, but the few clothes she threw into a paper bag and her grandmother's worn Bible.

Lillian walked several miles in the spitting rain to a large horse farm located down the road. The farm was owned by the Kellum family who had always been friendly to Lillian and her folks. Her hands trembled as she banged the large, antique brass "S" knocker. A heavyset black woman opened the door, in what took forever, Lillian thought. She peered into the foyer, blinking her eyes at the bell chandelier and brass sconces on the wall, casting a warm and inviting glow throughout the entrance.

"Mays I help you?" the woman asked.

"Yes, ma'am. I'm lookn' for a job. I'll do anythin', anythin' at all," Lillian pleaded giving her name to the intimidating, tall, big-boned woman.

"I's could sure use some help 'round here. I ain't gittin' any younger. Let's go ask Miss Kellum if she hire you."

Mrs. Kellum heard her name, "Who's here, Mary?"

"Miss Kellum, it's the Dennis girl. She lookin' for a job and my arthritis is acting up bad on me lately. I's could use some young'un to take the workload off."

Mrs. Kellum, tall and thin with gray hair pulled back in a knot, was elegantly dressed in a pink blouse and gray, wool-lined pencil skirt. Wearing a single strand of pearls and pearl drop earrings, she was a commanding presence. Lillian had never seen such lustrous gems worn in the middle of the day.

"What's wrong, honey? You shouldn't be out here in the cold and rain. It's blowing a gale. Please come inside and have a cup of hot tea." Glancing at Lillian's protruding belly, she inquired, "Are you with child?"

"Yes, ma'am. I need work and a place to live for me and my baby. I'll do any kind of work you need doin'. When the baby comes, I want to be able to keep him warm and safe. I ain't got no home." Lillian began to sob.

"Oh, you poor thing. I think I know your people. Where's the daddy?"

"He's not from 'round here. I don't want nothin' to do with him or my mama either."

The Kellums were wealthy and compassionate people. Mrs. Kellum did not have to think twice about helping the little waif, helplessly standing in front of her with bowed head. "You can help Mary with all the household chores, which includes cooking, cleaning, washing, and ironing. In the meantime, you can live in one of the tenant houses, and after giving birth, the new baby is welcome there as well. It's not fancy, but at least you will have a roof over your head. We provide meals for our staff."

"Thank you, ma'am. I can't thank you enough." Lillian sighed with relief.

Lillian gave birth to Stephen with the assistance of the aging housemaid who had befriended her the day she appeared at the plantation door. No one realized that the birth of her child in the little tenant house would bring heartbreak and strife to Lillian until the day she died. Baby Stephen was born with a low IQ on the verge of mental retardation, which would not be diagnosed for years to come. He exited the womb screaming incessantly—already a tormented, possessed soul—crying at the top of his lungs most evenings. When the moon was full, there was no calming the infant as sleep eluded him. He rolled side to side in his hand-me-down crib that had been left behind by the other field workers. Lillian would carry him to the plantation on days she worked. Stephen never had any interaction with other children and spent most days whining and crying alone in the basket. His fate led to a socially underdeveloped personality later in his toddler years.

"That chile don't look jist right if you ax me. All he do is cry and holler. His eyes look jist like the devil hisself," Mary commented.

Lillian hung her head in shame, feeling as though she had truly given birth to a monster. *What should I have expected?* she thought, knowing her boy was a product of a violent rape by an abusive tormented soul.

Growing up on the Kellum farm, Stephen would exchange blows and grapple with any man smaller than he was. Marching through the pasture, the horses would glance at him with terror in their eyes, sensing he had cruel intentions. Lillian grew remorseful, realizing she would never be able to give her son a kitten or puppy. She could not take that chance of the pet being tortured. Her boy was ill, but she chose to ignore the signs. Stephen was spiraling downward as he became older with fits of anger and acts of violence.

"You're a hothead, boy," the farmhands yelled as Stephen pursued an altercation with the feeble and weakest among the laborers.

"No, I ain't. He done asked for it," Stephen said after yet another bout of fisticuffs.

Stephen dropped out of school at the age of sixteen. He had grown to a medium height — thin with dark beady eyes void of emotion, staring into the distance. Since the first day of grammar school, his classmates would constantly tease him about his pointed, protruding ears that were accentuated because he always kept his head shaved. They called him Satan's child.

After seeing pictures of himself, he pompously began to believe that he was indeed the devil. Lillian began attending the evangelical church in the country. She insisted that Stephen walk with her every Sunday morning, there and back on the dry, sandy road that had not been covered with the traditional oyster shells. Some mornings, in the heat of the July and August stillness, mother and son could taste and smell the dust in their mouth and nostrils.

During the testimonies at the Mother's Day service one Sunday morning Lillian—at her wit's end—grabbed Stephen's arm and dragged him up the aisle in front of Pastor Hatfield's lectern. "Please pray for my son. He thinks he is Satan himself, Pastor Hatfield," Lillian pleaded. "I do declare, there are demons in him that need to be released before somethin' evil happens."

"We'll get that wickedness and sin out of you, boy," Pastor Hatfield bellowed, placing his hands on the top of Stephen's shaved head. "Lord, help this boy known for his diseased disposition who has caused woe, misery, suffering, and sorrow to his mother, become saved. The evil in his nature has destroyed the good. Help him, Lord. Only you can help him in the name of Jesus."

"Get the hell off me! I'm the devil! I have power over all of you," Stephen spewed as his eyes shrank into narrow slits. There were frightened gasps from the congregation as he began to talk incoherently with rage that suddenly turned to demonic laughter as if he was possessed by Lucifer himself. A toothy grin spread over his face as Pastor Hatfield dropped his hands and stepped back to avoid direct eye contact. The Pastor asked everyone to bow their heads and pray, closing the service in a flurry.

"Stephen, you get so nervous and upset about everythin'. Please watch your temper and quit makin' your boss on the farm mad. You've had job after job and you are gonna have to settle down. I ain't never seen nothin' like you, boy. Now you have embarrassed me in front of

Pastor Hatfield and the whole congregation of the Emmanuel Baptist Church," Lillian said as they walked back to the little tenant house.

He ignored her lecture and watched her hang up her coat. She went to the barren cupboards, rummaging through them from top to bottom searching for a morsel to place between two slices of bread. Placing a peanut butter sandwich in front of him on the tiny kitchen table, she bent and kissed the top of his head. "Mama loves you son. Don't forget to say a blessin' over your food."

"This ain't got no damn meat in it," he cursed after taking a bite.

"We can't afford meat, son. I don't get paid until next Saturday. I had to buy my pills yesterday. There just ain't no money left. I'll ask Miss Kellum for some cured ham from the smokehouse."

"Go straight to hell!" He picked up the kitchen table where he was sitting and threw it across the room, crashing it against the wall. The ironstone plates and jelly jar glasses began to vibrate in the cupboards.

"That ain't no way to talk to me on Mother's Day. No way at all," Lillian cried.

Stephen knotted his fist and with all his might punched her in the stomach. Grabbing her arm as she doubled over in pain, he threw her out the door and locked it so she could not get back in.

There was a bottle of Jack Daniel's whiskey on the counter. He opened it with a vengeance and threw back his head gulping as much of the smooth liquid down as he could until he began to choke—tears stinging his eyes from the strong taste of distilled alcohol. Ignoring his mother's wailing, he rifled through an old suitcase hidden under the bed, searching frantically until he found the pistol stolen from Mr. Kellum's plantation several weeks ago. "I'm tired of being an old farmhand," he cried, aggravation bleeding into his words. Stephen pointed the pistol at his foot and pulled the trigger.

The gun shot was heard from the other side of the shack. Lillian screamed, "Oh my God, open the door!"

"I want to die, Mama. I'm goin' to die. Let me be."

Lillian ran to the plantation house with searing stitches of pain ripping her abdomen. Mr. Kellum, on horseback in the riding arena, saw her waving her hands frantically as she approached him.

"Lillian, what's wrong?" he called, dismounting his stallion.

"My son has done shot himself. Please, can somebody help him?" she wailed.

"I'll call for an ambulance. You get in the main house where you're safe," Mr. Kellum assured her.

"Lordy, Lordy Stephen's done shot hisself. Help us Jesus," Mary said, shaking her head as she heard Mr. Kellum give the operator directions to the farm. "That boy ain't been right since he was birthed," she continued. "I tol' 'em he had the devil in him. I tol' 'em."

Stephen Dennis was admitted to the hospital where he recovered from his self-inflicted gunshot wound. From there, he was sent to a Virginia state mental institution for psychiatric evaluation. The psychiatrist diagnosed him as being potentially dangerous, both a social disturbance and an alcoholic suffering from a severe mental deficiency.

Stephen enjoyed all the attention he was receiving from the medical staff. It occurred to him that the more bizarre he acted, the higher dosage of medication he would receive, causing a state of euphoria for hours. Detoxing from alcohol poisoning would take a week. On the farm he drank Jack Daniels, Budweiser, and the cheapest red wine he could find from the time he awoke in the morning until he staggered to bed. The Virginia State Mental Hospital released him after he detoxed seven days later. On the eighth day, Stephen was back on the Eastern Shore of Virginia in the dark, dank tenant house with his mother.

"Stephen, put that bottle down! You ain't supposed to be drinkin'. The doctor said it would cause you to hallucinate and have seizures. You're very sick, son. Don't throw your life away on booze," Lillian begged, walking out the door on the way to work at the plantation.

He waited until she was gone and chugged the bottle until the last sip of the silky, amber liquid had disappeared. Wiping his mouth with the back of his hand he began to devise a plan to return to the mental hospital where drugs and pretty, young nurses were at his beck and call. Spring fever was in the air this early warm day as the intense odor of manure wafted through the window from the newly plowed fields. The male frogs were singing their high-pitched peep alerting the silent females that they were ready for love. The croaks became amplified into an overpowering chorus in the heat of the day. Streams and ditches were brimming with the toads that surrounded the pungent foul smelling, fertile soil.

Donning a pair of ragged trousers and a thin shirt, he slammed the door of the tenant house and stomped with angry steps towards the stable. Entering the stable, he eyed a whip leaning against the wall in the tack room. Grabbing it swiftly, his mind seethed with anger towards all mankind. He felt as if he was a victim of society. *I'm cursed, jinxed, and doomed,* he thought. Often the farm hands would call him a retard loser. He didn't know who his father was, and his mother's irritating lectures were reason enough to eventually kill her.

Jake, the old black man who took care of Mr. Kellum's stables, was singing a spiritual that his mama had sung to him since childhood. He sang while he mucked the stall next to the tack room. Jake had grown feeble and hard of hearing throughout the years, but still insisted that he was in charge of the stables. He was known to have a special way with the horses, keeping sugar cubes in his pockets and taking the time to rub their noses. Once, when a mare dropped her new born foal, she had allowed Jake to enter the stall and pick up the little creature. She then followed her trusted handler to a clean stall where he had made a fresh bed of straw for mother and baby.

"I'm Robert Kellum. I own you and this farm, you old darkie!" Stephen shouted as he cracked the whip over Jake's back.

Jake fell to the ground, stunned and in pain. Stephen turned him over and pinned him down with his knees, punching him about the face—his fists pounding, pounding.

"Don't hurt me," the old man whimpered, raising his hands to protect his bloodied face. "I ain't do nothin' to you, boy."

The horses in the pasture pricked their ears toward the ruckus and became nervous. Farmhands in the fields sensed that these sensitive animals were trying to alert them to danger, and they started to run toward the stable. When they saw Stephen straddling Jake and hanging over his blood-soaked face, an ox of a man named Willy pulled him off the frightened old man. All the farmhands took their turn—one at a time, releasing their frustrations out on the bully that had caused havoc for them over the years—until he was beaten to a pulp.

Once again, Stephen found himself in the back of an ambulance—bloody and swollen—on his way to the emergency room. Later he would be transported to the Virginia State Mental Hospital where he would remain sedated for the next four weeks.

"Leave me be! I own this place! Everyone is fired!" he hollered in the back of the ambulance. The driver made his way down the long oyster shell driveway at a high rate of speed with a blaring siren and red flashing lights, feeling uncomfortable and alarmed with his passenger in the rocking vehicle. Robert Kellum never pressed charges against the farmhands; these men had been loyal to the Kellum family and Jake's condition and pride was a priority.

On arriving at the hospital, a round of tests was given to determine how the doctors would execute his medical treatment. Stephen was declared schizophrenic with numerous mental defects and orders were given that he be kept under surveillance twenty-four hours a day.

"Your son lives a hostile, aggressive life of fantasy, Miss Dennis. He acts on impulse. I'm going to prescribe Scopolamine and Methapyrilene to sedate him, which will help aid his sleep when he returns home," the doctor said.

"He ain't got no money, doctor. What will he ever do? He's got to work. Mr. Kellum has done kicked us out of the tenant house. Sycamore Creek is all me and my boy ever knowed."

Early in the spring of 1960, Alfred Eyre sat in the library at the antique, mahogany desk that once had been his father's—methodically figuring a budget for the hotel. *The summer season will be here before we know it*, he thought. Margaret was playing bridge at a neighbor's house and it wouldn't be long before she would be in full gear at managerial capacity in their beloved Virginia Beach hotel. All the maids, bell hops, and switchboard operators were returning for yet another year. The spring held excitement in the air as the beach season was rapidly approaching. Guests returned season after season to enjoy the Eyres' hospitality, which always included Margaret's homemade baked cinnamon rolls, shortbread cookies, and peach cobbler. This repast was available in the lobby at precisely three o'clock in the afternoon and was always accompanied with a pot of tea.

Alfred heard a sharp knock at the door and rose to see who was visiting so late in the day. Opening it, he saw Lillian Dennis standing before him, eyes moist with tears. She was known throughout the small town as the tormented mother of a troubled son.

"Mr. Eyre, I need your help. It's Stephen. He's gonna git out of the insane asylum today and he ain't got no job. Can you please help him? The doctor says he's real sick and has put him on some strong medicine for his temper," she said as tears streamed down her cheeks.

"Oh now, now, Lillian, come on in the library. Would you like a cup of tea?"

"No thanks, Mr. Eyre. I'm so upset I can't eat or drink a thing. I guess you heard what happened at the Kellum farm?"

"Yes, I did. Sycamore Creek is a small town, to say the least. I'm sorry, Lillian. It seems you have had a lot of hard knocks along the way with your son."

"Stephen will never git a job now," her sobs coming in waves, desperation in her voice.

Alfred could not stand to see a woman cry and Lillian was a sorry sight begging on behalf of her boy. He opened his ledger and figured he could employ and afford another maintenance man around the hotel.

"We could use a painter this spring and someone to run errands. We have rentals in the Norfolk area; some days I'm too busy with the hotel to collect rent, so I could give Stephen that job as well. Sammy, our bell hop, said last year he needed help because of his back problems. I guess he's growing older like the rest of us."

Lillian brightened with Alfred's every word. There was hope for her son, thanks to Mr. Eyre. Maybe now he would calm down and quit lashing out at her. She said a prayer under her breath that the new pills would do the trick and change his violent nature.

"Thank you, Mr. Eyre. You are Stephen's last chance for betterin' himself. He'll make you a good boy. He means well."

"You're welcome, Lillian. I think I can help him. He's never had a father figure in his life. Let's hope and pray he comes to his senses in a new environment."

With that, Lillian was gone. Alfred was pleased that he had been a true humanitarian that afternoon remembering two of the Commandments he had learned and was drilled in his head as a child reading the Episcopal Book of Common Prayer: *Hear what our Lord Jesus Christ saith: Thou shalt love the Lord thy God with all thy heart, and with all thy soul, and with all thy mind. This is the first and great Commandment. And the second is like unto it: Thou shalt love thy neighbor as thyself. On these two commandments hang all the Law and the Prophets.* As he finished reciting, he crossed himself.

Margaret was coming in the kitchen door as Alfred handed her an afternoon sherry. He had poured a Virginia Gentleman for himself—a reward—and basked in the goodwill that he had performed. He began to explain to Margaret what had just transpired.

"Alfred, I never in all my life. The Dennis boy is mentally ill. The girls at bridge club were talking about all the ruckus he's brought to Saddle Creek. They don't understand why he hasn't been institutionalized years ago. The Kellums call him a mad dog after all he has put them through on the horse farm."

"Oh, Margaret, relax. He just needs some attention, that's all. Someone to give the kid a chance, a little self-esteem, a bit of confidence."

No background check was done in 1960. Alfred Eyre had good intentions that he was doing the right thing for this poor woebegone. After all, Stephen was a Sycamore Creek boy.

That evening the telephone rang after the dinner hour.

"Thank you for givin' me a fresh start, Mr. Eyre. I'll make you a good man. I can do anythin'. I ain't gonna let you down."

CHAPTER THREE

Suzanne couldn't believe how time seemed to fly. Late spring announced the arrival of her parents to Virginia Beach for the season. She loved this time of year and the promise of new birth it brought to nature. The Azalea Festival would coax the city out of its long hibernation. The shrubs were as tall as small trees, full of red and pink blossoms that would fall off the branches all too soon.

Edward loved to judge the "Miss Azalea Queen" contest held every year at the Norfolk Yacht and Country Club. She knew her husband had a roving eye which she had finally accepted. They had separated twice in the past, but their attraction kept pulling them back together like a magnet. Suzanne opted not to address the flings and gambling that persisted year after year. Edward lived the high life and she was along for the ride "till death do us part." Living without her true love was not an option until this past year when she caught him with Laura. Of course, she could find somebody else; men were available in this Navy town, two-to-one. Yes, she enjoyed flirting, but that was as far as it had gotten until Bill. *I blame Eleanor for all this mess and strife in my life*, she thought with amusement.

Eleanor Johnson was Suzanne's cousin who was going through a bad divorce in their hometown of Sycamore Creek. She had suggested to Eleanor that a move to Norfolk would be a welcome change of pace. It would be healing and there was no shortage of men in the city, an added bonus.

Eleanor had moved in with the Barclays initially because Edward was on the road most weekdays, opening branches for his company throughout the state of Virginia. She would be much needed company for Suzanne. Eleanor was not only a cousin, but a friend and great fun. After two weeks, she had moved to an apartment in the Victorian house on the picturesque, historic street of Kent, leaving a lonely void in Suzanne's heart.

Her memory flashed back to the afternoon she and Eleanor walked into the Greek restaurant downtown. The restaurant was dim and quaint, but the aroma from the kitchen of garlic and beef was alluring; she could practically taste the scents in her mouth. There was a dark and handsome man that became totally attentive, displaying an aggressive and animated nature the moment they stepped inside.

"Please come in! I've never seen two more beautiful ladies in my life. You look as if you stepped out of a magazine," he said with a thick accent, seating them at a small round table by the window.

"Let me introduce myself: I'm Bill Callias," he said with flair, kissing both women on each side of their cheeks.

Suzanne and Eleanor reveled in his attention and politely sat down in the chairs facing the window that he pulled out for them.

"Would you ladies like a Greek salad? It's the house specialty," he inquired gesturing with his hands as if they were butterflies in the air.

"That sounds delicious," Eleanor, the new divorcee, cooed.

After he went into the kitchen to assemble what he needed for his culinary feat, Suzanne eyed her cousin, a petite brunette beauty. "I'm so glad we started apartment hunting today. I think our new friend has an eye for you."

"He's adorable. We don't have any Greek men in Sycamore Creek," Eleanor sighed, already smitten.

When Bill exited the kitchen, rolling out a table on wheels with a white linen tablecloth that covered it entirely, he stopped at the side of their table. On the top was a large wooden bowl with salad ingredients surrounding it. He bent over to retrieve from underneath the cloth the imported olive oil from the old country and poured it into the spinning bowl. With excitement for his craft, he showed his new audience each smaller bowl of seeded tomatoes, peeled cucumbers, red bell peppers, Kalamata olives, red onion, Italian parsley, and oregano. He assembled the salad crumbling feta cheese on the top.

Suzanne remembered how passionate he was demonstrating his art.

Bill took a bow after he tossed the salad and plated it for them, topping his masterpiece with freshly cracked pepper. A bottle of red wine was presented and uncorked at the table with flair. Bill poured the dark wine with precision stopping halfway up the glass.

"May I join you?" Bill questioned, not waiting for a reply before seating himself.

"By all means," Eleanor replied batting her eyelashes.

Bill was spellbound by the blonde across the table from him. When Eleanor walked to the ladies room, out of earshot, he asked Suzanne, "May I have your telephone number?"

"I'm married!"

"I saw your ring. When would be a good time to call?"

Suzanne wrote the number down on a cocktail napkin he had handed her, and the rest was history. The Greek urged her to leave Edward, but knowing she would live to regret it, she had cautiously chosen to live a double life. Bill was attentive and kind as he worshipped the young blue-eyed Southern-born beauty. Edward had yet to find out about her affair. She secretly prayed that he never would, knowing it would change the course of their lives forever.

As she gazed out the window, sipping a cup of tea, the phone rang breaking her daydream.

"Hi, honey. We arrived late last night catching the last ferry. Poppy and I would love to see you and Elizabeth this afternoon." Margaret sounded cheerful.

"We can't wait either, Mother. May I help you with unpacking or making the beds with new linens at the hotel?"

"No thanks, dear. Your father hired Stephen Dennis this spring to help us move and be an overall handy man around the hotel for the summer season. The boy's been in trouble from time to time around Sycamore Creek. Alfred is trying to keep him on the right track. I wasn't very happy with your father's decision, but Stephen seems to be polite enough. Maybe this work experience away from home will turn his life around," Margaret said, keeping her voice low and guarded.

"You say he's from Sycamore Creek?"

"Yes, honey, he lived on the Kellum horse farm. I don't think you know him. He dropped out of school when he was sixteen and I believe he's a couple of years younger than you are."

"That's just like Daddy, always trying to help the down and out." They ended the conversation and Suzanne began to dress Elizabeth for their reunion at the hotel.

"Nana and Poppy have arrived for the summer and we're going to spend the afternoon with them," Suzanne told her daughter, as she was packing a bag of toys for her six-year-old in case she grew bored during their visit.

"Nana and Poppy are here!" Elizabeth squealed, running around in circles and exploding with energy.

Suzanne ran a comb through her hair and squirted perfume from the infuser on each side of her throat before going out the door into the brilliant sunshine with her daughter in tow.

Alfred and Margaret were instructing Stephen which rooms to place all the bags and various sundries when Suzanne and Elizabeth walked through the back door of the hotel. Stephen stopped in his tracks as he saw Suzanne greet her parents. He was introduced to both mother and daughter by Margaret, and he stood frozen, unable to avert his eyes away from Suzanne's beauty. She had golden hair that reminded him of an angel's with the darkest blue eyes the color of the ocean. Wearing plaid pants and a matching knit twinset of soft white, her petite figure was accentuated as the sun's rays shone through the large bay window facing the sea. Suzanne was used to stares from the opposite sex as well as her own and had grown weary of all the attention her looks generated. When Margaret noticed that Stephen could not take his eyes off her daughter, a feeling of apprehension crossed her mind.

Margaret looked at Stephen with a steady eye. "Let's get to work.

There's only a few hours left this afternoon."

"I brought my camera with me, Mrs. Eyre. I'd like to take a picture of y'all, so I can always remember my first day on the job here." Stephen sounded upbeat and giddy.

"Congratulations, Stephen. I hope you'll enjoy the summer at the beach." Suzanne smiled in a friendly manner.

"Would you like a Clark bar, Elizabeth?" Stephen asked handing her the chocolate treat he pulled from his jacket's pocket.

"Yummy! My favorite. Mommy, may I?" Elizabeth squealed.

Stephen snapped the camera taking his first picture of Suzanne Barclay—but it would not be his last.

Suzanne returned on weekends to sunbathe in front of the hotel. Guests that checked in every summer were happy to see her, as she had a gift of enveloping people with her warm personality. Unaware that Stephen was snapping pictures from a distance, she laid her beach blanket on the white sand or took a dip in the waves. He always took his work break to coincide with Suzanne's visits. Sitting on the concrete boardwalk, Stephen would hide behind rows of horizontal gray pipes, which allowed him to become mysteriously obscure, clicking the camera and panting excitedly to capture the woman that intrigued him. He was persistently rushing to the drugstore to have the film developed; scotch-taping the pictures to his one-bedroom apartment wall became a fixation that summer.

In the evenings, Stephen would walk to the honky-tonk arcades on the south end of town. Striving to win the largest stuffed animal for Elizabeth became an obsession; he played until the pennies and nickels were depleted from his trouser pockets.

"I won a large teddy bear for Elizabeth last night, Mr. Eyre," Stephen boasted with pride walking in the back entrance of the hotel at dawn.

"When we go to Norfolk this afternoon, we can stop by Suzanne's and you can surprise Elizabeth. I'd like you to see where they live because in the fall, the rancher will need a fresh coat of paint. Edward's too busy with traveling for his company to take the time for house or yard maintenance. He spends weeks at a time opening branches around the state," said Alfred as he rambled on, giving Stephen much more information than was necessary.

Stephen gloated: now he knew Suzanne's husband was infrequently home during the week and he was about to find out where she lived. He was intent on learning any new information he could that pertained to the woman he was consumed with. Mr. Eyre instructed him to drive the station wagon, thereby making it possible to know exactly what direction to take in the future—for stalking.

On the way, Alfred continued to confide in him. "Stephen, I'm going to let you collect rent every Friday. I'll show you today where all the tenant houses are located. You'll have to knock on the doors and tell them you're collecting on my behalf. Sometimes, I run into a problem not being able to get my money. Here's my .32 caliber pistol to use for your safety. You'll be collecting lots of cash so keep an eye out as somebody may threaten to rob you. Usually, seeing the gun curtails their motive. Only shoot if it is a dire emergency." Alfred placed the pistol between them on the seat.

"Yes sir, Mr. Eyre."

Driving the company station wagon into Suzanne's driveway made Stephen's hand tighten around the steering wheel; his heart pounded knowing where she lived. Suzanne was surprised to see her father, not expecting him this afternoon.

"What a pleasant surprise, Daddy!"

"Stephen has won something for Elizabeth, so I thought we'd drop it off—a teddy bear as big as she is."

"Oh, Stephen, how thoughtful of you! You are so kind. She's at a little friend's house, but she'll love it when she comes home. Thank you,"

Suzanne's innocent replies to Stephen served only to stoke the flames of his desire.

"Welcome," he mumbled, barely able to contain his composure. No one had treated him with respect in Sycamore Creek, which caused his feelings to grow stronger each time he was in the beauty's company.

"Tomorrow we're going to the Norfolk Zoo. I'm going to pack a picnic for just the two of us. I have a feeling Teddy may be tagging along as well," Suzanne said. "Stephen, do you remember Eleanor Johnson? I think she was in your grammar school. I mentioned your name to her the other night and she remembers when you were in the sixth grade."

"I think I knowed her." He coughed hardly finding his voice—the idea that Suzanne was talking about him to someone else was proof she was interested. His endearment was growing. He thought to himself that he must remember to stop by the Norfolk Zoo tomorrow during his lunch break.

Alfred kissed his daughter good-bye and they were off to visit the tenant houses to collect the monthly rent.

"Your daughter sure is nice, Mr. Eyre. I hope someday I can git me a wife like her."

"There's a girl out there for you, Stephen, all in good time."

Exactly at noon the following day, Stephen pulled into the parking lot of the Norfolk Zoo. He was astute enough to realize he didn't want to draw attention to the company vehicle, so he parked on the opposite side of the lot where the zoo's maintenance trucks were housed. He wore a baseball cap pulled down over his forehead, shading his eyes. His hands shook with emotion when he saw Suzanne, Elizabeth, and the new stuffed animal sitting at a picnic table in the shade. He hid behind a thick green privet that the zoo's gardeners had planted around the grounds. Peeping through a dense opening, he brought the camera to his right eye, snapping frame after frame of his object of affection.

"Ah, mission accomplished," Stephen mumbled to himself. Yet another photograph of Suzanne Barclay was tacked to the wall among the gallery in a matter of days.

Stephen listened intently to every word Mr. and Mrs. Eyre would say regarding the whereabouts of their daughter. He would promptly cash his weekly check at the bank, heading directly to the drugstore to buy candy for Elizabeth. *That will win Suzanne's heart*, he thought.

"Suzanne's not answering the telephone this afternoon, Alfred. I'm sure she's shopping again," Margaret guessed.

"She owns half of Thalhimers already," Alfred chuckled shaking his head.

"Mr. Eyre, I ain't feeling so good. I have pains in my gut and I done threw up my lunch," Stephen spoke rapidly.

"You better go back to your apartment, son. You're hungover. Try to stop drinking every night; it's not good for your health," Alfred advised.

Stephen drove frantically to Thalhimers Department store. He had methodically scoped out all the fancy stores after Suzanne's mother commented that they shopped together at least twice a week. He knew exactly where the shopping district was and had an idea of Thalhimers main entrance.

It seemed like hours until, as luck would have it, he saw Suzanne and a brunette-haired girl walking out of the store with boxes in their arms. Stephen assumed the other girl must be Eleanor. He lowered himself in the seat hoping they would not recognize him. They turned and headed towards Eleanor's car while he snapped pictures of them as they walked away. They wore straight skirts with their blouses tucked in, accentuating their slender waists. Their high heels made them look taller than usual.

"This is a great one," Stephen moaned with delight and sped off.

The summer flew by as Stephen performed his assignments. Evenings he was quite content to open a bottle of cheap brew, lay back on his cot in the sparse apartment, and gaze at photographs of Suzanne taken from the early spring until late summer.

One Sunday afternoon in August, Edward and Suzanne walked into the hotel together holding hands and gazing at each other affectionately.

"Happy Anniversary, you two love birds. Give your suitcases to Stephen and he'll place them in your room," Margaret said welcoming them.

"Oh Mother, this is a gorgeous day. We're going to take a dip in the ocean, sit in the rockers on the front porch, and have a cocktail. Edward's taking me to the Cavalier Club for dinner tonight," Suzanne explained with excitement in her voice.

Stephen's face tightened as he picked up the suitcases carrying them to their room. Opening the door, he saw an arrangement of a dozen red roses on the bureau. He could not read very well and studied the card beside the vase. He struggled to read: *Happy Anniversary. I love you with all my heart, Edward.*

Stephen spent the rest of the afternoon obsessed with watching Suzanne and Edward frolicking in the ocean waves and sunbathing on the blanket in front of the hotel. Late afternoon, they came in to bathe and dress for dinner. When Suzanne descended the stairs, she had on a blue silk dress the color of her eyes. At a loss for words, he stared awestruck.

Edward was in the kitchen concocting a pitcher of martinis. He handed his wife a glass with three olives and kissed her on the lips. The Barclays then meandered to the porch sipping their cocktails and basking in their joyful day, Suzanne's head leaning on Edward's shoulder.

Suzanne Barclay had paid little attention to Stephen Dennis that day beyond a polite greeting as she was so wrapped up in the celebration of her spurious marriage. She was glowing with happiness. *This is the way marriage is supposed to be*, she lamented. Did she have the endurance to try again after Edward's affair with Laura?

Margaret glanced from her desk and caught sight of Stephen standing in front of her. He was frozen with anger, silent, and staring straight ahead at Suzanne. His sunburned hands were knotted into fists at both sides as he seethed.

"Stephen, are you feeling okay?" Margaret questioned, wondering if he was going to punch the wall.

He glared at her, and that was answer enough. "I'm fine." His voice was as cold as arctic ice.

Margaret's hand trembled as she tried to make an entry in the hotel's ledger. She could not pinpoint Stephen's mood swings, but what she had just witnessed with her own eyes made her feel sick at heart.

"Alfred, I have a very uneasy feeling in my stomach. Stephen cannot take his eyes off of Susanne. I truly feel he is smitten with our daughter. I am concerned for her safety," she addressed her husband as they were preparing for bed.

"Oh Margaret! You are such a worry wart. Suzanne's a grown woman. She can handle herself. She takes after you, for God's sake," Alfred insisted, running out of patience with his wife's constant anxiety about their daughter.

"Is he going back home to Sycamore Creek this winter?"

"No, he's picked up odd jobs in Norfolk, but he'll still collect rent for us on Fridays."

Margaret felt a chill crawl up her spine and a feeling of unease began to weigh her down. "Goodnight," she whispered, trying to keep the blame towards her husband at bay. *He seems so completely unaware*, she thought.

The next morning when Suzanne rose early, she knew her mother would be in the kitchen percolating coffee for all the staff arriving for the morning shift.

"Oh, there you are. How was your dinner?" Margaret inquired.

"Lovely, Mother. We had so much fun. Thanks for the hospitality." She accepted the cup of coffee Margaret handed her and gave her a peck on the cheek.

"I didn't sleep very well last night," Margaret relayed.

"Oh, what's wrong?"

"I'm concerned about Stephen Dennis and his infatuation with you."

"With me!"

"Yes, he's not normal and I feel it goes beyond friendliness," Margaret said keeping her voice guarded.

"Oh Mother, one look at him and you know he's just not right mentally, but I think he's harmless."

"Please be careful and not overtly friendly."

"I promise—not to worry." Suzanne rose kissing her mother on the top of her head as she poured another cup of coffee. She had too much to be concerned with between her failing marriage and the secret emotional affair with the Greek. *Oh, what a tangled web we weave*, she pondered.

September 15th turned autumnal early with cooler nights which forced Sammy, the older bellhop, to carry logs into the lobby and lay a fire in the massive brick fireplace. The evening flames were essential for warmth.

"I'm ready to rest my eyes on Sycamore Creek," Margaret exclaimed.

"I think we'll start making our traditional caravan across the Chesapeake this week. There are no more reservations on the books. Let's just take our time packing, but I plan to have the hotel cleaned and closed by the end of October," Alfred said with determination.

"Sounds good, dear."

Edward was in Richmond for the months of September and October, coming home only on weekends. Suzanne kept herself busy with Elizabeth's kindergarten schedule and baking for their tea parties during the late mornings.

Most nights Elizabeth spent with a babysitter, particularly late afternoon until early evening. Suzanne would meet Bill in a bar or lounge for a couple of drinks and romantic conversation. She hungered for this foreign, mysterious man to give her the affection she so craved. His gaze was constant as he was completely enthralled. Hypnotized. Their affair was growing towards one of the heart. The Greek had fallen head over heels in love.

CHAPTER FOUR

October 26, 1960

After her parents and daughter said their farewells and were on the road to Sycamore Creek, Suzanne busied herself washing the dirtied cups and saucers. The rancher seemed eerily quiet without the constant singing of a five-year-old and the million questions she asked throughout the day. She chuckled remembering the countless afternoons Elizabeth would mimic her telephone conversations word for word, gesturing in the same fashion as her mother did. Suzanne would center a stern gaze on her child until the little actress would grow quiet and the mocking halted.

I've been fortunate to have spent my days with my daughter. She is the light of my life, Suzanne thought, *I miss her already*.

"Come Thor. It's too pretty a day to be inside. Let's go for a walk," Suzanne called.

Thor was the Barclay's regal boxer and exceptionally obedient after attending training classes the past year. Fawn in color, his enormous white paws matched the apron on his chest as well as the tip of his tail. Whenever Suzanne spoke to him, he would cock his head to the side and gaze into her eyes as if he understood exactly what she was trying to communicate to him, her ever-faithful companion. Thor allowed Elizabeth to paint his nails and display a baby bonnet on his massive head, tying the pink satin ribbon under his chin. Edward had dubbed him a gentle giant. His soulful dark eyes always watching over Elizabeth and Suzanne, protecting them at all costs.

"Remember the day you won third prize in the dog show, Thor, even though only three dogs competed?" Suzanne chuckled, as she recalled the other contestants. "You'll always be *First in Show* to this family," she said as she observed him with affection. He began to pant with anticipation; afternoon walks were the highlight of his day.

She grabbed his lead off the hook by the back door and they were off for a jaunt in the warm sunshine. Wrapping her sweater tighter around her shoulders when the sun slipped behind the clouds, she had to stop at every bush as Thor was determined to sniff and mark his territory. "More sniffing than walking, huh boy," she smiled.

Spotting one of her elderly neighbors raking leaves four doors down from where she lived, she promised herself she would spend a little time talking to Miss Hannah on the way home.

Thor's tongue was protruding from the side of his mouth with exhaustion as they approached the neighbor, taking a slow gait back after the two-mile outing. Stretching and extending his front legs, he laid down next to his mistress and rested his head on the top of his paws, promptly falling asleep.

"Hi, Miss Hannah, you are going to town on those leaves," Suzanne called at the top of her voice to the hard of hearing lady.

"I try to get out in the yard at least once a day for a little exercise, if it's nice," Miss Hannah answered. Stopping and leaning on her rake, she welcomed the company of her favorite neighbor.

Suzanne lingered longer than usual, sensing she was lonely after her husband passed away only a year ago.

"My John made sure the yard was tidy even in the fall. Nothing was ever out of place, not a weed to be found—no matter what the season. He would be upset if I let it go to pot. Things are not the same when you are a widow. I miss him every day," Miss Hannah said, stepping back from the pile of leaves to observe her work.

"He'd be proud of you, Miss Hannah," Suzanne confided. "You know, if you ever need us, Edward and I are only a few houses away."

"You both have been so kind to me. I don't want to take advantage of your generosity. I try to be as independent as possible, but thanks, honey."

After their chat, Suzanne walked home with Thor, promising him he could play in the fenced backyard after a big bowl of cold water and a biscuit.

"Okay boy, you're a free man!" Suzanne said as she unclasped Thor's lead as they walked inside the fence. Thor scampered off as his mistress climbed the patio steps and entered the back door to retrieve his goodies.

Looking at the kitchen clock on the wall above the Frigidaire, she realized she had chatted with Miss Hannah longer than intended. It was nearly three-thirty and the neighborhood kids were walking home from school. They would run into their houses, drop the books on the kitchen table and quickly change clothes for a game of tackle football, taking advantage of the remaining light until dusk when mothers called them in for dinner.

Miss Hannah had enjoyed Suzanne's company, but had grown weary of tackling the leaves in her yard. The more she raked, the more they fell from the sky around her. Bending over the last pile, she saw out of the corner of her eye a blue station wagon drive slowly in front of Suzanne Barclay's house. The driver drove to the cul-de-sac and circled the neighborhood once again, coming to a complete standstill in front of the Barclay residence. Walking to her shed to put the rake in its place, she was able to hear the driver floor the gas pedal. The tires squealed as he sped toward the exit of the quiet avenue. *How odd*, she thought, buttoning the top button of her jacket as the late afternoon grew cooler.

Suzanne was in good spirits anticipating Eleanor's visit before long. They were going to meet Bill for drinks in his restaurant's lounge and he promised to demonstrate his culinary skills preparing an authentic Greek feast for them. Bill had changed; he had become more and more demanding of her time, suffocating her with ultimatums — demanding she choose which man she wanted to spend her life with. Eleanor was aware of their affair, but figured in the end Suzanne would come to her senses. There was no way she would ever leave Edward, knowing they were trying to reunite, remaining completely infatuated with each other. In the interim, Eleanor had begun dating a judge, and he was going to meet the three of them this evening as well.

Suzanne decided to take a leisurely bubble bath before Eleanor came prancing through the door. She meticulously laid her blouse, skirt, underwear, garter belt, and silk stockings across the bed. All she would have to do is style her hair in a French twist and select heels that would match tonight's suit. A strand of pearls laid across the vanity ever-ready to be clasped around her neck.

I hope I can keep my secret a little bit longer... I enjoy the excitement of primping for a man, she mused. Despite her efforts to break it off with Bill, she knew she had cast a spell on him too, one of mystique and romance.

The bubble bath felt luxurious as she scooted and sank to chin level in the bathtub. Standing up, wrapping a terry cloth robe around her and tying it at the waist, she walked to the vanity. Spending the next thirty minutes in front of the mirror, teasing her hair and twisting it up securing every strand with a bobby pin, she meticulously sprayed half a can of Aqua Net on the precisely coiffed hair style, making her feel glamorous. The finale included painting her lips red with Revlon lipstick—her signature color. She rose from the vanity bench and walked to the bed where she slowly dressed with care.

Deep in her thoughts regarding Bill, she realized the wonderstruck couple had not planned for it to get out of control. Her marriage had been on the rocks for quite some time, and the handsome Greek constantly flattered her with his desire, which she found irresistible. *Who knows if he's sincere? I've fallen for him,* she told herself. The man could only contain his lust for so long. One of these nights she would have to decide whether they would fall in bed together and give into their developing sexual tension, or end their exciting emotional affair. She whispered to herself, *I can read his mind and he's growing impatient. Will tonight change everything?*

Stephen Dennis could not shake the dream from his senses that had awoken him the night before. Attempting to woo Suzanne Barclay had overwhelmed him; his mind was twisted with confusion on how to make her his own. She had barely said two words to him since he saw her and her husband on the day of their anniversary in August. She had purposefully avoided all eye contact with him, exiting the room whenever he entered. He didn't deserve being treated like a second-class citizen. Thoughts of the happy couple kissing in front of him continued to fuel his anger, his irritation, and his resentment.

"Pretty girls like Suzanne Barclay don't deserve to live. She was nice to me once, now the bitch acts like I don't exist. I'm goin' to make her pay. I've made up my mind," he kept rambling on as he placed the .32 caliber pistol in his hip pocket and a vial of sleeping pills in his jacket just in case he needed to sleep later. The previous night's dream was so vivid and he came to understand it was the only way to accomplish his goal of revenge.

When dawn arrived on October 26, 1960, Stephen opted not to work. Instead, he drove the company station wagon to an all-night dive bar where he was invited to join the old sailors in a crap game. "Keep the beers coming," he yelled to the bartender over the juke box, indulging in several beers and a pint of whiskey. Later that afternoon, he was feeling a twisted sense of rightness, knowing it was time. He got back in the station wagon and headed toward Norfolk.

Stephen circled around Suzanne's neighborhood between 3:30pm and 4:30pm. The vision of his dream was growing ever stronger as a voice in his head told him it had to be done. He worked up the nerve to proceed. His hands shook uncontrollably on the steering wheel; with an aggressive impulse, he turned into the driveway and slammed on the brakes. He marched to the front door where he banged loudly.

Thor began a low growl sensing danger for his mistress. He scratched at the back door with his front paws trying desperately to gain entrance.

"Oh, hello, Stephen. What brings you here?" Suzanne inquired.

"Mr. Eyre told me to stop by today after five o'clock and give you a contract on painting the rancher. I have it in my jacket."

"Well, I'd like Edward to look at it first, before I give you the go ahead." She stared up at him as her mouth grew dry with unease.

Stephen's face tightened as he cast an angry glare towards Suzanne. "Can I use your bathroom?"

"It's right down the hall," Suzanne said pointing with her finger.

Stephen moved quickly to the bathroom, slamming the door with a bang. His mind was made up; he would follow through with the plan.

Suzanne went back to her writing desk where she started to tackle a stack of bills she had meant to pay earlier. *I'll put everything in order until he shows me the contract he's talking about. It's odd Daddy never mentioned Stephen would be stopping by. I'm glad Eleanor will be here any minute*, she thought fretfully.

Just as her thought dissipated, Eleanor walked through the front door, blowing Suzanne a kiss. "Are you ready for our big night out?" she asked. "Is that your father's car in the driveway?"

"Yes, but Stephen Dennis is driving it. He's in the bathroom. We'll go as soon as he gives me a price on painting the rancher. I'm anxious for him to be on his way. I am very uncomfortable with him in the house; he's unwelcome here. I think he's been drinking—he reeks of alcohol."

"He always was a little creepy. I'm in no hurry. It feels so good to be off my feet. The bank was extremely busy today." Eleanor sighed as she slipped off her heels.

Stephen emerged from the bathroom. "Oh, hello," he said, startled to see Eleanor in the house.

"Oh, hi, Stephen," Eleanor said as he walked by her, heading towards the front door as if he were leaving.

But Stephen abruptly turned around, drew the pistol out of his pocket, aimed it at her crossed legs and fired. The bullet seared through both of Eleanor's legs.

Suzanne screamed, "WHAT HAVE YOU DONE?!"

"Look you two, this was an accident!" Stephen yelled, slamming the door and locking it.

"All right, but I will have to call an ambulance," Suzanne said trying to remain calm, but realizing time was of the essence for Eleanor's sake. She jumped up from her desk and ran to the bedroom where the telephone was. Stephen followed, grabbing her. She struggled and screamed until she broke away from his grasp. Unable to get to the telephone, she ran out of the bedroom, past Eleanor and fled to the front door, frantically trying to unlock it. He ran after her and seized her arm, pulled her in front of Eleanor and fired three shots: one through the spinal cord, one through the right lung, and one through the left arm. Suzanne hit the floor and didn't move. Stephen turned the gun on Eleanor as she sat immobilized, and he fired once more, aiming at her neck over her left shoulder. The bullet struck the edge of the vertebrae, then traveled up through her throat, and lodged in the roof of her mouth. Eleanor could only see the upper portion of Suzanne's body as she slumped over helplessly in the chair that was filling rapidly with her blood. She was unable to move due to the wounds she had sustained. She heard Stephen ripping at Suzanne's clothing and closed her eyes—gurgling on her own blood.

Stephen felt empowered over these two defenseless, vulnerable women. He went to Eleanor, grabbed her by the ankles, pulled her out of the chair and slid her on the floor beside Suzanne. Viciously tearing at her dress and snatching the panties down to her feet, he raped her. Realizing this was not his quest, his true intention pounded in his mind as he turned to Suzanne and raped her as well. Suzanne was dead, but it didn't matter. He had finally accomplished his mission. Eleanor laid on the floor in shock, trying to feign death. Stephen violated Suzanne before returning to Eleanor and raping her a second time.

Standing and zipping up his blood-stained fly, he walked into the kitchen. Eleanor heard running water in the sink as he tried to open the two vials of Scopolamine and Methapyrilene. The pills hit the kitchen floor, he immediately scooped them up in his hand and gulped them down placing the glass of water on the counter.

Thor threw himself against the screen door with a high pitch bark of distress after hearing the popping sound of the five bullets coming from the living room. The dog had sensed distress for his mistress when the station wagon pulled in the driveway initially. The body language of the man stomping across the yard had alerted him to the trouble ahead.

"Shut the hell up, dog!" Stephen screamed from the other side of the door. Opening the interior door, his eyes grew wide with fear at the exposed fangs and the sound of a low throated growl from Thor. "I've heard enough—you're next." He managed to open the screen door wide enough to aim his pistol at the boxer who was about to lunge. Staring into Thor's eyes, his hand shook as he fired the sixth and last remaining bullet into his skull.

Thor fell backwards and was silenced forever.

He picked up the wall phone and called the police department. "You better come to Suzanne Barclay's house, 221 Sunset Avenue. I've killed two women, oh yeah, and a dog." Hanging up the phone, he repeated, "What have I done? I have killed two women and a dog."

Walking back into the living room, he stood over Suzanne as she laid on her back. Looking into her eyes, he said, "This one's dead, but this one ain't."

Eleanor worried that another bullet would pierce her body at any second even though she tried to remain perfectly still, believing she was doomed to die.

He loomed over her and asked, "Do you know where a hospital is?"

She tried to nod an affirmative response.

Stephen unlocked the front door and summoned a neighborhood boy who was playing football in the next yard to hold the door open for him. Picking Eleanor up in his arms, he carried her to the station wagon and drove her to St. Mary's Hospital.

Eleanor felt the world moving in slow motion as she heard the screaming sirens of police cars and an ambulance coming towards her. Attempting to attract their attention, she raised her frail hand trying to summon the vehicles as they sped by. *Where is he taking me and what is he going to do to me now*, she thought.

Stephen drove Eleanor to the entrance of the emergency room, threw the gear shift into park, jumped out of the vehicle, and ran around to the passenger side. He scooped her into his arms and promenaded into the hospital, dumping her on the first stretcher he saw. An emergency room nurse met Stephen in the hallway.

"I shot her accidentally. I shot two of them," he blurted.

"My God, what happened?" the nurse asked, eyes as big as saucers, staring at Eleanor.

"The gun went off. It was an accident—the gun went off four or five times," he stated.

Stephen was anxious to return to the crime scene because he didn't want to miss the chaos he had created. He felt like a movie star as he pulled up to the rancher where Norfolk police had surrounded the premise, flattered by the attention he had garnered—still on a high. Stephen walked up to the motorcycle officer and handed him the keys, and then found himself in the back of the police car. It was 5:30pm. The carnage had only lasted thirty minutes.

On the way to headquarters, he stated with pride, "If I couldn't fuck her alive, I'd fuck her dead. I dreamed last night I done it. Some people are just marked for death," he said as a slow grin crossed his face.

Stephen became drowsy at the station and told the detectives who were in the process of interrogating him that he had taken two vials of sleeping pills after the crime. He was then rushed to St. Mary's Hospital where his stomach was pumped of the Scopolamine and Methapyrilene and remained there overnight—the same facility where one of his victims was recovering from rape and attempted murder.

Sergeant W.E. Farley had arrived at the scene of the killing about five-thirty on October 26, 1960. The next morning, he saw Stephen Dennis after his release from St. Mary's Hospital.

Stephen freely and voluntarily described the events that took place at the Barclay residence. He told Sergeant Farley he drank a beer or two, bought some whiskey and after a trip to Virginia Beach and a little crap game, had another beer, came back to Norfolk, and didn't remember anything after that time. Sergeant Farley reminded Stephen he had left out the most important facts.

"Well, I will tell you about it," he said and then voluntarily signed the statement written by Officer Farley:

Q. *"Tell us, in your own words what happened at 221 Sunset Avenue, October 26, 1960, at approximately 5:00 P.M."*

A. *"About 5:00 P.M. I went to Suzanne's house and she let me in the front door. Eleanor arrived and came into the house. She sat down in the big chair in the livin' room in front of the window. I went to the bathroom and came out and stood by the front door. Suzanne was either standin' or sittin' at the desk by the door. I don't remember.*

I pulled the pistol from my hip pocket and started shootin'. A bullet hit Eleanor first and Suzanne run into the bedroom and grabbed the phone and I pulled her away from it when I reached her. She run back into the front room and I run after her and started shootin' again, but I don't know how many times I shot.

Suzanne run for the front door when I was shootin', and I pulled her away from the front door and I shot her then. After I shot her, I turned around and shot again. I don't know if it was Eleanor or Suzanne. Then I walked over to Eleanor and I raped her, and I walked over to Suzanne, turned her over. She was layin' sideways and opened her eye up. She was tremblin' then. I pulled her clothes down and I raped her.

I called the police operator and I came back and put Eleanor in my arms and carried her to St. Mary's Hospital. I carried her in and laid her on the stretcher. I got in the car and came back to the motorcycle officer and handed him the keys and the next thing I knowed I was in the police car."

Q. *"Stephen, you were treated for an overdose of sleeping pills. Tell us when you took them."*

A. *"After I realized what I had done, I wanted to die, and I took the pills."*

Q. *"Where did you get the pills?"*

A. *"I had them with me when I went there."*

Q. *"How much had you had to drink?"*

A. *"A pint of whiskey and four or five beers."*

Q. *"What time did you quit work?"*

A. *"About 3:00."*

Q. *"You refer to Suzanne. Do you mean Suzanne Barclay?"*

A. *"Yes, sir."*

Q. *"You refer to Eleanor in your statement. Do you mean Eleanor Johnson?"*

A. *"Eleanor. I don't know her last name."*

Q. *"Where did you get the gun?"*

A. *"Alfred Eyre."*

Q. *"How long had you had it?"*

A. *"Since last spring."*

Q. *"How much did you pay for it?"*

A. *"Alfred Eyre gave it to me to collect rent. I carry a good bit of money at times.*

Q. *"I show you a 32-caliber automatic Serial No. 878394. This is the gun used on Suzanne and Eleanor?"*

A. "Yes."

Q. "How long have you known Suzanne?"

A. "Twenty years. We growed up together in Sycamore Creek, Virginia, along with Eleanor."

Q. "What did Eleanor say to you before you raped her?"

A. "Nothin' that I recall."

Q. "Are you comfortable at this time?"

A. "You are treatin' me all right."

Q. "Why did you go to Suzanne's house?"

A. "I don't know. I just went there. I knowed her father and mother and I had been there with them."

Q. "Had you had intercourse with Suzanne?"

A. "No, sir."

Q. "Had you had intercourse with Eleanor before this happened?"

A. "No, sir."

Q. "Is this statement the truth to the best of your knowledge and given freely without threat of promise by us or any member of the Norfolk Police Division?"

A. "That's right."

Q. "Anything else you care to say?"

A. That's all I guess. I want to die. I ain't got nothin' to live for."

Officer Farley called two psychiatrists into the interrogation room, Doctors Ellis and Ott. "It could be observed that Stephen Dennis is at this time in practically perfect mental health and there's no disturbance of mental status," Dr. Ellis informed the police department in his conclusion of the examination.

The other psychiatrist, Dr. Ott, told the department, "I am of the opinion Stephen Dennis was in a psychotic state on the day of the crime, and I would not trust him not to kill Suzanne Barclay again if she were living. The same applies also to other persons. He has a sick, mixed up mind. Even the stress of normal living may bring out his hostile, aggressive impulses."

Stephen began to change his story after he had already signed Officer Farley's written statement. "I did not shoot that woman. I drove to the house with another man, and he got out of the car and went into the house and I drove off. I returned to the house and found the police there and I was arrested. I don't know why I was arrested. Mike done it; it was Mike," his diatribe continued. "I am trying to do a favor for someone, and I am not sayin' any more. I am goin' to fight until I die."

Stephen was ordered by the trial court to be delivered to the Superintendent of the Virginia State Mental Hospital at Jamesville, Virginia, for proper care and observation, and examined for a detailed report of his mental condition as of October 26, 1960.

A black hearse rolled down the ramp of the Norfolk City Morgue with metal, silver letters displaying Sycamore Creek Funeral Home in the side windows. Harvey Eyre had come to take his niece home. Maurice Murray, the medical examiner, was just finishing the autopsy when Harvey walked through the door. He immediately laid down his saw, took off his gloves, and walked toward Harvey embracing him. The two men had been friends for years.

"Harvey, I'm so sorry … so sorry." The doctor's tone was serious.

"How many times was she shot, Maurice?" Tightness gripped his chest as he looked at the exposed, open cavity of his niece's body.

"Three times," Maurice replied, pointing to the wounds of the spinal cord, right lung, and left arm.

An awkward silence followed as Harvey tried to regain his composure. His voice broke, "Was she raped?"

Rather than respond verbally the medical examiner could only nod then he said, "After … after she was shot."

"I'll wait in the office until you're finished. Please be thorough: we are going to nail the son of a bitch," he said, determined to seek justice for his niece.

Maurice patted his old friend on the back and gave a big sigh.

For the first time in all his years of funeral service, Harvey Eyre was at a loss for words.

CHAPTER FIVE

"Children should not attend funerals. I will need you to watch Elizabeth during the service and lay out dinner for all the guests in attendance. The mourners who are traveling a long distance will need a substantial meal. Make sure the Smithfield ham is sliced paper thin. It's been soaking in cold water for hours and hopefully won't be too salty for dinner. The sweet potato biscuits will need warming at the last minute," Elizabeth heard Nana order Blanche. "Oh, and be sure the fried chicken has a crispy brown crust and the meat inside isn't dry. I left my largest cast iron skillet on the stove. Let's see, the cornbread and greens are in the Frigidaire," she rambled incessantly opening the door. "You know, Blanche, from the mountains of Virginia to the Virginian Eastern Shore, there is a Southern way of life and it begins with hospitality and a proper emphasis on good cooking," she said sagely.

"Yes ma'am, Miss Margaret. I has a list you left me. The women from my church will be here by ten o'clock. Everything will be set out on the table by the time you get back from the grave," Blanche promised. She had been working since dawn getting the kitchen in order with precision.

Margaret, because of her upbringing, referred to lunch as dinner and dinner as supper, and evening began promptly in the late afternoon, causing Alfred to imbibe with a Virginia Gentleman cocktail in hand as early as four o'clock.

Margaret was in her realm organizing and instructing Blanche for the large repast. Old Southern traditions die hard and it was just part of her being to entertain family and friends with home-cooked feasts. "No time to grieve. That will come later," she repeated under her breath.

Having been raised on a large farm just outside of town, Margaret's mother and the farmhands' wives would start at daybreak cooking a large dinner to serve the workers at noon. The men spent their mornings walking behind a horse-drawn plow or performing the grueling, back-breaking tasks of picking cotton and scything tobacco leaves. They were starved by the time they entered the farmhouse kitchen. The long, oak table with random chairs of every size provided a place they could rest until the main meal of the day was devoured. The laborers' eyes grew wide with appreciation as they blinked and salivated over the expansive amounts of food. The table groaned with the weight of white ironstone platters piled high with chicken—fried in black iron skillets heated in lard until it sizzled. The birds had been slaughtered and plucked that very morning. Succotash of lima beans and corn was thrown in the pot with ham hocks added for salty flavor. The mix permeated the air as it simmered slowly. Vegetables would nourish the men who had planted, tended, and harvested the fields. Summer was the season to pickle the peaches and can the ripe, juicy tomatoes and green beans. At summer's end, red and green peppers were gathered for grinding to make canned pepper relish in Ball jars which lined the pantry shelves and joined the other colorful glass containers. When autumn arrived, Margaret and her mother would retrieve the larger stew pots from the pantry. A combination of chicken broth and water with handfuls of salt would boil on high heat until the hen was stewed. Dough was rolled out with a rolling pin until paper thin, cut in squares by the blade of a sharp knife, and dropped into the scalding pot. Chicken and dumplings boiling on top of the old wood stove would scent the farmhouse.

As a young girl, Margaret derived satisfaction from having people enjoy her cooking, but this day was different. Her daughter was gone. She couldn't think, being in such pain with all the confusing emotions running through her. It would be very easy to go to bed and grieve, just like her husband was doing. Pressing her hands to the sides of her head, she closed her eyes. "I'll think about that tomorrow, not now," she whispered, swallowing the lump in her throat.

"Thank goodness for you, Blanche. You have stood by this family through thick and thin, but this day is an absolute nightmare." Her expression pleaded for consolation from the girl that was her daughter's age.

"The good Lord will watch over us." Blanche gave Margaret a pained look in return.

Blanche was a four-greats grandchild to one of the women who had been with Margaret's family forever. Her ancestors had been manumitted after the Civil War but chose to rent the cabins on the farm and continue to work for Margaret's family. Blanche and Elizabeth had bonded immediately upon the second day of her arrival in Sycamore Creek.

Margaret called Blanche the night of the crime and asked her to stay with the Eyre's family and assist them with all the tasks at hand. Blanche also worked and lived at the funeral parlor where she cooked and cleaned for Alfred's brother, Harvey—watching over him like a mother hen.

The day after Elizabeth's arrival, Blanche prepared dinner—a southern lunch served at noon exactly. "Blanche, why is your place setting on the kitchen work table and not in the dining room with ours?" Elizabeth asked.

"That just the way it is. I don't make the rules. My mama always say if common sense was lard, most peoples wouldn't be able to grease the pan. Don't ask questions, chile. It make no never mind to me."

"It does to me. I don't want you to be lonely, Blanche," Elizabeth stated with conviction. She promptly moved her place setting from the dining room into the kitchen next to her new best friend.

They became inseparable from that day forward. Although Elizabeth had broken Southern protocol, Margaret never acknowledged that a new generation was now in the house. She graciously accepted that everything had its day even if it meant fracturing the rules of Southern standards.

"I knows I'm little, but I have a strong voice and grip. It makes up for my blew eyes—one blew east, one blew west. My mama say, I was no bigger than a minute when I was born," Blanche would throw her head back and laugh so loud that the china in the cabinet would rattle.

"Come here, Miss 'Lizabeth and let Blanche sing you her favorite hymn," she said patting the rocker as Elizabeth squeezed in beside her.

The song was "Amazing Grace."

"The story go like this: John Newton was a sea captain on the *Greyhound*, a slave ship. Journeyin' home he got caught in a violent storm and just know'd he was about to meet his maker. The waves was a comin' up over the ship as it rocked side to side. He was at the steerin' wheel, prayin' like there was no tomorrow, and with that the sea growed calm. The Holy Ghost touch him, and he went to his cabin and wrote the tune of a song the slaves sang all the way home. The captain had promised the Lord he would set the slaves free when they reached shore and that's what he done. My peoples have sung Amazin' Grace throughout the years. Lord, have mercy, chile, it be our song."

Elizabeth felt at ease as Blanche sang low and soulful, belting out the lyrics.

"That's pretty," Elizabeth raised her head smiling up at her. "Sing it again, please."

"White peoples cain't sing black gospel chile, I do declare," Blanche muttered under her breath, stroking Elizabeth's blonde curls. "When you grow up and want to feel closer to God, you remember the hymns ole Blanche teach you and they will calm your nerves," she promised as the two formed a sacred trust.

The four days after Suzanne's death had been a flurry in the Victorian home. Sets of china had been washed, the antique silver polished until it gleamed, and white taper candles were ready for lighting, all thanks to Margaret's Episcopal Church friends and the Sycamore Creek Garden Club. Blanche had hovered over the ironing board for hours, pressing tablecloths that would cover all the additional folding card tables the bridge club loaned Margaret.

"I'll make these linen napkins stand up on their own," Blanche huffed as she poured starch over them in the sink.

The morning of the funeral, Blanche was at the ready as her church choir members strolled through the back door. They went to their stations in the kitchen without a word of explanation or direction. Food was warmed and spooned into china bowls lined up in the butler's pantry. The meats were arranged on platters, garnished with kale and fruit. The ladies brewed sweet tea by the gallons and perked Maxwell House coffee in percolators borrowed from the parish hall. The dining room table groaned as the repast seemed to grow and expand in front of Elizabeth's eyes.

"Blanche, may I have a cookie, please?" Elizabeth asked as her eyes darted toward the sideboard, ogling the display. It was a child's delight laden with cakes, pies, and every type of cookie one could only imagine. Arranging the desserts last, Blanche and company executed the feat as though it were an everyday occurrence.

"Southerners can eat. Them white folks will fill their belly's free of charge today! You just wait and see." Blanche chuckled not acknowledging Elizabeth's question about the cookie.

"I don't know why I can't go to Mommy's funeral at the Episcopal Church? I can see it from my bedroom window. Why do I have to stay here? I don't know how to cook," Elizabeth pressed and began to whine.

"You're staying here with me, chile. You can trust me, talk to me, and come to me anytime you need to. Now come here and gimme me some sugar."

Elizabeth looked up to see her father walk down the massive staircase in his dark suit, starched white shirt, and Brooks Brothers small patterned tie. He had been subdued since his arrival, always with a rocks glass in his trembling hand. At night, Elizabeth could hear faint crying coming from his closed bedroom door.

"I love you, Daddy," Elizabeth said as she walked towards him.

"I'll take care of you for the rest of your life. Your daddy is here," he managed to say as a lump thickened his throat—it was the only reply he could manage to utter.

Alfred and Margaret descended the stairs behind Edward. Margaret had dressed her husband in his navy suit that he wore only to funerals. Alfred never dressed up and Elizabeth thought her grandfather looked older. His face was strained, and he avoided eye contact with everyone. He preferred to handle the heartache by spending the days leading up to the funeral in his bedroom alone. Nana had taken daily meals to him on a tray which he refused.

"I'm not hungry. Please let me be," Alfred would mumble as his granddaughter eavesdropped outside the door.

Elizabeth fixed her eyes on her grandmother. The knit black dress accentuated her salt and pepper hair, a pillbox black hat with a veil covered half of her face. Pearls, pumps, and nails were polished to perfection on the saddest day of her life.

"You look elegant, Miss Margaret," Blanche softly said.

Feeling uncomfortable, Elizabeth cast her eyes downward and pretended to play with her Barbie Dolls. Aware and tuned in to the conversations around her, she was ready for everyone to go home so she could have Nana and Blanche all to herself again.

"Your mother will be buried at the church. We'll be able to see her grave from the house. She'll always be watching over you," Nana said sharing the only detail about her daughter's funeral with her granddaughter.

Elizabeth's family left the house to begin the solemn walk to the church. Her mother would be buried in the Episcopal Church yard. The grave was on the right, in front of the church and marked with an old Celtic marble cross monument stained with mildew. Raised letters in Old English with the name Eyre protruded from the stone.

Elizabeth walked in the kitchen watching Blanche organize her choir friends quietly, instructing them with last minute details.

"We won't let your Nana down, Miss 'Lizabeth; this will be some good eatin'. I'll make this dinner Margaret style," Blanche assured her, proud of being an Eyre employee in front of her friends.

A lonely feeling enveloped Elizabeth as she climbed to the top of the stairs and entered her room. She went to the bookcase in the room where her mother had grown up and pulled *Grimm's Fairy Tales* off the shelf. She plopped down in the wing chair next to the turret. The autumn sun filtered through the window, casting a warm glow of quiet sacredness as her mother's Burial of the Dead: Rite One service was about to begin.

Elizabeth heard car doors slam up and down Market Street as the mourners strolled slowly to the parish. The attire of the morning was black suits and wool dress coats worn by the men and the ladies that accompanied them were stately adorned in black dresses topped with mink stoles. Squinting, she peered through the branches of the Sycamore trees, which allowed her a perfect view of the church entrance.

A large black vehicle arrived, and Uncle Harvey exited from the driver's side. Six men in dark suits walked to the back and Uncle Harvey instructed them to line up on either side facing one another. He opened the door and started rolling out a box that looked shiny as a new penny.

"I found this brand-new copper penny on the sidewalk today, Elizabeth. It will bring you good luck," Suzanne had told her daughter last summer. Elizabeth remembered the moment when her mother placed the coin in her tiny, outstretched hand.

Elizabeth was mesmerized by the scene unfolding in the pane of the window. Her nose pressed against the glass as she stared without blinking.

"That's my mommy," she said out loud to no one.

Edward, Alfred, and Margaret followed the shiny box into the parish. Elizabeth stood frozen—unable to move, afraid of missing any final connection she may have with the copper box. Unable to open the book to gaze at the illustrations or sit still, she nervously shifted from one leg to the other in front of the turret window.

Time seemed like an eternity until finally the red doors opened, and Father Henderson appeared leading the procession with the deacon carrying a golden cross in front of him. They both wore white robes and black stoles. Father Henderson was reading from an open book as he walked to the Eyre cross. The same men in black suits carried the shiny copper box to the open grave. Elizabeth watched her father and grandfather walk on each side of her grandmother. The two men were overcome with grief, sobbing and blowing their noses into their white handkerchiefs. Her eyes locked on her grandmother, head held high walking with dignity, refinement, and grace as she followed her daughter to her place of rest.

"I love you, Mommy," Elizabeth uttered under her breath as the bell in the church belfry tolled twenty-five times.

CHAPTER SIX

"Where is Auntie Eleanor, Nana? I miss her. She always smells pretty," Elizabeth whined.

Eleanor was family and Elizabeth could not understand why she hadn't been around the past week, among all the cousins, great aunts, uncles and the entire community of Sycamore Creek, coming and going through the massive mahogany door. The rockers on the large wrap-around porch were in constant motion occupied with people rocking with unease, a sweet tea or a stronger libation in hand, always communicating in hushed tones.

"Doesn't she know Mommy had an accident and is in heaven with wings, Nana?" Elizabeth inquired. "She's the only one that's not been here to see us."

"She's out of town on bank business. She'll come when she returns," she answered, gazing downward, voice just above a whisper. Elizabeth watched her grandmother intently, thinking that she would never see her smile or laugh again after this mysterious week.

"When?" Elizabeth asked.

"Soon," Margaret replied.

She was persistent. "Tomorrow?"

Margaret replied with silence.

Elizabeth had always believed her mother and Eleanor were sisters. When Eleanor had moved into the Norfolk rancher, she had hoped that she would live with them forever. There were numerous evenings in which she would cuddle in the arms of her Auntie Eleanor who read bedtime stories to her—one after another as Elizabeth always asked for more. The search for a job at the biggest bank in the city had only lasted two weeks, enabling Eleanor to rent an apartment. Elizabeth remembered climbing three flights of stairs in an old Victorian home to help her mother and Auntie carry what she could on moving day.

"I'll miss you, Auntie Eleanor. I know I'll live here sometime soon with you." she rattled on and on.

"Elizabeth, you can't leave home just yet." Suzanne chuckled as she hugged her daughter.

Suzanne was lost without her cousin and anticipated her stopping by every evening at 5:15pm sharp. She'd burst through the front door as Suzanne was garnishing her gin and tonic with a freshly sliced lime.

Like clockwork she would ask "Do you know where I can find a good gin and tonic around here? The bar wench service is slower than a Sunday afternoon."

"You came to the right place, so hush your mouth," Suzanne would tease. "Remember Elizabeth, never say shut up its impolite. You should say hush instead." She knew her daughter's little ears didn't miss a word.

Eleanor was a clotheshorse like her cousin, creating friendly competition as to who could accessorize with the most flair and delighting in the ensuing conflict. Her hair was a beautiful sable shade of brunette that made her hazel green eyes twinkle with naughtiness. Olive-toned skin made an attractive opposition to her cousin's fair prettiness. They were endlessly aware of causing a stir as they walked through the busy streets of Norfolk, turning the heads of sailors fresh on leave from the aircraft carriers.

Walking in from the bank, Eleanor was dressed in a suit, matching high heel pumps, clutch, and the strand of pearls—a necessity. Never for want of a suitor, she cherished girl time with Suzanne. "The next best thing to being with a man is talking about them," Eleanor mused.

With the ever-present twinkle in her eye and a soft smile, she would tease Elizabeth incessantly about her afternoon tea parties. Guests included Thumbelina, Chatty Cathy, and the ever-present Billy Bunny with missing tail who was always head of the table. It had been convenient for the toddler to drag him along by his tail as she learned to walk.

"Let me take Billy Bunny to my apartment and sew another tail on him. He'll look good as new," Eleanor teased, knowing she would not part with her faithful companion.

"Mommy, Auntie Eleanor is being mean again!"

Suzanne would intervene, and the teasing would begin again, cocktail in one hand, cigarette in the other. Eleanor would discuss the bank gossip du jour, but only after the heels were slipped off and feet tucked under her. Round two of stirring up trouble would start when Edward walked through the door making Eleanor's mission complete, the real agitation about to begin.

Suzanne and Edward loved martinis and would orchestra their mixology with panache and drama. It was an evening ritual that began with chilling the martini glasses, placing them in the freezer an hour before cocktails were served.

Susanne always made hers first, arguing she liked it stirred, which was the proper way of mixing the gin and adding a splash of vermouth. Edward, however, was a James Bond fan and preferred his martini shaken, not stirred. It was a constant battle between the two of them, with Suzanne proclaiming that Edward's mixology bruised the vermouth. Eleanor reveled and enjoyed the theatrics by putting her two cents in, knowing that the show was for her benefit.

Five o'clock sharp the silver shaker, v-shaped stemware, and the crystal bowl of olives displayed on a silver tray were brought out of the kitchen and placed on the coffee table, looking magical and adding to the ceremony. The couple would toast each other clinking their glasses and kissing on the lips. Things were not so romantic by the third glass as disputes—about nothing substantial—would rise along with voices, for which Eleanor would gleefully act as referee.

"Please stop fighting!" Elizabeth cried.

The three of them would stop abruptly and all was well again until six o'clock the following evening.

All in good time, the mystery of the missing Eleanor was solved when Margaret proclaimed that Auntie Eleanor was moving back to Sycamore Creek to be closer to the family, particularly Elizabeth.

While mourners continued to stream into the Eyre's home, Eleanor was recuperating in St. Mary's Hospital where Stephen Dennis had dumped her. She was miraculously able to whisper the details of her ordeal to the surgeon in the emergency room as the blood still dripped from her wounds. As she was slumped over in the chair at the crime scene, she remembered a second bullet entering her neck and heard an explosion as it lodged in the roof of her mouth, breaking her jaw and loosening her teeth. She tried not to choke on the blood.

"I was shot and raped twice. Please help me. I've been raped," she pleaded trying to give details.

"I will," the young surgeon assured her.

The wounds where the first bullet pierced her crossed leg, entering one and exiting the other, had to be stitched.

"I've been raped," Eleanor repeated as she grew paler in color.

"I'm going to examine you and take you into surgery," the doctor stated. Not once had he ever seen anything of this magnitude so early in his career. He prayed, full of faith, that under no circumstances would he make any mistakes because he knew this patient's tribulation was going to become a court case. The surgeon executed a pelvic examination and swabbed a sperm specimen from her vagina.

Upon awaking the next morning, nurses, as instructed, gave her a liquid sedative to keep her calm. Eleanor's mouth had been wired shut due to her broken jaw.

"If you do not start your menstrual cycle within the month, we will transfer you to the Jewish hospital a few blocks away where an abortion will be performed immediately," said the surgeon.

Eleanor just gazed at him, sedated, confused—in absolute and total shock.

Evelyn and Richard Johnson, Eleanor's parents, were constantly by her side. They continued to wait for her in a private room where she began the recovery stages after the intense surgery. When she became coherent enough to remember what had happened, she began to ask questions.

"Where is Suzanne, mother?

"In the hospital."

"How many times was she shot?"

"Multiple."

"Where."

"Several places. Now, you get some rest, honey, and we'll talk tomorrow."

"She's dead, isn't she?"

No one spoke.

"Isn't she?"

Evelyn and Richard looked at each other and replied, "Oh, honey, she's gone."

"Stephen Dennis killed her," Eleanor sobbed.

The evening before, while Eleanor's parents waited in the lobby of the hospital, the Norfolk Police Department detectives began to brief them: "Mr. and Mrs. Johnson, we are sorry to inform you that at five-fifteen this evening your niece, Suzanne Barclay, was shot multiple times and died of gunshot wounds at her residence. Your daughter was shot in the legs and back of the neck. She was raped twice. These are words no parent should ever have to hear. We are sorry about the passing of your niece and the trauma inflicted upon your daughter. Stephen Dennis has been booked and is in the custody of our department. We will keep you informed."

A kind nurse stopped to ask, "May I bring you anything, something to calm your nerves or a cup of coffee?"

As they sat stunned, shocked and nauseated, wondering how in God's name this had happened and why, the operating surgeon emerged.

"Are you Eleanor Johnson's parents?" he asked.

"Yes," they said as they rose to their feet.

"Your daughter is stabilized. I have removed the bullet that was lodged in the roof of her mouth. Her jaw will be wired shut for the next few weeks. I assure you, an oral surgeon can repair the teeth and bite in the next several months as she recovers. I have stitched the wounds, and as her legs heal, she will slowly begin to walk again. Your daughter has been traumatized and needs to be confined to bedrest during the next six weeks or more depending on her speed of recovery. Her whole system is in a complete state of shock."

"How can she lead a normal life after what that bastard did to her? There will be no normalcy in her life again. Suzanne's the lucky one—God bless her heart. She won't have to live with the memories. I will kill him!" Richard said between forlorn sobs.

At that point, the detectives decided to place Eleanor's father under surveillance to avoid another felony. He would remain under scrutiny until Stephen Dennis was permanently incarcerated to avoid a father's wrath.

Eleanor's young age of twenty-three worked in her favor during the healing process and she was released from the hospital after seven days. Nurses and doctors kissed her goodbye, giving her a round of applause as she walked—refusing to sit in a wheelchair—as she left the hospital.

"I love you all. Thank you from the bottom of my heart," Eleanor responded as she limped to the car on crutches.

"God bless you," a nurse called back. She had been the one in the emergency room the day Stephen Dennis brought his victim in. A day on the job she never would forget.

Eleanor's father sat in the driver's seat and her mother stayed by her side in the backseat for the journey home. On the ferry, crossing the Chesapeake Bay, she asked her mother to walk with her to the lady's room. Constantly looking over her shoulder and aware of everyone around her, she realized this was just the beginning of the paranoia that had set in and would last a lifetime. In the lady's room, she discovered she had started her menstrual cycle. "I started my period, Mother!" she yelled from inside the stall.

"Oh, thank God, honey!"

Eleanor bowed her head and thanked the Lord she was not pregnant with Suzanne's killer's baby. Her cousin's death had left a hole in her heart. She refused to bear a reminder of that tragic day by looking into the eyes of a child whose father was a cold-blooded killer. When she emerged from the stall, Eleanor's mother held her daughter in her arms as the ferry rocked and swayed in the turbulent bay, tears streaming down their cheeks.

Turbulence was just beginning for the entire family. The next nine years would involve battling the legal system, which only brought more havoc into their lives. Eleanor was not capable of living alone and moved into her childhood home with her parents, eventually making her home in Vermont, estranging herself from Sycamore Creek.

"Eleanor is having nightmares constantly. She wakes up the entire household with her terror-stricken screams. She repeatedly yells, 'Run, Suzanne, run!'" her mother confided in Margaret.

"May God have mercy on this family," Margaret replied.

"I'm going to kill that bastard if it's the last thing I do," said Richard.

CHAPTER SEVEN

The morning after her daughter's funeral service Margaret had an odd feeling of being disconnected from all that was familiar. Her world had been turned upside down and now she had a five-year-old to raise.

"Hail Mary full of grace," she said, feeling as if Mother Mary understood her plight.

Blanche had stayed until late in the night washing dishes, wrapping the silver in gray silver cloth, and running the Electrolux across the oriental rugs until the house was back in order. Margaret thanked her as she left, slipping an envelope of cash in her coat pocket before she walked up the street to Sycamore Creek Funeral Home. Their eyes had met, both blinking back tears of sorrow with an understanding of the shared loss.

Buttoning up the collar of her coat, Blanche held it to her neck with one hand, stepping off the porch onto the brick sidewalk. The fog had rolled in off the creek as the night's autumnal wind grew colder in contrast to the warm sunny day. Private thoughts of Suzanne started to flood her mind and it was her turn to weep for the girl she had grown up with. She remembered when she was little her mother would bring her to work at the Eyre's house. Suzanne had been thrilled to have a playmate and they spent afternoons in the boxwood maze perfecting their skills of hide and seek. Miss Margaret would stir homemade cocoa on top of the stove, serving it with a large marshmallow for an extra special treat. They sat at the oak table and giggled. It was just like she did the other day with Elizabeth. These were precious memories. Waves of grief enveloped her as she walked into the church graveyard and found herself in front of the Celtic Cross that was now Suzanne Eyre Barclay's final place of rest.

"I'm fixin' to watch over your chile. She be safe at Sycamore Creek, Suzanne. I intend to help Miss Margaret raise her up to be as nice and kind as you was, bless your heart, as long as there's breath in my body.

I know you looking down on me; please ax Jesus to help us." Tears ran down Blanche's face.

"Blanche, I do declare, what takes you out here this time of night? I thought to myself I better check up on your whereabouts when I realized how late it was."

"Mr. Harvey! You done scared me to death, sneakin' up on me in this fog. It be thick as my mamma's pea soup out here."

"It's time to come home; you'll catch a cold in all this Eastern Shore dew. I don't need you to do anything at the funeral parlor tonight."

They walked to the funeral home in silence except for Blanche's sniffles in the cold air of the night. Entering the back door, Harvey walked into the foyer and climbed the massive staircase to his bedroom. Blanche had a room off the kitchen pantry with a twin-size bed and small table and chair. Here she could sit and read her Bible by a milk glass lamp with a matching glass hen. The hen's top could be removed for storage at the bottom. It was a perfect receptacle for her bobby pins, safety pins, and sewing needles complete with a spool of black thread cotton for emergencies.

"Goodnight, Blanche, Thanks for all you have done for this family in the past several days. Go ahead and sleep late in the morning. I'll fix my own breakfast," Harvey called from the stair landing.

"Thank you, Mr. Harvey," she called back gratefully, hoping to finally get some rest. Suzanne's death had taken a toll on her. Every bone in her body ached, but nothing compared to her heart.

Margaret's mind was going a mile a minute as she contemplated the tasks she would need to complete during the next couple of weeks. There were copious amounts of thank-you notes to write and send to all the generous people who gave flowers, food, and their time assisting the family at the service and reception. A Garden Club friend had meticulously kept track and written down in a condolence record every kindness the community had performed for the family. By nature, Margaret was always in control of events surrounding her, but this crisis had left her dazed and confused. Taking time to send a handwritten thank-you card was the ultimate display of proper breeding and it had to be done before the week was over and in her handwriting.

However, her main focus was on Elizabeth's future. She needed to talk to Edward about Suzanne's estate and advise him to set up a trust fund for Elizabeth's future as well as college education. *I know he'll remarry. He's such a playboy. Elizabeth needs to be enrolled in St. Paul's Episcopal Day School immediately*, she thought to herself. Her mind was jumping from one thought to another. The sharp pang of reality set down upon her and it was almost too much to bear. She quickly sat down in a kitchen chair as a wave of dizziness came over her. Holding her head up with her hands she allowed the spell to pass.

"Please Lord, give me strength," she prayed out loud as she filled the percolator with scoops of coffee.

"You're up early," Edward said standing in the doorway. "How's Alfred?"

"I ... I don't know. He was sleepless and filled with anxiety in the night. The funeral was practically unbearable for him. All he does is cry. He feels so guilty. Dr. Lewis is making a house call this afternoon. I expect him after dinner. What are your plans, Edward?"

"I think I'll stay until Elizabeth wakes up and leave for the office from here. Hopefully I'll catch the late morning ferry."

"Edward, there are a few matters we need to discuss. The District Attorney wants to meet with us this week. The indictments should be handed down soon, I can only hope and pray. There's no question in my mind that mad dog should be executed soon," Margaret said in a low tone. Her mouth grew dry.

"Don't worry, Margaret. I have connections in Norfolk. He won't last for long in that town."

"Edward, I beg of you to let the courts handle it. I don't want anything else happening to this family, no matter what connections you have."

Margaret placed two cups and saucers of coffee on the kitchen table, and they sat in silence, sipping. With the first cup swallowed, Margaret poured a second and said, "Edward, Suzanne always asked me if anything ever happened to her would I raise Elizabeth in my home? I know you were married and are Elizabeth's father, but I promised my daughter I would be Elizabeth's caregiver and raise her in Sycamore Creek. Please don't fight me on this."

"Margaret, I'm glad you brought the subject up. I travel extensively on business, and a motherless young girl needs to be with her grandmother. I don't know the first thing about how to raise a child. I will pay for her needs, of course. I want her to have a good education and be exposed to the nicer things in life, like her ... her mother. Suzanne's Will and Testament states that Elizabeth will inherit the house and all its contents when she turns eighteen. I'll take care of having it professionally cleaned. I saw blood everywhere, walls, chairs, floor, and bloody fingerprints in the kitchen."

Margaret raised her hand so Edward would stop talking. She didn't want to contemplate the carnage and aftermath of the gruesome crime. The less she heard and knew, the better—vowing never to step foot in the rancher again.

"Isn't your name on the house?" she looked at Edward with a puzzled expression.

"Margaret, I have something to tell you." He looked down sheepishly. "Suzanne and I divorced over a year ago."

"But you celebrated your anniversary last August at the hotel. She was radiant and so happy. I don't understand ... Suzanne would have told me. We were close!" She glared at Edward as her disbelief grew from shock to anger. Years of avoiding her son-in-law's cruelty had finally come to a head and she erupted, "You were never true to her—out most nights cheating and gambling with money that should have been given to your family. All you ever cared about were fancy sport cars, clubs, and whores! You mistreated my daughter, even the wedding ring on her finger was won in a poker game," Margaret spewed.

"I'll make it up to Elizabeth. Our divorce was a secret from her as well. We wanted life to be as normal for our child as possible." Edward hung his head in shame.

"Suzanne confided in me that you often came home in the wee hours of the morning drunk with lipstick on your collar!"

"I'll talk to my attorney and the life insurance company to make sure everything is in trust for my daughter." Edward rose slowly from the table and made his way upstairs to Elizabeth's room, hoping the confrontation with Margaret was final. *If I could only turn back the clock*, he thought with regret.

Margaret sat stunned, trying to absorb Edward's words. *Why in the world would Suzanne keep their divorce from me?* It broke her heart thinking her daughter was living a lie, being too ashamed to come to them for help, emotionally and financially. She saw it in his eyes; it was obvious Edward did not want to discuss the matter. He had avoided Margaret's questioning gaze.

"Honey, are you awake?" Edward rapped softly on Elizabeth's door.

"Yes, Daddy."

"May I come in?"

"Yes, sir."

Edward sat on the edge of the bed and looked into his child's eyes. "Daddy is going to leave this morning. I must be at work. I'm way behind on my accounts. I promise you I'll visit on weekends and holidays. You'll be living here with your grandparents and attending St. Paul's Episcopal Day School. I know you'll be happy here. Your mother was."

"Yes, sir." Elizabeth had already made up her mind she was never leaving Sycamore Creek—ever. She had Nana, Poppy, and Blanche. Her father leaned over and kissed the top of her forehead.

"Oh, Daddy, guess what? Nana says I'll be in Miss Yvonne's ballet class. I'm supposed to start next Saturday for my first dance lesson. Miss Yvonne's coming this week to measure my feet for ballet slippers." Elizabeth raised her arms over her head in a circle as if she was a ballerina already.

"Just like your mother," Edward murmured.

Edward quietly slipped out the front door, avoiding contact with his former in-laws. *After all*, he thought, *there is nothing left to say*. Margaret would do things her way, and he would be lucky to see Elizabeth on his terms now that she knew Suzanne's and his secret. He started the car and looked up at the turret where Suzanne had grown into a lovely young woman and wished the same for his daughter. Backing out of the driveway and onto Market Street, a wave of grief engulfed him. He began to weep.

Driving down Market Street, Edward dried his tears, turning his head toward the graveyard where the only woman he had truly loved was buried. He stopped the car when he saw a dark haired man standing at Suzanne's grave, his collar turned upwards against the mist of the morning fog. In the crook of his arm rested an enormous bouquet of red roses. The stranger knelt at the grave on one knee and placed the flowers at the head of the freshly dug mound of dirt, burying his face into his hands as waves of uncontrollable sobbing wracked his body. Edward turned the ignition off and hastily exited the vehicle, walking towards the mysterious man.

"Hello, Edward," the man said looking up.

"Bill ... Bill Callias. What are you doing here?" Bill had been a client of Edward's in the Norfolk area for several years.

Bill blew his nose in his white handkerchief and with a pained expression considered whether to tell Suzanne's ex-husband the reason. "The night Suzanne was murdered I was going to ask her to marry me."

Edward felt the ground give way from underneath him for the second time that week. He glared at the foreigner, abruptly turned and with an angry stride reached his car. Squealing the tires, he sped towards the ferry.

"Goddamn Greek," he muttered.

"Alfred, are you getting out of bed today?" Margaret asked as she walked into their bedroom. The curtains were drawn shut so no light could enter the room. Turning on the brass lamp atop the night table, she studied her husband: blanket over his head and lying in the fetal position.

"I'm really worried about you, honey. Please try to get your robe on and meet me in the kitchen for a cup of coffee. Dr. Lewis is stopping by this afternoon to give you some medication and maybe a shot to calm your nerves."

"I don't need Dr. Lewis or anybody else," he said as he adamantly shook his head. "Go away and leave me be!"

Margaret turned her back on Alfred and exited the room, full of worry that she had lost him as well. Feeling alone, she wondered how she would manage raising her grandchild without the support of Alfred or Edward, the only two males in her life except for Harvey and she contemplated what the future had in store for their family regarding Stephen Dennis. She hoped she could hold up for everyone who was counting on her strength.

She feared the magnitude of it all was more than she could bear.

Then and there, Margaret made up her mind: she was the only one with a strong will and the endurance to show Elizabeth that life could go on. Any outward displays of sadness and grief in front of the child were unacceptable. With a rush of adrenaline, she felt in high gear and began planning activities that would preoccupy her granddaughter's time. *Harvey will help me*, Margaret reasoned as she picked up the receiver with a newfound sense of purpose.

"Hello, Sycamore Creek Funeral Home."

"Harvey, do you mind taking Elizabeth to the Aspirin Horse Farm this afternoon? She starts her riding lessons after ballet class on Saturday. I'm trying to keep life as normal as possible around here for the sake of that child."

Harvey could hear the anxiousness in her voice. "I'll call Betty Aspirin as soon as we get off the telephone. I'm free this afternoon and Elizabeth and I can have uncle and niece time together."

"Oh, thank you. Elizabeth adores you. Your brother is still in bed and refuses to shower and shave let alone come downstairs and eat a little something. Yesterday after the funeral he went straight to our room and never greeted any of the guests in our own home."

"As you know, Margaret, depression runs in the Eyre family. Suzanne's death will be a real setback for Alfred. To be honest with you, I don't know if he'll ever get over it."

Margaret swallowed hard. "Dr. Lewis will be here in a couple of hours. I have so much to do I don't know where to start. I feel so overwhelmed," she said.

"You have not allowed yourself time to rest or properly grieve, Margaret. Please take care of yourself."

With that, the conversation ended and Margaret went into the kitchen to prepare breakfast for Elizabeth, her favorite—cinnamon toast and hot cocoa.

Harvey felt a pang of dread cross over him. He had planned a day trip to Richmond, spending the afternoon and early evening with his lover, Bernard, before heading back to Sycamore Creek. Bernard worked for a funeral home in the city and today was his day off.

Bernard takes poorly to change, Harvey reflected. *I guess I better get this over with and give him a ring with my change of plans*, he thought, worried that the conversation would not go smoothly.

"Hello," Bernard answered the phone matter-of-factly.

"Hello, darlin'. How have you been?" Harvey asked, trying to prolong the conversation and not wanting to state the reason for his call.

Bernard responded with a sigh, "I'm so tired, running all over hell's half-acre. We have had seven calls at the funeral home this week. That averages out to one a day and, of course, they all wanted to make funeral arrangements with me. Our morgue rat has put in overtime for embalming and dressing, so I had to work in the prep room as well. The owner of the funeral home is so pleased with me; he thinks I'm the reason for his business doubling. I've made such a difference here, and I don't know why he won't give me a raise. After all, he'll never have another employee of my caliber that cares as much as I do."

Harvey listened patiently as Bernard jabbered on. *One thing he's not is humble. Maybe it's because he's twenty-five years younger and must prove himself to me*, Harvey considered.

"I had a rough week with the unexpected death of my niece," Harvey interrupted. "Alfred and Margaret wanted to view Suzanne privately. It took me a long time to get the swelling down from her face. They had posted the head and body. The medical examiner dotted his I's and crossed his T's, knowing this would be a court case. I'm exhausted as well. I tried to make her look as beautiful as she did in life, but I failed. I did the best I could."

Bernard grew quiet as Harvey had taken the wind out of his sails.

"Listen, it doesn't suit me to drive down today. Margaret is counting on me to babysit Elizabeth for the afternoon. We are driving to the Aspirin Riding Stables today. The sooner she gets acclimated to Sycamore Creek the better, bless her little heart."

"So, Elizabeth is going to take precedence over me now. I see how it's going to be. I get one day off a week and you can't drive down here for a fabulous gourmet dinner. I shopped at the finest market last night and bought filet mignon. We were going to dine on filets with béarnaise sauce, scalloped potatoes, asparagus, and pot de crème for desert. I've spent a fortune, a fortune! Maybe that cute little tart Sydney would enjoy my cooking. He's the up and coming designer for all the bluebloods in the city now."

"For God's sake, Bernard! It's just this one time. Quit making a mountain out of a mole hill," Harvey stated, feeling at his wit's end.

"Put yourself in my shoes, Harvey. The funeral home would have to close permanently if I wasn't here. I have a lot on my plate keeping these old families in Richmond satisfied."

"I'm sorry, darlin'. You know I can't invite you to Sycamore Creek. The townspeople don't know I'm an old queer. You're so flamboyant—the farmers here would suspect something odd right away. If the Creek knew about my lifestyle, business would shut down immediately. They would be sure to boycott me, and I just can't take that chance."

"If you lived down here you would be free as a bird. There's a whole community of us," Bernard sniffed.

"I'll call you later tonight. You're about to have one of your hissy fits," Harvey said. He wanted the conversation to be done and over with, but Bernard ended it by slamming the receiver down on its cradle, finalizing the scene to his self-perpetuated never-ending drama.

"Arrogant little twerp. He's always been so self-absorbed," Harvey muttered under his breath. Harvey had experienced tornadic years since he and Bernard had been lovers. It was like living in a hornet's nest. Lost in deep thought about his family's plight, he steadied himself to become Elizabeth's father figure.

CHAPTER EIGHT

The Superintendent of the Virginia State Mental Hospital and Dr. Charles North, its clinical director, reported to the court that Stephen Dennis was considered mentally competent and able to testify in his own defense. They further stated that they found nothing in the history of his behavior in jail to indicate the presence of any psychosis, and in their opinion, he was without psychosis during the period of his incarceration.

Dennis's trial would move forward.

On February 1, 1961 at the request of Stephen Dennis, the court appointed William Schiff, an experienced attorney, as his counsel, Stephen had been indicted for the murder of Suzanne Barclay. Five days later, four other indictments were found against Stephen Dennis: one for malicious shooting with intent to maim, disfigure, disable and kill Eleanor Johnson; two for committing rape on Eleanor Johnson; and one for committing rape upon Suzanne Barclay.

The trial date was set for April 17, 1961.

In a letter to his mother, he wrote: "I'll fight till the end. I ain't ready to die no longer. I may be dead in a year, but you can help me, Mama. Yes, I done it, but my attorney says anyone who did what I done is insane. I told him I dreamed about it and would go do it again. I would. Some people are just born to die. I know I put you through a lot in your life, but you can tell them how sick I was growin' up. I've been in a hospital just like this one before. It ain't so bad. It's up to you, Mama."

"Oh, thank you Dr. Lewis for coming to the house once again," Margaret whispered so Elizabeth wouldn't hear her. She was just returning from first grade. "I don't think the drugs you prescribed are working. He won't get out of bed, only to go to the bathroom. I bathe and shave him every day. He stares at the ceiling or covers his head with the bedlinens."

"I cannot believe he's lost so much weight in a month. I've never had a patient so severely depressed. It's obvious he is overwhelmed with Suzanne's untimely death," Dr. Lewis said, shaking his head. He was standing behind the closed door of Alfred's bedroom.

"It's guilt. I'm at my wit's end with Alfred's condition. I've met with the Commonwealth's Attorney in Norfolk and it seems there's a possibility a trial date may be set as early as this spring. If he's still ill by then, I'll have to attend the trial by myself. It's also up to me to make Christmas as normal as possible for Elizabeth." Margaret's eyes pleaded for some type of help. Her words were barely audible.

"Margaret, I hate to ask this question, but has Alfred ever talked about taking his own life?" Dr. Lewis bit his bottom lip. He was afraid of how Margaret would respond.

Margaret nodded, not making eye contact with her old friend. "Alfred said he would rather die than live in this black hole. It's as though he's paralyzed, unable to think, eat or sleep. He says sometimes his heart beats so rapidly he feels as though it will jump right out of his chest. The sheets the next morning are wringing wet from his body sweating profusely. His sleep is tormented, fitful even. I have to roll him from side to side and pull the sheets out from under him."

Fresh bedlinens became an everyday occurrence. Alfred was adamant that Margaret be the only one allowed in the room to attend to him. His room became an ominous dark cave with only one lamp illuminating the heaviness and despair permeating the air.

What could she do to bring normalcy back into his life? She was sinking along with him at times: her dizzy spells were returning more frequently. *I must get hold of myself,* she thought, *Elizabeth has nobody. She needs me.*

She turned her attention back to Dr. Lewis with eyes welling with tears. They did that so often lately.

"Margaret, I suggest that before Christmas, Alfred be admitted to Johns Hopkins for electroconvulsive therapy."

"I beg your pardon?"

"It's sometimes called electroshock or shock treatments," The doctor explained. "The convulsions that occur are not as violent as they were in the thirties and forties. Shock treatments are generally administered in the morning before breakfast. Alfred would be given anesthesia and a muscle relaxant prior to the actual treatment. Two paddles would be placed at his forehead and an electric current applied that causes a brief convulsion. Minutes later, he will awaken confused and without memory of events surrounding the treatment. Treatments usually are repeated three times a week for approximately one month. The number of treatments varies from six to twelve. I highly recommend twelve in Alfred's case. Then we will continue the medication to reduce the chance of a relapse. I think he will be in better shape to attend the trial if he participates in this therapy. Otherwise, I personally feel he should not be subjected to the drama of the courtroom."

"I guess Harvey and I can take turns driving him to Hopkins for the day of treatments," Margaret said. "I need to be here at night for Elizabeth and I know Blanche will help me as well. Should Alfred be admitted for long term hospitalization instead?"

"No, in my opinion Alfred does not need to be isolated from his family and all things familiar," the doctor said. "I recommend because of the pending court trials, he begin electroshock treatments immediately. The treatment is known to last for four weeks, enabling him to participate in Christmas festivities. Of course, I will need Alfred's consent."

"Let's talk to him about it now," Margaret said, wanting this latest nightmare over with. *Maybe he will listen to his family physician*, she told herself.

Dr. Lewis entered the bedroom and walked to the side of the bed.

Alfred realized they were moving in on him; he only wanted to be left alone. He felt immobile. Dr. Lewis turned on the lamp by his bed and Alfred covered his head as if the light pained him. Darkness, silence, and sleep were all he needed. The doctor and his wife began asking him a bunch of strange things. He thought to himself, *how can I answer all these questions?*

"Yes, yes, yes," Alfred groaned in response. It was all a blur, just a blur of two people hanging over him.

Margaret leaned down and kissed his bald head as she tucked him securely under the covers. "You sleep now, dear. It's going to be much better by Christmas. We have to make the holidays a happy time for Elizabeth." Margaret's eyes bore into Dr. Lewis for answers as they quietly left the room.

"I'll take care of all the scheduling, Margaret. The sooner we start treatments the better."

Elizabeth stood in the doorway of her room wondering what treatments Poppy was about to start. Nana had already informed her she would be spending a great deal of time with Uncle Harvey and Blanche after Christmas. It seemed that her visits to the funeral parlor were happening more and more often, requiring her to pack in a great rush.

"Norfolk business, Norfolk business," Nana repeated, always in an extreme flurry.

The afternoon of December 23rd, Blanche's brother brought a huge pine tree through the front door of the Eyre home. Alfred held the door open for him with his pipe in his mouth and newspaper tucked under his arm. "I declare, what do we have here? That's a beauty," he stated.

"Don't you remember, honey? Blanche said Roger was going in our woods and cut a Christmas tree big enough to fill the bay window," Margaret rambled on. She was elated to have Alfred home after trips to Johns Hopkins. *Don't expect miracles*, she thought as she realized his memory had faded with the series of shock treatments.

Huffing and puffing, Blanche and Margaret made numerous trips to the attic, climbing the three flights of stairs. Boxes of glass ornaments individually wrapped with tissue paper and placed in a cardboard sectional container caused Elizabeth's eyes to widen with wonderment. Jewel tones of green, red, purple, and gold shimmering glass were luminous on their own.

"I bought these to match our Tiffany lamp. I thought they were elegant. The sales lady in Norfolk told me they were based on an artist's glass originals. I wished I had written the name down, but it seems like I can't remember anything these days. Look Elizabeth, there's a little manger in this hollow one with the baby Jesus inside. They are all so lovely," Margaret explained smiling.

Spiked and round ornaments were unpacked and handed to Margaret as if they were too fragile for anyone else to maneuver or hang correctly on the branches.

"These are my favorites. They look like birthday candles," Elizabeth squealed as she held up a cord of traditional bubble lights.

"I'll plug them all in so when the liquid warms, you can see them bubblin'," said Blanche.

"How does that happen?" Elizabeth questioned.

"Christmas magic, chile, Christmas magic."

The largest spiked ornament was fitted over the top of the pine tree by Roger, who was standing on a stepladder. Mitch Miller and his band played on the stereo and the mood for all, just this one cloudy afternoon, was festive in spirit.

Margaret was in her glory as she unwrapped small villages of architectural wonder, glittering silver against their white frames. The houses had steep roofs and gingerbread details just like Sycamore Creek in miniature. Margaret placed the village on fluffy white cotton and opening a bag of faux snow, sprinkled it over the entire scene. The village had been delegated to a small cherry table and Elizabeth had the honor of placing the high-steepled church in the center.

"We need a cross in front of the church where Mommy is buried."

Margaret's face tightened as reality set in and broke the temporary feeling that maybe Suzanne was not dead after all and they were a whole family again—one without tragedy.

Blanche witnessed immediately the change of mood that Elizabeth's statement had brought, just like a dark cloud passing over the glare of red and green lights on the tree. "Chile, I tol you jist the other day your Mommy is with you all the time. She's lookin' down on us right now, laughin' 'bout how crooked Roger placed that big ole ornament on top of the tree. Lord a mercy, I never."

"The other day in school Miss Hilda and Mr. Herman stood behind my desk and talked about me."

"What did they say?" Margaret questioned her granddaughter.

"Mr. Herman asked my teacher if I was doing okay after all the family had been through and if I ever said anything about my Mommy. They both said such a shame and started to whisper. I couldn't hear the rest of it."

Margaret glanced at Alfred who sat in his chair, mesmerized by the Christmas tree as if he was in his own little bubble like the tree lights. Blanche hummed "Amazing Grace" as she made her way back to the attic with empty boxes. Looking past Margaret intentionally, realizing the spell of Christmases past had been broken, Blanche wondered if their world would ever right itself again.

"Come help Nana drape the tinsel on the branches. Make sure you separate them now," Margaret was directing her command towards

Elizabeth. *I'm determined to have Christmas as it should be*, she prayed to herself.

"When's Daddy going to be here, Nana?"

"After work Christmas Eve."

"He's not going to miss Santa, is he? Mommy said I have to be asleep for Santa to come."

"He's never missed us yet, and now that you're here, I bet he will be a while with all the presents he has to place under the tree."

"Let's not forget his pipe, cookies and eggnog, okay, Nana? Mommy puts carrots out for Rudolph too."

Margaret dabbed her eyes with the Kleenex she now carried perpetually in her pocket. Tears were always close to the surface as she moved through her day. Angry, sorrowful, and happy memories surfaced at any given moment. She opted to stay home from service on Sunday mornings, unable to bring herself to walk through the doors, seeing in her mind the copper casket that Suzanne was laying in—forever silenced. Bridge club friends had called begging her to return, reminding her it would be good to get out of the house when Elizabeth was in school. Margaret felt obligated for Alfred's well-being and could not bring herself to leave him alone. *When will I run out of excuses?* she asked, deep in thought.

Father Henderson paid a visit every week. Some visits were eerily quiet, while in others Alfred talked incessantly. He prayed for them as they opened their mouths for the wafer. Margaret refused to participate in Holy Eucharist at times, feeling conflicted, asking God how this could have happened to her innocent, precious daughter?

On Christmas Eve morning, Margaret decided to bake a hot milk sponge cake—a holiday tradition. It was important to stay busy so that she didn't have time to think about their first Christmas without Suzanne. Elizabeth sat on the counter watching her pour scalded milk in the mixer, the batter rising with a comforting scent of vanilla extract sweetness.

"When's Daddy coming?"

"I told you honey, after work," Margaret reassured her.

"I'm going to watch for him in the living room by the Christmas tree."

"I'll let you know what time he should arrive," Margaret promised.

Five o'clock rolled around and the glow of Christmas lights strung across the street lamps, pole-to-pole, and electric candles in the windows pierced the darkness of Sycamore Creek. Margaret was comforted to see Alfred in his chair, Virginia Gentleman in hand. He seemed dazed and confused most of the time, but more like his old self than she had witnessed in weeks. Elizabeth was constantly sitting on his lap listening to ghost stories, begging for her grandfather to tell her about Blue Baby just one more time.

"Is Daddy on his way, Nana?"

"I haven't heard from him honey."

"You said he'd be here after dark."

Margaret had a knot in her stomach. Her compassion for Edward dissipated rapidly by the day. He never called his daughter unless he was inebriated and always after her bedtime. She was in the process of making turkey gravy as the lumps fell victim to her frustration. *How many years are ahead of having to make excuses about Edward's late appearances,* she wondered.

Catching the last ferry in the nick of time, Edward drove his car into the hull. He had spent a little longer than anticipated at the office party. Downing coffee, cup after cup, on the way to Sycamore Creek, he drove in the stillness of the night. His intentions were to portray a sober father as he carried presents from the car trunk into the Charles Dickens decorated home where his daughter now lived.

"Come now, Elizabeth, you need to go to bed before Santa arrives. If he sees you're still awake, he'll pass us over. It's really late and you've been at that window for hours," Margaret pleaded.

"Daddy's coming. I just know he'll be here any minute," Elizabeth said defiantly.

Car headlights flashed and crossed the bay window.

"Daddy's here before Santa!" Elizabeth squealed. She jumped up and ran to the door.

CHAPTER NINE

"Ah, spring finally," Harvey muttered to himself while on his way to pick up Elizabeth and drive her to the Aspirin Riding Stables for the first English equestrian lesson. Margaret had decided the fall and winter seasons would be too cold for her to ride. She was overly protective and had misgivings about her only grandchild on horseback.

Entering the back door to the kitchen, he spied his niece sitting at the table testing Margaret's Tollhouse cookies. With a smile on his face and a twinkle in his eye, he exclaimed, "Don't you look like an equestrian, decked out in your jodhpurs and boots?"

Elizabeth was dressed as if she was performing dressage, albeit it was going to be her first day on horseback.

"Elizabeth, I've been thinking, how would you like a pony of your very own? I happen to know that Mrs. Aspirin has one for sale."

"Now Harvey, we don't need a horse to take care of. We have Norfolk business the next few months and the maintenance of a horse would be all too consuming of our time," Margaret said.

"All my own, Uncle Harvey? Yes sir!" Elizabeth said, ignoring her grandmother's anxiousness.

"I'll pay Betty Aspirin to board it, Margaret. Just relax," Alfred reassured her.

Harvey and Elizabeth sat in the front seat of his black station wagon as he drove. *These back roads go on forever*, she thought. The road wound around bare cotton fields with only a hint of cotton bits left from last fall's harvesting.

"Uncle Harvey, look at all the horses!" Elizabeth exclaimed. She was enthralled and spellbound by the way they were running, vigorously kicking up their hind legs with spring fever.

"The ponies will be in a pasture by themselves. Mrs. Aspirin will have yours in a riding ring."

They turned off the road onto an oyster shell driveway. It was the longest lane Elizabeth had ever seen. With her face pressed to the passenger car window, she continued to watch the majestic animals, wishing she could jump out of the car that very minute and hop on the pure white stallion she had spied.

"I'm going to ride him today, Uncle Harvey," she exclaimed, pointing in the horse's direction.

They approached a large, white, brick Georgian house with a circular driveway that led to the stables behind the mansion.

"Mrs. Aspirin is waiting for us at the first riding ring," Harvey explained. Parking the black wagon, they stepped over piles of horse manure on the way to the ring where Mrs. Aspirin was standing. She held the bridle of a beautiful chestnut colored pony.

"You must be Elizabeth. I'm Mrs. Aspirin. How do you like your new pony?"

"Hello Mrs. Aspirin. I love him! Can I ride him now?"

"No, honey, not until you start your lessons. The other girls are in the stable. I'll teach y'all from the ground up how to take care of a horse. There's a lot to learn on grooming, saddling, and overall maintenance before you mount."

Harvey saw Elizabeth's puzzlement and the disappointment clearly on her face. "What will you name your pony, darlin'?" he asked.

"Virginia Peanut. I love them and eat them very day. When I lived in Norfolk, Mommy would take me by the plant where Mr. Peanut lived on the way to nursery school. He waved to me in the mornings and Mommy would always slow down so he could see me, waving until we were out of sight," Elizabeth rattled on with exuberance.

"Virginia Peanut it is," Uncle Harvey stated with teary eyes.

Mrs. Aspirin said, "Come now and meet Peanut, but be gentle and just rub his nose. Let him get to know you."

Elizabeth approached gingerly and stood on the tip of her toes reaching for the soft skin. Peanut eyed the child in front of him and lowered his head to meet the tiny hand. Sensing the need in her, they would become inseparable for years to come.

"I'll give you a check for the pony, boarding, and the attire before we leave, Betty," Elizabeth heard Uncle Harvey say as she gently stroked Peanut's nose. This was her pony—forever.

"You're a good man, Harvey."

"I'll see to it she never goes without," he said in a hushed tone.

They headed for the stables where Elizabeth was about to meet the new students who collectively would embark on their first lesson.

"Hi, my name is Elizabeth and that's my very own pony, Peanut," Elizabeth said, pointing at him through the open door as he was being led into the barn.

"He's pretty. My name is Jacki," a petite little brunette said with a smile.

Elizabeth and five little girls filed into an empty stall, up to their knees in hay. They were dressed identically: white shirts, tan jodhpurs, brown riding boots and perfectly braided pony tails underneath a riding helmet.

Earlier that morning, Blanche had arrived to assist with Elizabeth's hair, but mainly she had wanted to see how she looked in her riding attire. "Now keep still, honey chile, if you want a smooth braid," Blanche said, as she fussed with the plait.

"Blanche you're killing me. That hurts!" Elizabeth pouted. She could not take her eyes off the mirror as she watched Blanche plait her long blonde hair. She seemed to pull all three plaits so taut that Elizabeth felt her eyes would bulge.

"Hold still," Blanche demanded as she heavily sprayed the perfect braid.

In the stalls, Mrs. Aspirin barked, "The first thing you young ladies will learn today is how to muck the stalls. Each girl will have her own pitch fork. The wheelbarrow will be in the middle of the stall since all the horses are in the pasture now, so you will be filling it with horse manure. Then on to saddling your horse." With that, Mrs. Aspirin left the stall.

"Aren't we going to ride today," Elizabeth questioned the girls who would all later be future ribbon recipients.

"I'm telling my parents," said a little girl who resembled a Barbie Doll. She was very disgruntled about all the manual labor. "This poop is big, and it smells," she continued and stomped her boot for emphasis.

Elizabeth realized she was the only one enjoying the scent of horse manure and sweat. *Peanut really needs me*, she thought.

Mrs. Aspirin herded the girls into the ring, walking in front of them with Peanut by her side. The gentle pony would be used as demonstration for the lesson. "Gather around girls, but don't stand behind him. A horse can't see you if you do, and he may get spooked and kick. The mane and tail are for protection from insects. Whiskers around the muzzle are for feeling things. If you are scared, your horse will be scared of you being scared. Be confident; horses are very smart. Sometimes your horse will buck—this means that there's a reason why. His saddle might be pinching or he is having a bad day. And always be nice to your horse."

As she mounted Peanut, she said, "Keep your heels slightly lower and your feet will not slide through the stirrups. Keep your eyes and head up and remember you should always look first towards where you want to guide your horse. If you are looking nowhere, your horse should be going nowhere."

She clicked her tongue and slowly rode Peanut around the riding ring. "Next Saturday we will learn how to care for your pony: what they like to eat and how to brush them."

Harvey stood in the background chuckling to himself at Betty Aspirin's commanding presence and the look of terror on the children's faces, all except for one—Elizabeth's. As she walked toward Elizabeth after the lesson, she looked at him with a questioning gaze.

"Can Virginia Peanut come home with us? I don't think he likes Mrs. Aspirin," she whispered.

"No, darlin'. Mrs. Aspirin is boarding him for us. Peanut cannot live in town."

"But he doesn't like her." Elizabeth started to cry.

"Now, honey, dry your tears. We should go home and tell your grandparents about today's riding lesson and how much you learned."

Elizabeth scuffed her boots through the sandy dirt as they headed back to the station wagon. She blew Peanut a kiss.

"I'll miss you, Peanut. See you tomorrow and the next day and the next day."

"I guess I've started something now, I declare," Uncle Harvey said, patting Elizabeth's head as they drove home.

Elizabeth bolted into her grandparent's house talking a mile-a-minute about the new pony. "He's beautiful and I love him. Uncle Harvey is going to take me every day to the barn where he lives."

"Please be careful around him. Horses are known to be mean. They bite and kick. Scarlett O'Hara's daughter, Eleanor, fell off a horse when she attempted a jump and died in the movie *Gone With The Wind*. I remember that scene like it was yesterday. I don't want to lose you because of a horse, Elizabeth," Margaret warned.

"Don't worry, Margaret. Elizabeth is a natural," Harvey reassured her.

"Thanks, Harvey, for all you've done for us," Margaret said as the spring sun shone through the windows. "We must leave town Monday morning, as things are progressing rapidly. Can you and Blanche please watch her? Norfolk business."

CHAPTER TEN

Margaret stared at the photo of Stephen Dennis for several moments. He was grinning sheepishly for the camera as he left the courtroom after the first day of trial. The local newspaper sensationalized the story portraying the two victims as Eastern Shore beauty contestants.

The newspaper had been delivered to the hotel room in Norfolk along with the Eyres' morning coffee. They did not have to arrive at the courthouse until ten o'clock.

"I have lost my appetite, Alfred. Do you want breakfast before we go to the courthouse?"

"Not at all. I feel nauseated with all this medication I'm taking. I can't bear the thought of eating before going in that courtroom. I'm ready for this trial to be over and done with. Coffee will be just fine for now."

Margaret took a sip and extended her hand to her husband as she read the headlines out loud to him.

"Petite, twenty-four-year-old, olive-skinned, brunette woman, relayed to an attentive all-male jury a bloody tale of murder and rape. A story of being brutally shot and attacked, her cousin slain as she looked on, helplessly wounded," Margaret's voice quivered as she glanced at Alfred. "Do you want me to continue reading? It will only upset you more and we have another day to go through," she lowered her voice as if she was afraid of being overheard.

Staring into space, Alfred responded, "I couldn't sleep last night, Margaret, not a wink. My mind kept seeing Eleanor quietly sobbing on the stand as she reiterated what happened to them. I tossed and turned for several hours, unable to get the picture of Suzanne in the last minutes of her life out of my head. It was sometime after three o'clock that I finally dozed off. Did you see the look on that bastard's face? I just knew he would plead not guilty by reason of insanity to avoid the death penalty—I would have bet my life on it. Poor Eleanor, the charges of shooting and raping her twice. Those are going to be heard sometime down the road. She'll have to testify all over again. How much more can the girl take? Suzanne, may her soul rest in peace, doesn't have to go through this, she was raped after..." Alfred started to cry and abruptly cut the conversation.

Margaret was relieved that Alfred had begun to finally express his emotions and talk to her about the murder of their daughter. Feeling like the weight of the world was entirely on her shoulders over the past few months, she welcomed his rambling. It was imperative to share her fears and concerns with her husband because he was the only one who could understand.

"It was chilling to hear the account again. Eleanor will be traumatized for the rest of her life. It is just a miracle she's still alive. She told me she doesn't want to see Elizabeth for quite a while yet. You know Alfred, Elizabeth looks just like her mother. I don't think Eleanor could bear it," Margaret sighed.

Alfred held his breath for several seconds before confiding to his wife. "Margaret, I just can't get the scene out of my mind, it literally gives me chills when I think of our daughter witnessing Eleanor being shot in the legs and seeing the terror in her cousin's eyes as she raced towards the phone in the bedroom. I didn't realize Suzanne and that worthless bastard struggled as she picked up the receiver. Why did he chase her into the living room, slinging her backwards as she tried to escape through the front door, shooting her with my pistol? Why, why, why? I could just strangle him," Alfred broke down and buried his head in his hands—again.

"It's okay, honey, yesterday was a day I dreaded and today won't be any easier. When I glanced at the devil himself, he was chewing the end of a ballpoint pen, pretending to scribble notes on a piece of paper. Did you notice how nervous he was during the selection of the jury? It seemed as if he quieted down after that."

"I did. I understand he asked a jailer to shave his head before the trial—whatever that is supposed to indicate. When his attorney made the statement that Stephen Dennis had a diseased mind and has had a diseased mind for some time, I knew it was just another tactic to spare his life. How in the hell can his attorney represent him after he confessed his guilt? Damn politics. I wish I had taken those three bullets myself. I would do anything to have my daughter back."

"Please Alfred, we can't turn back the hands of time. Let's put our faith in what the Commonwealth's Attorney said yesterday, that justice demands the death penalty. That's what we must focus on. He actually signed a statement confessing to the murder and rape of Suzanne, and Eleanor is the living witness. It's cut and dry, honey."

"I do feel comfortable with Todd Wynn. He's been a thorough attorney so far. Thank God the judge said we could be excused before the slides were shown to the jury. I just couldn't bear to see the photographs of our dead daughter sprawled on the floor. It was a good decision to leave the room, at least that portion of hell is over," Alfred reflected.

Margaret recollected meeting in the winter with the Commonwealth's Attorney who had informed her of his intent to show the gruesome photos. "Mrs. Eyre, I plan to introduce another element which may be damaging to the defense. A set of fifteen photographs were taken by the police at the scene of the crime. I don't intend to make this anymore difficult for you, but they show Suzanne dead on her living room floor. She is partially nude. Her clothes are in disorder and there are bloodstains on the furnishings."

She had, with much consideration, opted not to share his plan with her husband. His frail mental state was always in the back of her mind. Margaret sat stunned, shocked, and unprepared during the meeting. *Could things get any worse?* she thought.

The jury was allowed to see the photographs over the strenuous objections of the defense attorney who argued, "that since a living witness to the crime had testified, the photographs were unnecessary and would serve only to inflame the jury. In fact, the pictures were made with just that thought in mind."

Stephen eyed the jurors speculatively as they filed into the box the first day of trial. Eight prospective jurors had been stricken from the rolls, seven because of sentiments against capital punishment. *Will these twelve men determine whether I live or die?* he thought, believing his days were numbered.

Minutes before the court adjourned, Stephen made a decision to testify on his own behalf the following day, the second day of trial.

Margaret folded the newspaper and tucked it into the side compartment of her suitcase. Alfred had incessantly tossed and turned the night before. Like her husband, she had experienced insomnia as well. The distress encapsulated them as she pressed her forehead against his back, laying in the fetal position together until daybreak.

After Alfred drank his coffee, he decided to shower and dress for another dreadful day. He closed the bathroom door so abruptly that Margaret flinched and began to pray.

"Dear God, please allow justice to be done today for all our sakes. This cold-blooded killer who murdered our daughter deserves the death penalty. Be with our family as we listen to the accounts again with the strength that you enfold upon us. Amen," Margaret whispered and then began to rise from her kneeling position by the side of the bed.

Dressed in a navy suit and pearls, Margaret walked into the courtroom on the arm of her gaunt and frail husband whose suit hung on him due to the extreme amount of weight loss. They joined Edward, Eleanor, and her parents at the bench where they were saving them seats.

Psychiatrists from the state mental hospital took their turns testifying that on the morning of the crime, Stephen Dennis knew right from wrong and was not psychotic when he shot and killed Suzanne Barclay.

Stephen, who indicated at the conclusion of the first day of testimony that he would take the stand in his own defense, surprisingly chose not to as the defense rested its case.

Two additional doctors from the same mental hospital rebutted a defense claim that Stephen Dennis was sane. The defense pleaded not guilty by reason of insanity.

The doctor who examined Stephen Dennis after the incident testified, "My impression was that he was not psychotic at that time."

Dr. Lankford, the initial analyst who had conducted four examinations since the beginning of the year, took the stand and said, "Stephen Dennis was suffering from schizophrenia and has a mental defect. On the day of the crime he was in a psychotic state," the doctor proclaimed. "He lived a hostile, aggressive life of fantasy. He dreamed the night before of killing Suzanne Barclay. My study indicates he acted out a dream. He awoke with the thought and carried it out."

"How do you account for him raping Eleanor Johnson when he didn't dream about her?" asked the Commonwealth's Attorney Wynn, on cross examination.

"He was acting out on impulse," he answered. Dr. Lankford continued that Stephen told him that if Suzanne Barclay were still living, he would do it again.

"Do you think he would?" the attorney questioned.

"I wouldn't trust him not to," the doctor replied. "He was unable to prevent himself from doing so," he added.

In his closing argument, the defense attorney tried to enhance the picture of Stephen's instability, asking the jury to spare him because, "We shoot mad dogs not madmen." Stephen Dennis's murder trial had become a battle of psychiatrists—sane versus insane.

During the hour-and-a-half wait for the jury's decision, Stephen sat and talked uneasily with his mother. "I'm afraid I've lost," he said as his nervousness visibly increased as the minutes ticked by.

The all-male jury found him guilty of first-degree murder and fixed his punishment as death. On hearing the verdict, he paled slightly and shrugged. The victim's families sighed, relieved and exhausted.

"Justice prevailed," Margaret said, thanking God.

CHAPTER ELEVEN

Lillian Dennis clenched a tissue in her hand and brought it to her eyes. "It's hopeless, hopeless. I'm goin' to lose my son! He's the only thing I got! Help me Lord, help me," she began to wail at the top of her lungs, attracting attention.

"Shut up, Mama. I ain't dead yet." Stephen rose and was escorted out of the court room with a large grin on his face as he passed the jury box.

Margaret Eyre pressed her hand on top of Alfred's clenched fist as she glanced at her husband. *He's aged tremendously in the past six months*, she thought. "Honey, let's leave now. We may be able to make the early afternoon ferry," she said as she extended her hand to support his lack of balance. Together, they rose from the bench with dignity and silence.

A soft smile crossed Margaret's face as she made eye contact with Eleanor and her parents. "We'll talk on the ferry," she whispered nodding to them.

Turning to Edward, she felt obligated to voice her feelings, not knowing the next time she would see him. "Please be in touch Edward. You're welcome in our home at any time. Elizabeth misses her father," she said quietly.

Edward only sighed. He had become a functioning alcoholic, the rims of his eyes were always red and the whites constantly bloodshot since he lost the love of his life. "You've been wonderful raising Elizabeth. I am so appreciative. Oh, by the way, there are good tenants in Suzanne's house. I mean Elizabeth's house. They are unaware of the crime that took place there. I have a realtor in the area managing it and taking care of the maintenance. I'll send you the rental check every month so you can deposit it in Elizabeth's educational fund."

"Edward, I was unaware that you rented Suzanne's house. Blanche was kind enough to pack all her things and then she scrubbed and cleaned it from top to bottom with the help of her brother Roger. It took them several trips to Norfolk, but I wanted to save everything that was hers so that Elizabeth would have the opportunity to go through her mother's items when she was older. Accessories of Suzanne's are packed and stored on one side of our attic." She eyed Edward with interest. "So, when did you lease the rancher?"

"January," he mumbled, not making eye contact in return.

"I've not received a check from you for Elizabeth's support. So, it's about time for you to buckle up and mail two checks. One for child support and the rent check as well. That money is hers, Edward. I have opened an account for her at the bank. See to it that monthly deposits are made."

Edward's eyes rounded and then went back to normal. "Yes, ma'am," he replied.

The Eyres walked past the press keeping their eyes focused on the front door of the courthouse. Reporters walked beside them and yelled questions on how they viewed the verdict. Alfred lowered his head as his wife directed them out the door and into the parking lot. All they wanted was to get in their car and escape the hard, cold reality of the past two days.

"Can you drive Alfred or do you want me to?"

"I will. I feel so relieved this is all behind us. I don't think it will be long before that bastard is sentenced to die in the electric chair. I wish I could be the grim reaper, the one to pull the switch."

"Now honey, please try to relax. The execution will take place sometime this summer, I suppose. It certainly won't be soon enough."

"Did you hear his attorney? As soon as they fixed his punishment as death he immediately moved to set aside the verdict. It was a first-degree murder charge, for God's sake!" Alfred reiterated the day's scenario. "What more proof does that jerk want?" Margaret realized her husband had not allowed a word to escape him during the sentencing and prayed he would not relapse.

The ferry ride home was long as the exhausted passengers were eager to return to their quiet village of Sycamore Creek. Stopping abruptly as if frozen in time, the townspeople from all walks of life had accompanied "their own" giving them love, courage, and support during the two-day trial. School teachers and local policemen that had problems and incidents with Stephen in the past filled the ferry. Clergy and their congregations of all religions were asked to pray for Eleanor as a constant prayer chain remained in full effect. Harvey Eyre had opened the doors to the funeral parlor, so the community had a place to congregate and ascertain information before the press did. Sycamore Creek had banded together—except for the one attorney in the next community on the Virginia Eastern Shore.

One month later, William Keller from Burley, Virginia entered the case of Stephen K. Dennis, twenty-four, who was convicted of first degree murder and scheduled to die in the electric chair. William Keller informed the presiding Judge in Corporation Court Part II that he had been retained to represent Mr. Dennis.

The court-appointed attorney withdrew from the case.

A hearing on a motion to set aside the jury's verdict had been slated for May 16th. From the court, Keller requested a continuance to June 15th which would allow him time to review the transcript and prepare argument. The motion was honored. But still, Stephen Dennis was set to face trial for the charges of raping and wounding Eleanor Johnson.

Lillian hugged her son's new attorney as she sat in his office. The lawyer had decided to take on the case—pro bono—of a man who was on the verge of mental retardation and had been sentenced to death.

"He ain't ever been right since a baby growin' up till now. I couldn't do nothin' with him. He tried to shoot hisself four times," Lillian pleaded her case, still in a state of disbelief that this attorney was willing to help her son.

"There's a changing mood of the time—no human being should be sentenced to death if they are insane. Insanity is a mental illness. I believe in justice for the mentally retarded criminal. This case caught my attention from the beginning. I plan to fight for justice. Thank you for seeing me, Miss Dennis. I'll see you in court on Monday."

Attorney Keller was quite confident that, at only thirty-two years of age, he was about to make a name for himself with the Norfolk murder case. He wanted partnership in the prestigious law firm so bad he could taste it. The young counselor firmly believed if he could save this man from the electric chair, then he had a chance to make that goal become a reality.

The phone rang loudly as Margaret was arranging peonies in an antique rose medallion bowl by the large kitchen sink. "Get the phone please, Alfred. My hands are wet," she yelled while placing the stems in the glass frog.

Alfred was making an inventory list for the hotel as he sat at his desk in the library. The Eyres had come to the decision that working at the hotel for the summer season would keep them productive, and seeing their old guests could be a chance to heal, getting their minds off their enveloping grief.

"Hello. I hope this is good news," Alfred said as he heard the voice of the Commonwealth's Attorney on the other end of the line.

"Mr. Eyre, I regret to inform you that Stephen Dennis has retained an attorney from the Eastern Shore and is going to bid for a new trial. Sentencing is scheduled for Monday. Now, I just want to warn you that the country is becoming very liberal with regard to the death penalty. But I promise to do all I can to see him duly punished. You have my word."

"Thank you," Alfred's words felt like a heavy weight. Hanging up the phone, he called for his wife who was now standing in the doorway of the library, wiping her hands on a tea towel. Alfred had grown pale and a worried expression came across his face as he locked eyes with hers. How could he say this to her, his wife, his rock?

Dumbfounded, he pushed his chair away from the desk. "Stephen Dennis has a new attorney and he is going to bid for a new trial."

Margaret walked to the wing chair beside Alfred's desk hoping her knees would not buckle from beneath her before she reached the chair. Now was not the time for Alfred to see her come unglued; her reaction would only prove detrimental to his frail condition.

"I don't understand. Like I've said hundreds of times before, he confessed and signed a statement of guilt. Eleanor is a living witness! This cannot be happening. I thought it was final and justice would be done. It's an atrocity if he's allowed to live. What is happening in the world today? Everyone has gone crazy and the law is being bypassed!"

"I have some more bad news, Margaret."

"More, what more? How can there be any more?"

"The new attorney is from the Eastern Shore of Virginia. It's like rubbing salt in our wounds. He's not a local boy, but never-the-less, for God's sake."

Margaret's head dropped. In a matter of minutes, she found the strength to stand—she was obligated to a six-year-old. "Elizabeth will be home from school any minute. Harvey's picking her up today. They are as close as close can be," she could not stop rambling, not wanting to think. As she entered the kitchen, one of her dizzy spells washed over her; she could feel her head spinning and, with caution, she maneuvered her way to the kitchen table. The daily blood pressure pills were not as effective as they once were.

"Nana, I'm home!" Elizabeth called entering the kitchen from the back door.

Margaret uprighted herself at the table and sat stoically, hoping Elizabeth would not notice her posture or demeanor.

"Nana, you look pale. Are you all right?"

"Yes, honey, just fine. How about cookies and milk for an after-school snack? I baked oatmeal this time."

"Yummy!" she squealed as she gave Margaret a hug.

As she placed the cookies and milk on the table, she said, "Elizabeth, I have to tell you something."

Elizabeth eyed her grandmother with crumbs on the side of her mouth and a thin milk mustache lining her upper lip. "I guess I'm going back to Uncle Harvey's soon so Blanche can babysit me."

"Norfolk business," grandmother and granddaughter spoke in unison.

Driving through Norfolk, the red azalea bushes, purple rhododendrons, and pink dogwood trees bloomed in harmony with tulips in various colors along the streets.

"I used to think Norfolk, Virginia was the most beautiful city in spring time," Margaret said, casting her eyes on the riotous shades of Mother Nature's art from the passenger's window. "I had absolutely no desire to go to Virginia Garden Week this year."

"What is that, honey?" Alfred questioned with the perpetual gaze of confusion on his face he so often had anymore. "I've forgotten."

Margaret glanced at Alfred realizing the memory loss was more frequent than expected. Dr. Lewis told her he didn't think her husband would need any more treatments. In time, his memory would slowly return and with daily medication, the doctor believed he could keep his patient stabilized if the depressive cycle ever returned.

"Remember helping Sycamore Creek Garden Club park cars for the house tour that takes place the third week in April? You and George have supported us for years. The girls work extensively cutting flowers from their gardens and arranging them in the houses that are open for the two days. Our house was on the tour for several years. It was a lot of work making sure it was in tip-top shape. Talk about getting your house in order." Margaret knew she was babbling, but her intentions were to keep Alfred in a good frame of mind as they drove to the courthouse. She continued, "The Federation of Garden Clubs preserve Virginia's public gardens. It's a great cause and we raise a huge amount of money that week. I'll never forget when we had a warm spring one year and Pearl's tulips began popping up prematurely in her garden. She had Roger bring in a pickup truck full of ice to dump on the tulip beds to retard them from blooming before garden week. It's just amazing that the tradition has gone on since 1929."

"I do vaguely remember Garden Week. Didn't George Thornton help me park those old biddie's cars?" Alfred chuckled, not realizing Margaret had just mentioned George.

Margaret laughed as well thinking, *maybe . . . just maybe, someday his sense of humor will return.*

Convicted murderer Stephen K. Dennis averted his eyes from the judge presiding directly in front of him. He remained speechless after being sentenced to die in the electric chair, after the motion for a new trial was overruled by the judge in Corporation Court Part Two. The date was set August 26, 1961 for execution, ten months to the day from the murder of Suzanne Barclay.

Stephen Dennis's new attorney, William Keller, said after the hearing he would apply to the Virginia Supreme Court of Appeals for writ of error. Keller was hoping it would be granted, allowing him to argue the motion before the Supreme Court of Appeals.

At his trial on the murder charge of Suzanne Barclay only, Eleanor Johnson was a key witness for the Commonwealth. Dennis pleaded not guilty by reason of temporary insanity.

Keller in arguing for a new trial contended Stephen Dennis was denied a fair initial trial because certain evidence was included improperly while other evidence was excluded improperly. He also charged that two of the judge's instructions to the jury as well as closing arguments by the Commonwealth were improper.

Stephen fidgeted next to his mother as she sat perplexed as to what this new flamboyant attorney was arguing about. *Just save my boy from death*, Lillian prayed to herself, unable to remove her eyes from him, unable to blink. *This man's gonna save my boy.*

William Keller wore his black shiny hair parted on the side and slicked down with grease. His white shirt was heavily starched, showing French cuffs with solid gold cufflinks. An equally starched white handkerchief was tucked in his breast pocket.

Not letting any details of the trial go unnoticed, he was about to transform Stephen Dennis's conviction. His sights were on the political arena and this case would help prepare him for when he was ready to throw his hat into the ring. *The times ... they are a changing*, he smiled to himself.

Margaret glared at Keller, determined his disastrous speech would not change the judge's mind. *Show biz*, she thought, *out to make a name for himself. All show biz. How did our suffering become such a mockery?* She glanced at Alfred who was alert and focused on Mr. Bigshot, as she would later dub him on the way home while discussing the events of the day with her husband.

William Keller's chief point about the trial was that testimony on the rape of Eleanor Johnson, which occurred after Suzanne Barclay was shot, was inadmissible because it had nothing to do with the killing of Mrs. Barclay. He highly objected to Eleanor Johnson's testimony and to photographs of the crime scene.

"The photographs of Suzanne Barclay's partially nude body and bloody objects inflame and prejudice the jury against Dennis while being irrelevant to the charge of murder," Keller stated theatrically.

Eleanor fixed her eyes on Margaret and mouthed the word "unbe-lievable"; Margaret rolled her eyes in agreement.

Arguing against the motion, Commonwealth's Attorney Todd Wynn rebutted, "The photographs characterized it as an attempt by Dennis to seek justice when in fact, he has gotten justice."

The judge in overruling Keller's motion said, "I am convinced there had been no error in exclusion or inclusion of evidence and no error in instructions to the jury. I do not believe the closing arguments by the prosecution were improper."

The Eyre and Johnson families left the courthouse believing August 26th would be the day of Stephen Dennis's demise.

CHAPTER TWELVE

"Roger, please help the Caseys with their luggage. Their room is 18," Margaret said, checking in her favorite guests. The Caseys were an older couple from Roanoke that she had grown fond of through the years. They had a standing reservation for the first week of June—their anniversary. Spending their days rocking on the porch, watching the sunbathers, and catching up on the past winter occupied their week with the other guests. Margaret smiled to herself as they rocked in unison, holding hands. The Eyres had returned to the Virginia Tide with the hope that a season of keeping busy and being around other people would ease their constant heartache. Blanche had mentioned that her brother had expressed an interest in working for them at the hotel. Roger joined the staff and had taken over where Stephen had left off. Margaret trusted Roger and her entire work family, and she realized as Alfred declined, she was becoming more dependent on them.

The phone rang at the switchboard where Margaret sat as Roger lifted the suitcases and helped the Caseys negotiate the stairs. "One at a time," he warned, keeping an eye on their canes.

"Good afternoon, the Virginia Tide," Margaret answered with her professional voice.

"Mrs. Eyre, Todd Wynn. I wanted to let you know that Stephen Dennis's date of execution has been denied. Keller is seeking habeas corpus and taking the case to the Supreme Court of Virginia. He's just not going to let this drop. The Commonwealth will do everything we can. Take care of yourselves."

Margaret did not retain anything that Wynn said except that the date of execution had been denied for now. Keller was appealing once again; Dennis was not guilty because of insanity. *I wonder how he would feel if his daughter had been killed. If Alfred holds up to this bit of news, it will be a miracle*, Margaret speculated. His mental health was growing more and more fragile with each passing day. She had made up her mind if he had not shown improvement by August, she would try to convince him to put the hotel on the market. She was beginning to regret their decision to work this summer. It had been less than a year, albeit a life changing one.

Once the hotel had an afternoon lull, she asked Alfred to join her in the quiet of their office.

"What's wrong, Margaret? I can tell there's something on your mind."

"Stephen Dennis's execution date has been delayed." Fraught emotion bled into her words.

Alfred grew quiet, and quiet he would remain for the duration of the summer. "I'm drained with this constant burden of politics. I'm going to take a walk on the beach. I need to be alone and think," he muttered.

Margaret went back to her desk as the Caseys descended the stairs, refreshed and ready for their afternoon cocktails. Bertha, one of the Eyres' maids for the past eighteen years would be serving them. Elizabeth entered the front door straight from the beach, brown as a berry, hair encrusted with salt water and sand, followed by Constance Medes, her seventeen-year-old nanny. Constance relished her job spending days in the sun with Elizabeth.

"Look how you've grown, Elizabeth! You're so pretty, just like your mother. How is Suzanne, Margaret?" Mrs. Casey inquired.

A chill shot down Margaret's spine. "Suzanne is no longer with us. She was in an accident last October," Margaret said, determined not to go into gory detail with anyone ever. "We'll talk later."

The Caseys hands flew to their mouths simultaneously. "We are so sorry." Mrs. Casey hugged Margaret, then Elizabeth and walked out of the hotel lobby, speechless, followed by her husband.

Margaret wrapped her arms around Elizabeth with a protecting grip so tight her grandchild struggled for breath. The two of them would survive the years ahead—she was determined. "There will be a lot of questions about what happened to your mother, Elizabeth. Nana will take care of them for you."

"I'm sorry, Nana," Elizabeth tried to console her grandmother.

Margaret swallowed hard. "I'm fine, honey. Let's get you ready for dinner."

Margaret's suspicion was correct as she spent the summer days continually explaining that Suzanne had passed away due to an accident. The guest's reactions proved too painful for Alfred to endure so he shunned the public, hiding in his room for the duration of the summer. When he tried to speak, his throat tightened and tears constantly stung his eyes.

Margaret knew in her heart this was the last summer they would be at the hotel. This would be yet another loss for them. And so, immediately after Labor day, the Eyres packed and closed the Virginia Tide.

"I'm not coming back this fall for anything else. I want to be in Sycamore Creek on the anniversary," Alfred stated. They had taken Elizabeth home at the end of August to her Uncle Harvey's. Blanche began preparing her for another school year.

Margaret's voice softened, "We feel what we feel, Alfred. It was a very difficult summer for both of us, and Elizabeth for that matter. You have every right to be upset with the magnitude of our loss. The sale of Virginia Tide is cutting connections with things familiar to us, people that we use to enjoy in the past. Suzanne loved the beach and the hotel, but I don't think we should subject ourselves to another season. It's just too difficult and there is no need to put ourselves through it. I've spent the entire summer answering questions about Suzanne. If I had only known..."

Woman's intuition told Margaret that Alfred was failing daily, and she often wondered if he would be with her for another year.

On March 4th, 1962, the Virginia Supreme Court upheld the death penalty imposed by an Norfolk jury on Stephen K. Dennis for the murder of Suzanne Eyre Barclay on October 26, 1960. The court did not set an execution date.

A month later, Stephen Dennis was back in Corporation Court Part Two, where Commonwealth's Attorney Todd Wynn called the Eyres and relayed to them that three counts of rape and one count of malicious shooting against Dennis was denied. He would not be brought to trial on these charges due to the decision of The Virginia Supreme Court.

"I cannot tell you how sorry I am that you both have to go through this political circus. This needs to be finalized so you can obtain peace of mind. The Commonwealth will continue to pursue justice," Wynn promised.

Margaret hung up the phone and climbed the stairs to the room where her husband lay in bed.

"I brought coffee, honey," Margaret said, setting the tray on the ottoman in front of the tester. She had placed the silver coffee pot, china cups, and vase with one of her prized yellow jonquils that had just bloomed from her garden. It was all an attempt to lift Alfred's spirits. They sat in the still of the room as the March raindrops hit the windowpane with angry force, which reflected their mood.

"Todd Wynn just called. No date has been set for execution. There's a possibility there may be another rehearing on April 19th," Margaret informed her husband.

Bringing the steaming cup to his lips, Alfred searched Margaret's eyes wondering how they were going to survive one piece of devastating news after another pertaining to the legal system?

"There are no words," is all he could say, frowning with discomfort.

"It doesn't seem to end, but we have a granddaughter that needs a normal upbringing. Please try to get up in the mornings and be a part of Elizabeth's childhood. She wonders why you're always in bed." Margaret's eyes burned, and she was out of sorts. The world seemed to be always on her shoulders. Tears filled her eyes with the pressure of her husband constantly in a dejected state and the responsibility of a child. Life had changed in a blink of an eye.

Finishing her coffee and placing the cup and saucer back on the tray she went to her husband. Cupping his cheeks in her hands, she looked into his eyes. "I promise you we will fight this to the very end, as long as there is breath in my body. Our only daughter did not die in vain. She was an angel that walked this earth for only twenty-five years and we were blessed to have her in our lives."

"What is it, honey? Tell me what's wrong!"

Margaret turned on the lamp next to the bed as she saw Alfred clutching his chest and moaning. Glancing at the clock it was twelve-fifteen as she picked up the receiver and placed a call for the ambulance.

"I think my husband's having a heart attack! Please hurry!"

Sitting on the side of the bed, Alfred sputtered, "Can't breathe ... chest pains."

Margaret remained upstairs, keeping her husband calm until she heard the siren approaching. Wrapping her robe around her, she hurried down the steps to let the two local volunteer firemen in the front door. The men raced up the stairway and Elizabeth showed them which room her grandfather was in. She stood in the doorway, watching him gasping for breath, as one man placed the oxygen mask over his mouth.

"Can you walk downstairs, Mr. Eyre?"

Alfred nodded, slowly descending the stairway. He was then helped onto the stretcher that awaited him.

Margaret had called for Blanche to come immediately to stay with Elizabeth. Then she rushed out the door to follow her husband to the hospital, remaining at his side. The physician on duty informed her that

Alfred needed heart surgery immediately and that he no longer would be strong enough to survive electroshock treatments.

Margaret didn't need to be told that the treatments had led to the weakening of his heart. This was yet another obstacle in the vicious cycle that plagued her.

After the surgery, a hospital bed was set up in the library at home. Alfred spent his days recuperating, as he watched birds on the feeders that Margaret kept full of seed. She made constant trips to the local library, checking out books on the rich history of the region. Elizabeth sat on the side of her grandfather's bed, sharing her days in school or the most recent lesson she had with her beloved Virginia Peanut.

"Guess what Poppy!? Mrs. Aspirin says I'll soon be ready to learn how to jump," she exclaimed enthusiastically.

"By God, don't tell your Nana, dear heart. She'll call Mrs. Aspirin. You know she won't allow it. She worries about every lesson you take." Alfred smiled.

April 19, 1962

"Good news, Mrs. Eyre," Todd Wynn exclaimed on the other end of the line. "Stephen Dennis was denied a rehearing!"

CHAPTER THIRTEEN

Christmas Eve, 1964 - 11:58 P.M.

Pop!

Margaret jolted upright in bed. She had not slept peacefully since Alfred's first heart attack several years ago. His bedroom had been moved to the library, permanently. Due to a weak heart, he was discouraged by his surgeon to climb the stairs or exert himself in any manner.

Edward opened the door of the guestroom and bolted down the stairs with Margaret following behind him. "What was that? Has Alfred fallen out of bed?"

Alfred had turned on the lamp next to his bed, placed the .38 caliber pistol at his temple, as he sat on the edge and pulled the trigger. His body fell to one side as the pistol hit the floor.

"Go upstairs to protect Elizabeth. I don't want you two to see any of this," Edward said, crying as he opened the library door.

Margaret peered in at the scene blinking her eyes in disbelief. Blood poured down the side of her husband's face from the bullet wound. She focused on his eyes wide with the finality of life. "My God, he's shot himself." Whipping around abruptly, she ran upstairs to her granddaughter's bedroom.

Edward, in a state of shock, looked down at his father-in-law who just an hour ago had wished him goodnight. Visiting his daughter for Christmas, Edward and Alfred stayed up extra late to chat while drinking eggnog. When Margaret had whipped up the homemade eggnog that afternoon, she made sure there was plenty of Alfred's favorite libation—Virginia Gentleman bourbon.

"Why didn't you talk to me Alfred? We all loved you. Why? Why?" Edward rambled, trying to cover Alfred's tormented face with the bedsheet. Out of the corner of his eye, he spotted the .38 caliber bullet which had exited the other side of Alfred's skull and lodged in the horsehair plaster wall, splattering brain and blood on the mahogany desk.

Sobriety hit Edward as he picked up the sealed envelope on which Alfred had neatly penned the words: *My Dearest Margaret*. Placing the letter of farewell back on the desk, his hand trembled as he picked up the receiver and called Harvey.

"Sycamore Creek Funeral Home," Harvey answered in a groggy state.

"Harvey, it's Edward. I have some bad news. Alfred has shot himself. Margaret and I heard it at the same time. He's gone."

"Oh my God! Where is he?"

"In the library on his bed. We've been laughing all night. I thought he was fine—like his old self. We were going to make an effort to go hunting tomorrow afternoon. I just don't understand."

"I'll be right there."

Opening the door to Elizabeth's room, Margaret walked to her granddaughter who was feigning sleep. "Honey, honey wake up."

"What's all the noise about, Nana? Daddy was running down the stairs."

"Poppy has passed away. Your daddy is with him. I think he had another heart attack."

"Can I say goodbye to Poppy, Nana?"

"No. I just say a little prayer for his soul. I will stay up here with you until Uncle Harvey comes. Try to get some sleep, there's presents under the tree to open in the morning."

Harvey hung up the phone. "Oh God, my brother. Why didn't you talk to me? I thought you were improving with each day. I guess I didn't do enough. All this could have all been avoided. Why?" Harvey questioned out loud, blaming himself as he dressed in his dark suit.

Edward met him at the front door and offered a quivering hand. "When I arrived this afternoon, he seemed so jovial and high-spirited. We spent the evening joking and bantering. It was just like old times. I can't believe this has happened."

"Where's Margaret?"

"She's with Elizabeth upstairs," Edward whispered, feeling Harvey's pain as he placed his hand on the back of the undertaker as they walked to the library.

"Oh brother, nothing was worth doing this. My God..." Harvey said. "Do you mind helping me put him on the stretcher, Edward? I didn't call my man Charlie since it's Christmas Eve. Alfred's so thin, I think we can handle him. I'll check on Margaret after we've made the removal and placed him in the hearse."

Harvey went outside to the hearse and rolled a stretcher from the back. He then brought it into the library to remove his brother's body from the homestead they had grown up in. Edward assisted him, grateful to be busy. Together, they placed the body in the black vehicle. Harvey had just begun; he had a night of tidying up the scene ahead of him. He rolled up all the bloody bedlinens to discard at the funeral parlor; he then took his handkerchief and wrapped the pistol for the local police. *I'll call them later, not from here*, he thought. Walking to the desk, he spotted the envelope that Alfred had written to his beloved wife. His hands shook as he retrieved the suicide note that hopefully gave an explanation and tucked it into his coat pocket.

Harvey knocked on Elizabeth's bedroom door and opened it peeking inside. Margaret sat on the bed, stroking Elizabeth's blonde curls.

"Come in, Harvey."

"How are my girls?" Harvey asked, walking towards them, arms open for an embrace.

"We're fine," Margaret reassured him. She stood up to receive his hug. "Let's go downstairs and talk. Elizabeth, try to get some sleep. I'll see you in the morning. Christmas morning."

Elizabeth cuddled down underneath the covers wondering why everyone in her family was dying. She never closed her eyes as Christmas Eve faded into daybreak.

Edward was percolating coffee in the kitchen as Harvey and Margaret shuffled in, taking seats at the kitchen table to discuss yet another tragedy in the family—four years after Suzanne's murder.

"I thought he was making progress and on the road to recovery. When we got word last spring that there would be another trial he seemed despondent, but this summer and fall, it was if he had rebounded. He just couldn't take going through another trial that's scheduled for January. Stephen Dennis has more blood on his hands." Margaret moaned.

"I noticed this evening he was ebullient as we ate dinner," Edward chimed in. "As a matter of fact, he's been that way all fall when we talked on the phone. He asked me if I would like his solid gold cufflinks with the monogram E, and all his tie clips because he had no need to wear ties anymore."

"He kept saying he needed to get our books in order, pouring over them constantly making sure finances were gaining enough interest, becoming obsessed with money," Margaret lamented.

Harvey said, "You know, he mentioned to me this past summer that if anything should happen to him would I see to it that this house would remain in good condition and keep it in the Eyre family. He loved you so much he was preparing for this, even back then. I'll take care of all the paperwork and call the authorities. They owe me a favor. Do you want to see him again, Margaret?"

"No, Harvey, no fanfare. I don't want this to get out in the public. Nobody needs to be in our business. We've been through enough. Harvey, listen to me. I want a simple graveside service and bury Alfred next to Suzanne. He never healed from her death, taking responsibility for trying to help that lowlife. The shame ate at him day and night. Now he'll finally have peace."

"Margaret, I found a letter Alfred wrote to you."

Edward had poured three tumblers of bourbon on ice and placed them on the kitchen table. He didn't want Harvey to leave. *There's strength in numbers,* he consoled himself, not wanting to be left with Margaret alone as the gloom enveloped the home.

Harvey handed Margaret the envelope and her heart stilled as she quickly opened the last communication she would ever receive from her husband.

> *Dearest Margaret,*
>
> *I'm sorry I must leave you this way, but I could not go on with the pain and guilt for what happened to Suzanne for one more day. I was the one that gave Stephen Dennis a chance to better himself and look where it got us. I placed the gun in his hands that killed our daughter and wounded Eleanor. In December Stephen Dennis called his attorney informing him he wanted to change his plea to guilty by reasons of insanity, a desperate move to get off death row. I have lived with this for three weeks. It's more than a father can bear. By the time you read this I'll be out of my misery and with our daughter. I've thought everything through. You and Elizabeth will be financially taken care of. Thank you for loving me through the years. You were the best wife a man could ever wish for, and I love you with all my heart and soul. I'm sorry. This is not your fault.*
>
> *Forever and a day, Alfred*

Margaret laid the linen stationery on the table as tears dripped down her face and stained the page. She began to sob and was incapable of speech. Edward and Harvey sat at the table unable to move.

"I'll call the priest," Harvey murmured.

CHAPTER FOURTEEN

Stephen K. Dennis's 1961 death sentence was argued again January 5, 1965 and reversed in May of 1965 by the U.S. Fourth Circuit Court of Appeals on grounds that a true test was not made of his sanity. It would begin a year of hearings and psychiatric tests for the prisoner.

The Corporation Court's late winter session of 1966 protested the commitment order even though a psychiatrist's report stated: "Stephen Dennis should be considered extremely dangerous for a great many years to come."

Stephen would disregard the advice of his attorney and take the stand. "I was prevented from hiring a lawyer and the Commonwealth's Attorney has no right to prosecute the case in the first place," he said. Pointing an accusing finger at Todd Wynn, he continued, "The Commonwealth's Attorney went out the night before with the girl I killed. He had no right to prosecute the case."

"I've been married since 1955 and considered a pillar in the community," Wynn stated, laughing off the accusations.

Judge Lawrence Hudson was obviously irritated by Dennis's charge against Wynn. "The commitment fell within the law. As of this minute you are committed to the Virginia State Mental Hospital," he said as he glared at Dennis. "Earlier this year, I ordered a local mental examination on Stephen Dennis," the judge continued. "In February, Dennis was examined by Dr. Frederick Whitman, a local psychiatrist. The report by Dr. Whitman states: 'I examined the man for over an hour and felt satisfied at the end of this time that he was mentally ill, suffering from a schizophrenic reaction of paranoid type, severe in degree and that he was lacking in insight. He expressed absolutely no remorse for the killing, justifying it on the basis that some people are just marked for death. Dennis gave a vivid description of how he shot Mrs. Barclay and wounded another woman in Mrs. Barclay's home. He claimed his father was a member of the Cosa Nostra, which he pronounced *Casa*

Nova, had killed twenty-three men, wounded two and was a member of the Ku Klux Klan, but never served any time. He also claimed that members of his family were psychic and could regulate events by merely blinking their eyes.'"

Pausing for a brief moment, the judge continued, "Further, Dr. Whitman gave the following summation, 'It is my impression that this man is mentally ill, legally insane, incompetent to stand trial, probably permanently incapacitated and because of lack of insight and control, he should be considered extremely dangerous for a great many years to come.'"

William Keller who had remained with Dennis the past five years rose in the courtroom. "My client wants to address the court, but I have advised him against it."

Stephen took the stand and with a smile on his face stated, "I want to hire a lawyer."

"You already have one of the best lawyers in the state. Get this man out of my courtroom!" Judge Hudson ordered.

Elizabeth lived to cantor and jump. Margaret would drop her off after school so she could spend time with Virginia Peanut. The Aspirin Riding School was her second home.

"Now please be careful around all those horses. They can be mean," Margaret called out as Elizabeth dashed into the stables.

The uniform of jodhpurs and riding boots was worn with pride. With blonde braids flying in the wind on her very own horse, she felt she could breeze through life just as easily. Never missing a lesson or afternoon of practice, Peanut and mistress were disciplined and in sync.

The warm Saturday, the first of May in the brilliant Virginia sunshine, was perfect for the jumping competition. Peanut and Elizabeth with both manes braided to perfection readied themselves before entering the field.

Standing by her horse while holding his bridle, Elizabeth kissed him on his soft velvety nose. "I know we're going to win a ribbon today Peanut—I can just feel it. The others don't know what they're doing. They can't even control the reins. I just know we'll be unbeaten," she sniffed.

Sycamore Creek's horse set had turned out to cheer the teenage Barbies on. The mothers of Virginia descent never missed a chance to wear a wide brim hat in the sun, sipping their sherry as they watched their daughters giggle with nervousness.

Peanut and Elizabeth trotted onto the field, picked up the pace as Elizabeth leaned forward for their leap over the horse jumps, a maneuver they had accomplished with great finesse time and time again. This day however, Ole Peanut had other ideas. He decided he would come to an abrupt stop, take a bow, and let his costumed mistress plunge and tumble out of her freshly waxed saddle. Elizabeth leapt over the horse jump, but Peanut did not.

The ladies gasped, but not as loudly as Margaret. Jumping up from her seat, she rushed to get as close to her granddaughter as possible. Elizabeth had landed and tumbled resulting in a sore neck. Pride and dignity hurt beyond words with the aborted jump by her stubborn Peanut, who just wasn't in the mood that afternoon for entertaining the Mom Belles of Sycamore Creek.

Mothers became frantic with worry as they looked for their own daughters about to perform. Elizabeth scuffed her boots in the sand as she strolled to Margaret, head bowed with tears rolling down her cheeks.

The ambulance was called, and the volunteers checked her for injuries, concluding the only damage they could ascertain was ego.

"We need to sell that horse. I won't bury another child," Margaret said with determination, driving Elizabeth home.

"No, Nana, not ever! I love Peanut." It would not be the first or last of spills off his back, unbeknownst to Margaret. *What she doesn't know won't hurt her*, Elizabeth thought.

Ambling in the back door, Margaret and Elizabeth began to inform Blanche what had happened that afternoon.

"Oh Lord a mercy. I'll cooks you anythin' your little heart desires, honey chile."

Those are the sweetest words one could ever wish to hear, Elizabeth thought. She soon would be recuperating on the couch propped up by down-filled feather pillows. "Don't forget a dollop of whipped cream on top, Blanche, pretty please," she called. Quite enjoying all the lavish attention as she stuffed her mouth with homemade pecan pie, she managed to give Blanche a wink.

September 13, 1966

"I'm insane; I can't be tried for murder," Stephen Dennis insisted. His retrial was scheduled for that morning in Corporation Court, but was delayed.

"Dennis claims he is insane, and under state law, cannot be tried. The law says a defendant must be mentally competent to plead and stand trial," the judge explained.

At the sanity hearing, Lillian described her son's younger years as ones of confusion, delusion, and attempted suicide. She had been instructed by Keller on exactly what to recite on behalf of her son. Lillian spent hours poring over the typed pages he had given her, struggling to pronounce words that were strange to her ear.

"I noticed a difference in Stephen when he was ten or twelve years old. He was very nervous, and he'd have those horrible dreams. At age fourteen to sixteen, he was always askin' for sleepin' pills. I was forced to hide the household medicine. He was goin' to kill himself. He said nobody loved him. He said he had a brain tumor and was goin' to die. He shot himself in the leg in July of 1957, and the same month was committed to the Virginia State Hospital for the insane. He was furloughed in August of 1958 and after attemptin' suicide in December of that year in Sycamore Creek was recommitted. My boy was discharged in April of 1959 to come to Virginia Beach to work as a bellhop in a resort hotel. His difficulty with Suzanne and Eleanor followed."

Lillian sat wringing her hands, as pieces of wadded Kleenex fell from her lap like swaddling. "I visited him on death row several times a year. He'd be all mixed up. Often, he'd ask me if I'd seen Suzanne Barclay. He acted like he didn't remember what happened. I think Stephen is a very sick boy."

Stephen sat at the table throughout his mother's testimony with his head slightly bowed and his hands shielding his eyes.

Lillian continued, "If he couldn't get his way, he'd pick up chairs and throw them, walk the floor and say he was goin' to kill himself. He once owned a car, along about 1957 and frequently bought accessories for it."

The judge interjected, "He did all right for himself. Most of them around here steal them." The comment brought chuckles from the courthouse, and Stephen who had been passive, allowed a smile to cross his face.

A police officer traveled all the way from Sycamore Creek to testify as well. Stephen looked at him. The officer was familiar with the attempted suicide and told the court, "His actions do not surprise me. I always thought he was incompetent."

The hearing would continue the following day in the battle of psychiatrists. Smiling to himself, Stephen knew he was returning for mental testing, and if he played his cards right, then he might just save his own life.

September 14, 1966

DENNIS RETURNED FOR MENTAL TESTING
POTENTIALLY DANGEROUS

The headlines of *The Daily Norfolk* were bold, and the article followed suit:

> Yesterday's hearing was an effort by Stephen Dennis's attorney, William Keller, to have the court rule that Dennis was not mentally competent to stand trial at this time.
>
> Physicians at the Virginia State Hospital had already said Dennis was sane and competent to stand trial, the latest appraisal having been made in March.
>
> The presiding Judge said the physicians at the state hospital would now have the benefit of reports made by Keller's team of psychiatrists. They testified he was insane, mentally incompetent to stand trial, and potentially dangerous to the public.

For his part, Keller briefed the newspaper, saying "I'm disappointed that the judge chose not to make the decision himself on the basis of the evidence presented. I question the wisdom of recommitting him to Virginia State Mental Hospital. The physicians at Virginia State could be miffed that their decision has been questioned. I asked if there wasn't another hospital available and the judge said absolutely not. I already stated that the state hospital system for the criminally insane have facilities and staff that are inadequate—they release patients for trial without a full evaluation. I hope this hearing has done one thing. I hope it brings these hospitals to task in their examinations."

During the hearing, Keller got the doctor who had examined Dennis the day after the crime to admit the patient was under the influence of tranquillizers.

Commonwealth's Attorney Todd Wynn argued that the public is unaware of what would happen if Dennis was judged insane and sent back to the hospital.

"He's going back to a hospital where physicians have already said he is sane. They would have no recourse but to turn him out. If we say this man can't stand trial, it's tantamount to freeing him. The public should know that. This is the day in court for the defendant; I say the public should have its own day in court," Wynn stated.

He continued, "One thing is for certain, the courts haven't seen the last of Stephen Dennis."

CHAPTER FIFTEEN

"You're doing what, Edward?" Margaret inquired.

Elizabeth heard her grandmother's angry voice coming from the library; she heard a tone that made her come to a complete standstill, rooting her feet to the floor by the front door. She had planned to walk to the public library this unusually warm March day. Forsythia bushes bloomed with vivid yellow flowers against the barren landscape. Mother Nature had yet to realize spring was still around the corner as freezing temperatures prevailed most evenings.

"I'm building a duplex on the beach. I'll rent the first-floor year-round and live on the second. The builder said he could start next week. Elizabeth can spend the summers with me and I can get to know my daughter better. I've joined the Cavalier Beach Club recently. It has an Olympic size pool with an outdoor grill, and a bar you can swim right up to. She'll love it," he said with nervous tension in his voice.

Margaret pressed her ear against the receiver, trying to comprehend what Edward was describing. *Too big for his britches*, she thought.

"You've not sent any child support or rent from Suzanne's house this entire year. I have been patient long enough. How in the world can you afford a place at the beach, Edward?"

"Well ... I cashed in Suzanne's life insurance policy and I'm using that."

"You did what?! That's Elizabeth's money for her college education! I cannot believe this!"

"Margaret, please calm down. Her name will be on the deed to the property. It will be worth a fortune someday, at least a million as real estate values rise. It'll be all hers; I promise you."

"Edward, you are a poor excuse for a father. You're responsible for Elizabeth's college education. It's a parent's obligation, after all. I'm so upset right now. I don't want to talk to you until I think this over!"

The phone went dead.

"What's wrong, Nana?"

"Nothing that I can't handle." Margaret went in the kitchen and put the kettle on the stove for tea. She needed time to mull this over.

"I'm going to the library," Elizabeth yelled, exiting the house at breakneck speed. The one thing Elizabeth could not withstand was confrontation and controversy, particularly between Nana and her father. She missed her father's presence as he was always away on business. On occasion he would attend her ballet recitals, but he would always walk into the auditorium at the last minute. At the last recital, he had the audacity to bring an attractive lady who clung to him all evening. The visit was very short-lived as Edward claimed they had to drive back to Virginia Beach the same night, only to end up in a hotel on the shore. Elizabeth and Margaret were relieved; it was hard to witness Edward's attempt to replace Suzanne.

Standing on the top floor of the beautifully decorated duplex, Elizabeth looked out the bank of glass windows towards the Atlantic Ocean. Edward had painstakingly decorated the upper floor with Suzanne's furniture from the rancher. The blood-soaked chair had been reupholstered and a few new pieces were now a part of the collection. When she entered the duplex, her eye traveled to the large fireplace on the right and then to a long bar on the left side of the massive room. A narrow hall lead to two bedrooms on opposite sides. Varying colors of beige dominated the quintessential bachelor's pad.

When Elizabeth visited her father, they would spend hours in art galleries and fine antique stores, hunting for just the right piece of marine art to hang over the fireplace. On one sojourn, Elizabeth saw a beautiful oil painting of a Chinese junk, the moody colors of green and blue as the ocean met the sky spoke to her.

"Look, Daddy, I love that painting of the oriental ship. It would be perfect in the living room."

"If you like it, I'll buy it," Edward said reaching for his checkbook— that at all times seemed limitless.

Although she was only fourteen, Elizabeth could feel her father's loneliness. He had become a functioning alcoholic. Cocktails began immediately when he walked through the duplex door from the office. A pitcher of martinis was concocted which brought back vivid memories of his special happy hours with Suzanne. Edward sat at his bar sipping and creating ads for the Reuben H. Donnelley's yellow pages. His only social interaction with women was at the Cavalier Beach Club, where he frequented drinking and dancing the night away.

There was once a serious relationship with a girl named Beverly, but as time went by she realized she was unable to compete with a ghost ... one which was a constant age of twenty-five and beguiling, a memory that would never die.

Edward lived longing.

Elizabeth was packing for the last week of summer vacation, looking forward to days spent around the pool at the Cavalier Beach Club. Tying her string bikini over her developed breasts, she realized she would need a new one next summer. The top barely covered her, making her look much older than she was.

"I worry about you in Virginia Beach. Please be careful and stick with your girlfriends you've made there when you are around the pool. Are you sure your father doesn't leave you alone at night?" Margaret asked.

Elizabeth threw her clothes in the suitcase, wishing her grandmother would for once stop worrying. It seemed she fretted over every single thing as she matured.

"I love it there, Nana. I may spend all of next summer. I'll be fifteen, old enough."

"I don't think so, young lady. Uncle Harvey wants you to start working at the funeral parlor, learning the business."

"Yuck!"

"We'll discuss this later. Your father just pulled up," Margaret said, glancing out the window at Edward's latest purchase of a luxury vehicle.

Edward loaded up Elizabeth's luggage and off they drove in the Cadillac convertible, wind flying through their hair.

Elizabeth spent the last week of August swimming in the pool and performing numerous cannonballs. Her competition was her crush, Ricky, who always made the biggest splash. The sandy-haired boy with the golden tan flirted only with her and never once with the other girls.

"Stop untying my top," Elizabeth hollered, holding the front of her swimsuit with one hand and splashing water in his face with the other. He laughed and dunked her head under the chlorine water until her eyes stung, finally relenting and tying the string in a perfect bow as it cascaded down her bronze-colored back.

Picking up Elizabeth from the pool on his way home from work, Edward said, "I'm really going to miss you tomorrow. Let's come back to the club this evening and have dinner. I heard there's a good little jazz trio playing tonight."

Elizabeth was thrilled, thinking that just maybe Ricky would show up with his parents.

Elizabeth felt special in the white-eyelet shift dress that emphasized her tan. Her hair was nearly white after a week of Sun-In and chlorine. *I look like all the other Virginia Beach girls*, she thought gazing in the mirror, enamored with herself.

Edward and Elizabeth dined on filet mignon and lobster tail as she sipped her Shirley Temple. They danced the cha-cha as the trio played with a Latin beat, receiving a round of applause walking back to their table. Elizabeth recollected watching her parents cha-cha, tango, and rumba the hours away in the evenings when she was a child, often including her in their dance routines. Tonight, she saw her father's pride, and she felt guilty leaving him after such a happy week.

"I'm going to take you home and come back to talk with some of my friends," Edward said as he eyed a striking redhead at the bar.

"Yes sir. I need to pack for tomorrow. What time did you say we were leaving?"

"Around 'leven." Edward slightly slurred after too many martinis.

Elizabeth felt relieved to be back in the duplex. Her father's alcoholism had grown scary as the years progressed, the constant feeling of unease she remembered experiencing as a child.

She turned on the television and began to pack, wondering if she would return for Thanksgiving. It was different here. She could do what she wanted without the constant worrying of her grandmother. She thought to herself, *after all, where could I find such complete freedom, but here?*

Packed and still excited from all the attention of a couple of hours ago at the club, she decided to jump in the shower and wash her hair. *One more thing I won't have to do tomorrow,* she thought. She had just turned on the faucet when, much to her great shock, the bathroom door opened and a hand on the shower curtain appeared, pulling it to the opposite side.

"Give me a kiss, Suzzzanne," Edward slurred, trying to keep steady on his feet as he stepped over the tub. Elizabeth gasped—he was nude! Never had she seen a naked man before, and she frantically searched for an exit from the shower before her father staggered and fell on her. He seemed determined to kiss her as she grabbed the other side of the shower curtain and ran to the door, not being able to take the time to grab a towel. Running to her room, she slammed and locked the door, looking for something to wrap around her soaking wet body. She grabbed the blanket off the bed, covering herself. She was shaking uncontrollably.

After a few moments, Elizabeth collected herself and got dressed. She laid on top of the bed listening. After an hour, she assumed her father had passed out from drunkenness in his king size bed. She didn't sleep at all that night.

The following morning, she unlocked the door and waited in the living room until her father readied himself for the drive back to Sycamore Creek.

The convertible top was down, which made conversation against the wind inaudible, but there was no conversation to be heard. Only silence and traffic. Elizabeth knew life for her and this stranger she couldn't trust had changed forever.

Pulling into the oyster shell driveway of the welcoming Victorian home, she hopped out of the car, brushing past Margaret who stood on the porch to greet her with a hug.

"What's wrong? What's happened, Edward?" Margaret asked as her granddaughter raced by her.

"Teenagers." Edward rolled his swollen bloodshot eyes as he put her luggage in the living room.

"You can believe that I will find out!" Margaret exclaimed.

"I have an appointment this afternoon. Tell Elizabeth I'll call her."

As she watched the Cadillac speed away, Margaret's womanly intuition told her something nefarious had happened.

She went up to Elizabeth's room and asked her granddaughter if she was feeling ill. Elizabeth had unmade the poster bed and sunk down in between the covers. Margaret noticed the dark circles around her eyes.

"I don't want to talk about it Nana."

Margaret never knew what happened during Elizabeth's visit with her father. It remained a dark secret. That visit would, however, be the last one for years to come.

CHAPTER SIXTEEN

I done it! Stephen smiled to himself as he waited for his new trial to begin. A nine-year fight against avoiding death would end soon. He was confident that his life would be spared, and according to his attorney, he would be eligible for parole after fifteen years.

"Stephen, you will automatically be credited for time served since 1960. This case is simple," Keller assured him with a slap on the back.

Stephen's pleas, in effect, were the same he entered in a jury trial in April 1961, but with one important difference. In 1961, he said he was not guilty because of insanity—a plea that he did it but wasn't blameworthy. When he was asked at this trial, he simply said, "I did it."

Eleanor was ready to testify once again, hopefully for the last time. She had moved to Weston, Vermont where she rented a small Cape Cod cottage. She was painting and selling her art, and had become a recluse—painting at night and sleeping during the day. Nights were terrorizing, caused by heightened anxiety attacks. Natural light made her mind calmer, but still she was only able get five hours of sleep or less daily. She was very rarely in public, and when she was, she was constantly looking over her shoulder, always leery of people around her. A constant state of heightened alert had become a way of life. The paranoia had paralyzed her ability to succeed in the professional workplace she had once loved so well. Relationships suffered except for her constant companion, a rescued mutt from the humane society. A kind, elderly couple lived next door. Eleanor wondered how long they would be able to help her with chopping wood for the fireplace, which was the only means of warmth. She guessed she would have to bite the bullet eventually and install some form of heat for the quaint dwelling. The monthly check from her parents was meager, but she was becoming well-known as an artist that could capture the landscape of Vermont.

Taking the stand, Eleanor began her testimony. After nine years, she was a more confident woman. She glared at Stephen Dennis.

"I visited the home of Mrs. Barclay, my cousin, about five-fifteen in the evening, on October 26, 1960. I sat in the nearest chair and asked Suzanne whose car was in her driveway. She was paying bills at her writing desk. I saw Stephen entering the living room from the bathroom down the hall. Suzanne and I grew up with Stephen in Sycamore Creek. I spoke to him, noticing a puzzled look on his face as he glanced at me.

"Stephen walked past us and pulled out a pistol. I was sitting with my legs crossed and he shot me through both legs. Then Suzanne screamed, and Stephen said it was an accident slamming and locking the front door. She said she would have to call an ambulance.

"Suzanne ran into the bedroom and was followed by Stephen. I heard a scuffle and they ran back into the living room. Suzanne was apparently trying to get out of the locked front door. He slung her backwards and shot her several times. Then he shot me in the neck. It went in here," she said indicating the entry over her left shoulder. "It struck the edge of a vertebra and came up through my throat and lodged in my mouth."

Eleanor continued, "I witnessed Stephen removing clothing from Suzanne's body. Next, he removed some of my clothing and raped me. Then he moved to where Suzanne's body was, then returned to me and raped me again.

"He went in the kitchen and started running water. I heard him say, 'What have I done. I have killed two women.' I heard him holler at Thor, her boxer, and then the gun was fired again. After that he called the police." Eleanor spoke without emotion—her tears had dried up years ago.

"He went to Suzanne and looked into her eyes. Then he looked into mine and said, 'This one ain't dead.' Stephen asked me if I knew where a hospital was. I said yes. He summoned a neighborhood boy to hold the door open while he carried me to the station wagon. He drove me to St. Mary's Hospital and dumped me on a stretcher in the hall and left. He was arrested by police when he returned to the crime scene."

Eleanor's eyes bore into Stephen's as she stepped down from the stand. She wondered if he knew the magnitude of heartache and altered lives he was responsible for. As she left Virginia on a flight to Vermont that evening, she vowed never to return.

Dr. Maurice Murray, the state medical examiner in 1960, took the stand. He testified, "About six-fifteen in the evening, on October 26, 1960, I went to the address of the home of Mrs. Barclay. There I saw Mrs. Barclay's body. My later examination showed she was shot three times, once through the spinal cord, once through the right lung, and once through the left arm. The cause of death was multiple gunshot wounds."

Throughout the proceedings, Stephen sat staring at the floor. He responded in very short answers to questions from the judge.

"Do you have anything at all to say after entering your guilty plea?"

"No."

The Commonwealth's Attorney recommended life imprisonment. Defense attorney Keller asked that the recommendation be adopted and with that, the judge sentenced Stephen K. Dennis to prison for life. Further, he said, "I am permitting the prosecution to drop the remaining indictments: two counts of rape and one for the wounding of Eleanor Johnson as well as one count of raping Suzanne Barclay."

Two state psychiatrists were summoned to the witness stand ironically after the sentence. Both said they had reviewed Dennis's record and had viewed Dennis in the courtroom. They were of the opinion that he had been capable to plead and assist in his own defense.

The trial ended a little after eleven o'clock in the morning and Stephen Dennis had been sentenced to the state penitentiary for the rest of his natural life. It had lasted less than 20 minutes.

Afterwards, Stephen posed and smiled on the steps outside the courthouse. "Send me a copy of the photograph," he said to the reporter. A police officer escorted him away to jail.

"Mr. Keller, Mr. Keller. Will you grant us an interview?" the staff writer of *The Daily Norfolk* called out.

William Keller seemed moderately at ease sitting across the table in the conference room, happy to be interviewed—excited to have his picture in the press! He knew there was precious little to take pleasure in about a life sentence, but he still loved the limelight.

"I have fought for this man. Stephen Dennis might be on death row at the penitentiary—or dead. Perhaps the changing mood of the time that Dennis killed in 1960 and was sentenced to die in 1961—might have saved him. Some observers speculated the U.S. Fourth Circuit grasped at a straw in 1965 and granted him a new trial, ostensibly because of flaws in the trial, but in fact merely to save Dennis from the electric chair.

"I have been on this case during its most trying times. Twice up the ladder of appeals. We won the argument against Dennis's execution in the Fourth U.S. Circuit Court of Appeals in 1965 and preserved the victory later in the U.S. Supreme Court. Since the spring of 1965, I have guarded the case jealously when at times it seemed that Dennis might hazard himself before a jury and get back on the road to the death house.

"This has literally been a battle of psychiatrists from the beginning. The state had their crowd and of course the defense can get psychiatrists to sustain their position," Keller said, enjoying his diatribe.

"Just three months ago," he continued, "Dennis sent for me and informed me that he would plead guilty. The assumption was that a life sentence was in the offing and not the death penalty. Today, after the guilty plea, the state made the agreed sentence—recommendation of life imprisonment.

"Dennis's case is a good argument for a public defender in the state. I was on the case as retained but a low-paid private counsel. Later I was court appointed but still a low-paid lawyer. I have a negative view of the death penalty as a device for law enforcement. The death penalty is a lot of damned nonsense and barbaric. The legislature ought to go one step further and just abolish it.

"Obviously, with a fellow sitting in death row the case is more critical. You hold yourself out as a trial lawyer. What else do you do?" Keller crowed to the reporters.

"Miss Margret, I just saw Lillian Dennis uptown. She said her boy would need a place to rent. He'll be out of jail soon. She asked me if I knew of any place he could go?"

George Thompson had leased the Eyre's farm land for years, growing cotton, corn, and wheat. He knocked on Margaret's backdoor immediately after his conversation with Lillian. George's face was red, and he was out of breath as he relayed the current news.

"We don't want that murderer in Sycamore Creek. There must be something the town folks can do." George shook his head, regret in his eyes. "I hate to burden you, Miss Margaret, with this news."

"I've not been notified of Dennis being set free by the Commonwealth. I'll call Ray Morton, the District State's Attorney. He's a local boy. He'll help us out," Margaret muttered. "I thank you for coming to me, George."

After George left, Margaret's eyes slammed shut. *No, this can't be happening.* Taking a slow breath, she walked to the phone. Picking up the local phone book, she found the number for Ray Morton's office and slowly dialed with a trembling finger. She explained to him the information George had just given her—her voice tight with concern.

"Miss Margaret, you have nothing to worry about," Ray advised her. "I will circulate a petition in Sycamore Creek that we don't want Stephen Dennis back in this town. You have my word. I believe the information you heard was a rumor."

Margaret began to breathe easier. Feeling the tension release from her shoulders, she said, "Thank you, Ray."

"Are you all right?" Ray inquired.

"I'll be fine," Margaret said with a false sense of bravado.

Margaret hung up the phone and looked at the clock on the kitchen wall. It soon would be time to pick up Elizabeth from school. *How much longer should I keep all this from my granddaughter*, she wondered. *After all, Harvey has plans.*

CHAPTER SEVENTEEN

"Hello," Margaret said as she answered the phone beside her chair. Her favorite program, *The Dean Martin Show*, was on television. She had waited all day to watch Dean in his tuxedo and was irritated by the interruption. It was late, after all, and she enjoyed Thursday nights with the sexy TV swooner.

"Hell...looo, Margaret. I want to talk to my daughter." Edward slurred more than Dean.

"Edward, she's asleep. Elizabeth doesn't want to talk to you. She won't tell me what occurred during her last visit. So, I want to know exactly what transpired?"

"I...I don't remember."

"Yes, you do. Please stop calling here."

With that, the phone went dead until two in the morning.

Margaret sat up in bed, removed her sleeping mask, and turned on the lamp. Reaching for the phone on her mahogany table, she yawned into the receiver, "Hello?"

"You have a telegram from Western Union," the operator announced.

"What? Go ahead."

"Dear Elizabeth. Stop. Your grandmother won't let me talk to you. Stop. Please call me. Stop. I love you. Stop. Daddy."

"Thank you." Margaret placed the receiver back on the cradle. "Oh, for heaven sakes. Edward is a noose around my neck," she grumbled under her breath, pulling the covers over her head. Margaret had her suspicions, but she also had a gnawing feeling that under no circumstances would she ever know the reason for the estrangement between father and daughter. They had not seen one another in two years.

Elizabeth had blossomed into a lovely young lady. Days were spent with Virginia Peanut, ballet, teas, and finishing classes. Margaret was adamant that her manners would remain those of the Southern Belle. Her purpose in life was to keep busy, at no expense, with her granddaughter's maturity and refinement. This did not allow time to grieve for Suzanne, Alfred, or get caught up in the legal system where Stephen Dennis had oddly become the victim.

A set of new circumstances had prevailed due to politics.

Elizabeth had become quite the bookworm. Confining herself to her bedroom, she sat in the chaise and read the hours away. Last summer she received an award from the library for reading sixty-four books, more than any card holder in town. But on this day, she was on her way out the door to the library for the second time that week.

"I'm going to the library, Nana," Elizabeth called.

"Elizabeth, I need to talk to you. Come in here for a minute."

"Um, what did I do?" Elizabeth asked in reply to Nana's seriousness.

"Have you thought about a job for the summer? You need to start contributing to your college education and job experience wouldn't hurt. It builds character and structure."

"Uh, I guess I could get a job at the library organizing the card catalogue. I'll ask Miss Hazel today," she replied, but her heart wasn't in it. Her goal was to be galloping on the back of Peanut for the entire summer. Trying to go through the motions of being social had waned since the unfortunate circumstances with her father. Guys kept asking her on dates, but she just wasn't interested. She preferred one girlfriend and one girlfriend only, avoiding complications.

"Well, your Uncle Harvey wants to talk to you about testing the waters at the funeral parlor," Margaret spoke gingerly, carefully selecting her words.

Elizabeth's mouth dropped open, unable to comprehend what her grandmother was trying to explain. Life had been so utopic and then BAM! She felt as though Nana had hit her upside the head with a three-day old hushpuppy.

"Are you informing me I have to earn my keep?" she asked with an attitude.

"No need to overreact, young lady. You'll thank me some day," Margaret said, matching her tone. "Your Uncle Harvey wants to meet you for an interview this afternoon."

"Why? I already know him."

"He wants to explain what goes on behind closed doors to operate and maintain a funeral parlor. Funerals don't just happen overnight, you know. He's aging, and you could be such an asset with your personality. Your interview is at three o'clock this afternoon."

"Ha, ha." Elizabeth wasn't amused.

"You'll need to wear a dress and fix your hair," her grandmother spoke with authority.

Sitting at her favorite table in the library, Elizabeth began to reflect on all her visits to the Sycamore Creek Funeral Home throughout the years. She considered it her second home. Blanche and Uncle Harvey were her favorite people, and to her it really was no big deal they lived in a house of the dead. She was intrigued at an early age by all the exquisite antiques Uncle Harvey had acquired from fine galleries and shops throughout the South. Just last year, Blanche warned her to be careful of the china, glass figurines, and accessories on the mahogany Chippendale and Queen Anne tables.

"Everythin' all up in here is the real thing. Goin' back to the eighteenth century when my peoples was slaves," Blanche stated, as if Uncle Harvey had made her his own personal curator.

"Mr. Harvey spent lots of money on his things and takes great pride in them. The oriental rugs are handmade wool from Iran." Blanche swooped her hand down and up as if she were on stage.

There had been many facets that Blanche had educated her on as she grew older. Blanche knew the fine arts and loved the opportunity to enlighten the next generation with her knowledge. Admiring the oil paintings, silver, and furniture, Elizabeth pondered if the people in the funeral business were in some type of cult, or the mafia, to acquire such treasures.

Uncle Harvey's bedroom reminded Elizabeth of an English king's she had once seen in the movies. The large, four-poster canopy bed was dressed in raspberry silk damask with a bedspread to match. Waterford lamps constantly illuminated the room covered in dark wallpaper. There was an oil portrait of an English gentleman over the bed. A picture lamp shone on the young man's face giving him a girlish look. Elizabeth would stare at the painting, trying to ascertain if it was a female when all was said and done—rosy cheeks and blonde ringlets.

Everything in Uncle Harvey's home was immaculate. The local florist had a standing order to deliver a large arrangement of calla lilies twice a week, which were then placed on the piecrust scalloped table in the foyer. A large crystal chandelier hung from the ceiling, shining on the massive oak stairway.

Every time she visited, she would think, *I want to live with beautiful things surrounding me someday*. The finer things spoke to her. *His house is fancier than Nana's, but Nana's was homier*. Decorated with furniture and lamps from her mother and mother-in-law, taking on a mismatched look, she contemplated the difference.

Glancing at her Timex, Elizabeth decided to hurry home for her appointment with Uncle Harvey. Maybe she would be able to collect antiques of this quality just like her uncle. *Better not be late*, she thought.

Blanche had her white blouse pressed and navy skirt hanging on the door hook of her closet. She was allowed to wear makeup since she turned sixteen, but only soft pink blush and lipstick. Nana had held her ground and not given in to pierced ears yet. Being extra careful she made sure the mascara was applied lightly. Her blonde hair was pulled back in a ponytail with a navy, satin ribbon bow that Blanche tied perfectly.

"You look so pretty. I want to take a Polaroid of this special day," Margaret said. Elizabeth felt as if Nana knew something she didn't and rolled her eyes with impatience.

Uncle Harvey met her at the door of the funeral parlor and merrily gave her a squeeze. "Come in, come in, darlin'," he greeted her. Gesturing his hand toward his office he instructed her to have a seat in front of his desk.

"First, I'd like to give you a little history lesson on how I ended up in this business," Uncle Harvey said, sitting down in front of the massive mahogany desk.

Elizabeth knew it would take a while. Uncle Harvey loved to hear himself talk. It seemed the older he got, the more he repeated stories, particularly about his younger years. She settled in the wing chair and waited for him to begin.

"I was once a banker, but even in those days, I was a very frustrated undertaker. I worked part-time in this very funeral parlor when I was your age. My father, your great grandfather, was friends with the president of the bank. They also hunted together. After my stint in the Navy, I returned home and was promptly placed in the First Bank of Sycamore Creek. There was no doubt I'd work my way up to president. It was a given. However, I was like a cat on a hot tin roof and could not get the scent of formaldehyde out of my sinuses." Uncle Harvey laughed low and loud. Growing serious he continued, "I broke my father's heart, hung up the business degree and bought the funeral parlor from Mr. Wilson, the old bachelor I had worked for since I was a lad. I have no heirs to leave the funeral parlor to except my niece. I'll cut to the chase. Are you interested?"

"I guess so," Elizabeth whispered. She had no idea where this was leading as her mind drifted back to the exquisite antiques and his wealthy lifestyle. "Yes, Uncle Harvey. Yes, I am," she said, batting her eye lashes.

"God bless your little heart."

With that, Harvey began barking orders on what he expected from her. "You'll be weeding the flower gardens, washing the coach, and manning the guestbook at all viewings and funerals this summer. Be sure to bring a change of clothes to wear in the yard."

Elizabeth swore she saw a twinkle in his eye. A tour of the funeral parlor was not necessary since she had practically made it her second home. The mood had changed; Uncle Harvey had morphed into a tyrant.

She was madder than a wet hen during the short walk home. *He expects too much manual labor from me. That's what he has Roger for. Maybe after school I can enlist for a tour in Vietnam*, she thought. Contemplating the idea, she grew concerned about central air conditioning in the barracks. "I do not want to experience any climate more humid than the summers in Virginia. I can't run away because Peanut and I don't know where to go," she said under her breath. *Oh well, I might as well join them. Uncle Harvey didn't seem too impressed that I was going to have a career as a Rockette anyway*, she lamented to herself.

"How did it go?" Nana questioned before Elizabeth had hardly stepped a foot into the kitchen.

"Uh ... I think I had the job before I was even interviewed."

"Congratulations!" Margaret grabbed Elizabeth and hugged her to her soft bosom. Elizabeth thought she would choke to death on the scent of Estee' Lauder's *Youth Dew* perfume, Nana's signature fragrance for years.

"Thanks, but I'm still going to be a Rockette." Elizabeth was aware it irritated her grandmother that she would ever consider leaving Sycamore Creek, let alone move to a big city, such as the likes of New York City.

"That's enough of that kind of talk. I have a surprise for you on your bed."

"Like what, Nana?"

"You'll see."

They both climbed the stairs to Elizabeth's room. Margaret beamed as she watched her granddaughter pick up the little black dress and hold it up to her body. Gazing in the mirror, she said, "Nana, I love it."

"Oh good. I bought it at Feinstein's in Salisbury. It's very conservative. Try it on, I think it will fit. There's also a pair of little black kitten heels in the shoe box."

Elizabeth removed her skirt and blouse and donned the black dress. It was a perfect fit. Slipping on the kitten heels, she gazed at herself in the mirror and liked what she saw. *I look sexy*, she thought, admiring the view.

"Don't you look pretty," Nana said, smiling with delight. "You favor your mother so much. You know what you need?" she continued not allowing Elizabeth to answer. "Your mother's pearls. She had a strand of real cultured pearls with earrings to match. I think they are packed in the attic somewhere. I placed all her things in the front on the right of the window. Everything of hers belongs to you and you can go through them anytime you wish."

"I'm going to look for them right now."

"Change your clothes first," Margaret chuckled.

"Oh! Right!" Elizabeth hung up her black dress with care. Slipping on her jeans and Oxford shirt, she placed the heels back in the box, then dashed to the attic. Opening the door and turning on the light switch, she had to duck to get in the low entrance. The steps from the second floor led to the third behind the door to the attic. The scent of mothballs and musty collections of old household items entered her nostrils. Lightbulbs with pull chains hung from the rafters. Elizabeth had always loved to spend afternoons browsing through the antique books her grandparents had saved from their parents. The pages had yellowed with age and silverfish lived quite contently among the binders. Hurrying to the boxes on the right, she was on a mission to find her mother's pearls. "This will be like icing on the cake. I'll start with this small one," she muttered out loud. Crouching down and eyeing the box, she opened it with a vengeance and examined the contents. Staring back at her was a picture of a grinning man. A man with a shaved head, protruding ears, and overlapping teeth.

DENNIS PLEADS INNOCENT
PETITE WOMAN TELLS TALE OF VIOLENCE

The newspaper article headlined above the photograph. There was a stack of articles, carefully cut with scissors, and stacked in chronological order. Gathering the box in her arms, jumping up and banging her head on the rafter, she scurried down the steps. She closed the attic door and plopped down on the chaise in her room. In this moment, Elizabeth would learn in these articles the details of her mother's murder.

At first, Elizabeth felt too stunned to react, but once she collected her wits, she became furious—furious that this gunman could do such a thing to her mother. The mystery of the missing Auntie Eleanor from her life began to fit like pieces of a puzzle. Eleanor's name had not been mentioned in years, the estrangement deep-felt.

DIVORCEE TELLS OF MURDER
DOUBLE RAPE
DEFENDANT FAILS TO TAKE STAND
DENNIS TO DIE AUGUST 26
NEW TRIAL BID DENIED
DENNIS'S DEATH UPHELD
CALLED EXTREMELY DANGEROUS
DENNIS SENT TO HOSPITAL
DENNIS RETURNED FOR MENTAL TESTING
NEW SLAYING TRIAL SET FOR HANDYMAN
ACCUSED SLAYER CLAIMS HE'S INSANE
LIFE SENTENCE GIVEN IN SLAYING
LIFE TERM GIVEN TO DENNIS
DENNIS CASE, TRIAL GRIPPED LAWYER'S LIFE

Each article from *The Daily Norfolk* gave more details than the last. An increasing tightness formed in her stomach. Her mouth was suddenly dry, and the temples of her head throbbed so hard she could only hear the pounding in her brain. Her hands quivered as she put the box aside and grabbed the newspaper articles.

"Why didn't you tell me what happened to Mommy?!" Elizabeth demanded in a horrified voice as she barged into the kitchen.

Margaret closed the oven door where she was basting a roasted chicken for dinner. Harvey was joining them for a celebration of Elizabeth's new job. Placing the baster in a measuring cup, she glanced over her shoulder and lowered her voice. "We thought it was in your best interest, honey. It's been a nightmare and I didn't want you to go through what we have been dealing with all these years. I'm sorry you found out this way," Margaret glanced at the yellowed papers in Elizabeth's shaking hands. Motioning for her to sit down at the table, she swallowed hard and asked, "Do you have any questions for me?"

"Where is he, this ... monster? Am I safe to live here? Is he going to get out? What happened to Auntie Eleanor—it's like she just disappeared?" Elizabeth shot questions at Margaret like darts.

Margaret offered her an apologetic smile and deliberately answered all her questions in a quiet tone. It was time for the truth. Elizabeth was sixteen and Margaret knew sooner or later someone in Sycamore Creek would enlighten her granddaughter. *I'm surprised no one has said anything before now with details about the crime*, she thought.

With all the questions answered, Elizabeth stumbled back to her room. Preoccupied with the findings, she stayed in her room and missed her celebratory dinner in honor of her first job. Not able to sleep for the next two nights, she missed school on Monday. "The whole town knows, Nana. I can't look my friends in the eye."

"Sycamore Creek stood by us, Elizabeth. These are good people here. They don't want him back in this town. Your mother was loved here. Now get yourself together. I'll drive you to school."

Margaret tried to brighten Elizabeth's mood. "Uncle Harvey called. He has a funeral on Saturday. Would you like to work as a hostess?"

CHAPTER EIGHTEEN

Elizabeth was dressed and coiffed to work her first funeral as the guestbook attendant. Walking into the funeral home, her world as she knew it was about to change forever. The Grande Dame of Sycamore Creek or the Hawkins House as known to many, became Sycamore Creek Funeral Home in 1930. It sat on 239 feet of waterfront on the central branch of the creek. Elizabeth could view the water from every room. The winter porch had windows that Uncle Harvey had acquired from an old chapel in the country.

At one time, during the mid-nineteenth century, a shipyard was located at the back of the property. Schooners were built and deployed and plied the waters from Baltimore to the West Indies.

Uncle Harvey had told Elizabeth that the home used to be the First Bank of Sycamore Creek as well. The original safe was still located in the back of the building. Just like her grandmother's home, Uncle Harvey's had a gracious porch that wrapped around the structure. Elizabeth was instructed that if the funeral parlor could not hold all the guests, they could sit on the veranda in warm weather.

Always early, Elizabeth entered the front door and glanced into the secretary's office at Sadie. Recently, Uncle Harvey's secretary, who had been with him for years, decided to retire on her own accord. Ruby Belle was the town gossip. She had abandoned secretarial duties as bridge and sherry became her afternoon delights. The bridge club chattered the time away on who had what and who was running whom in their small hamlet.

"I guess I'll be fixin' to hire a new girl," Uncle Harvey had stated in the town diner. Sure enough, word got out and around Sycamore Creek and he was soon blessed with Sadie, an obtuse, forlorn Ruby Belle replacement whose appearance was comparable to a blown-up bullfrog or lumberjack, with personality to match. Surprisingly, Elizabeth would soon learn that Sadie despised all men except for Uncle Harvey. She gave the impression she knew a secret that Elizabeth didn't.

Sadie's general duties included submitting obituaries to the paper, typing death certificates, and overall paperwork.

"I've explained how important answering the phone is in our business—after all, it's our image," Uncle Harvey clarified in front of Margaret and Elizabeth one evening over dinner. "Depending on Sadie's mood, I never know how she's going to handle a grieving family. You know what she did the other afternoon?"

"What?" Elizabeth mumbled, with mouth full of mashed potatoes.

"Elizabeth, don't talk with your mouth full. That isn't very refined," Margaret instructed.

"Well," Uncle Harvey continued. "She placed a bereaved family who had just experienced the death of their mother on hold and forgot to retrieve or notify me and I was right in my office. They ended up getting in their car and driving seven miles to the funeral parlor. When they banged on the front door Sadie answered and informed them curtly, 'We ain't got no funeral director on call today.' She didn't want to be bothered because it was Friday. Needless to say, I lost the call to my competition the next town over. Nine out of ten times she's too lazy to get up and answer the door," he said, pouring another glass of Beaujolais from the decanter.

"I'll tell you what else happened earlier this week. She forgot to submit an obituary to our local newspaper. The family called incensed to inquire about their loved one. She was in one of her moods and snapped, 'It will be in the paper eventually because the editor only puts the important people in first.'"

"Oh Harvey, she doesn't sound like the caliber you want at the funeral parlor representing you. You have such a sterling reputation for being professional. The Eyre men were always credited with a laudable standing in this community."

"I know, Margaret, but she has nowhere to go. She's really quite pitiful; her family has abandoned her because of ... well ... her lifestyle. I gave her an allowance for clothing, so she could dress more appropriately. Hopefully the next time she comes to work she won't favor a lumberjack. Those red flannel shirts, I declare."

After he left, Nana said to Elizabeth, "Harvey has opened the door to another misfit. God bless him."

Elizabeth tried not to stare walking pass Sadie's office, but concluded this must be the woman that Uncle Harvey was describing over dinner recently.

Sadie glanced up and grunted something Elizabeth had trouble understanding. "You think you're cute," she said with a hint of sarcasm.

Elizabeth had never encountered such a caustic remark. Sadie seemed a bit daunting, but she was up for the challenge. *Uncle Harvey was right—gender was questionable*, she thought. Staring at her cropped haircut, smacking gum loudly, and sitting behind her desk decked out in a gray jogging suit, she thought, *Nana would have her hands full refining this one.*

"My name is Elizabeth. Pleased to meet you."

"I don't care what your name is, missy," she hissed.

"Uh ... where's Uncle Harvey?"

Elizabeth sensed her irritation. Sadie did not welcome her onboard. It was obvious that Sadie didn't realize Elizabeth had a job there, starting today. The woebegone secretary seemed determined not to relinquish any information to her. Elizabeth's jaw tightened, worried that this was the unkind way she would be treated for the entire summer. It seemed impossible that somebody could be so miserable.

"There's my girl. Are you ready for your first day on the job?" Uncle Harvey chuckled, walking out of his office.

Elizabeth glanced at Sadie. She seemed baffled as to what was going on. The ever-present scowl was etched on her face.

"Sadie, have you met my niece Elizabeth?"

Sadie's face reddened with embarrassment. Unable to make eye contact, she cast them downward to her desk. Papers were in disarray and she attempted to busy herself placing them in order.

Elizabeth was willing to let bygones be bygones as she extended her hand. "Pleased to meet you, Sadie," she said for the second time that day.

"Likewise," she muttered.

Harvey chuckled. "Elizabeth, let me show you what chapel the body is in. This one seats seventy-five people and we are expecting a big crowd today. Oh, here's your curb list." Uncle Harvey reached into his coat pocket and handed Elizabeth a typed paper of names. "My morgue rat Charlie is on the street. He'll be parking the family in order of relationship. He has a duplicate of the same list including the pallbearers and minister. If you can, study the list and familiarize yourself with the family, addressing them by name if at all possible. I've built my business on personalization. If anyone gives you a hard time, pull out your list and see if they are actually immediate family."

"Uncle Harvey what's a morgue rat? Are there really rats in there?"

Harvey laughed. "I forgot you don't know the verbiage of the death business. A morgue rat is someone who would rather be in the prep room working on dead bodies than around the public." Uncle Harvey brought his hand to his chin and thought for a moment. "Instead of going over everything all at once, we'll just take it slow and I'll explain as we go along. I wouldn't want you to become overwhelmed on your first day."

Elizabeth's brain was still stuck on morgue rat. "You mean Mr. Charlie likes touching dead bodies?"

"He loves it. He does all the removals, embalmings, and posts ... uh, autopsies."

"Oh, that's so gross. I've never touched a dead body before," Elizabeth said.

He smiled at her. "I need to check on Mr. Jenkins," he said.

Elizabeth followed Uncle Harvey into the big chapel where Mr. Jenkins was laid out, looking quite surreal in his opened casket. Uncle Harvey leaned over him to check his cosmetics. Turning up the torchier lamp one more notch, the pink light bulb cast a rosy glow on Mr. Jenkin's face.

"Oops, his lips have dried out a bit. I need to add a little more wax and touch them up with color," Uncle Harvey spoke with authority.

Elizabeth blinked and watched as Uncle Harvey performed his magic. Using a container of wax and a metal spatula sealing the lips together, he scraped off the remainder of the wax. Then he expertly applied a lip tint with a small lip brush to make sure the contour of the philtrum was perfect. "Wow, Uncle Harvey, you're an artist."

Harvey smiled at the compliment. "I get many accolades on how good the bodies look. It's the reason why people want to use this funeral parlor. If the corpse doesn't look natural, the family will be upset. When I bought the business, Mr. Wilson was only doing forty calls a year. Now I do seventy-five calls. I swear it's because of my bodies," he explained triumphantly.

Elizabeth nodded in agreement, not knowing how to convey her feelings on the matter. She assumed seventy-five calls meant funerals. The funeral business had a vocabulary all its own and it would take time to become educated in the lingo.

Standing back from the casket, Uncle Harvey muttered, "Now that looks better. I know you've never touched a dead human being before, darlin'. I'll make it easy. I'm going to put my hand on Mr. Jenkins' hands that I've crossed and placed just below his chest. His hands are very cold. When we die, our heart stops beating, which kept the blood throughout our body warm. At death our body turns cold. Now you put your hand on top of mine and when you are ready just ask me to remove mine underneath. My hand has made his warmer."

Elizabeth took a deep breath and did as Uncle Harvey had directed. After a few minutes she whispered, "Okay, Uncle Harvey, I'm ready." With that, he slowly removed his hand and watched his niece take another breath and relax. She looked at Mr. Jenkins ... really stared at his face. It was peaceful. "He could be my grandfather, Uncle Harvey." *This gentleman was a living breathing human being; he's not just a body*, she reasoned.

"See, everything's going to be fine," Uncle Harvey said with such confidence that she couldn't help but believe him. Showing her where to stand at the guestbook, he continued to instruct her as to what row the immediate family would sit. There were signs on the back of the chairs that read FAMILY as well as PALLBEARERS. "Details, my dear, details," he said as he pointed to the placards.

Blanche was busy arranging flowers in the chapel on accordion style racks with hooks. The Styrofoam backing of the flowers fit over the hooks as she lined up the sprays in an appealing array of matching rainbow colors. Elizabeth was in awe as she watched Blanche become an artist as if the funeral parlor was her canvas. When her task was complete, she moved onto arranging the baskets surrounding the casket with dark green stands at different heights. When she was through, she took several steps backward to admire her work. Uncle Harvey quickly came up behind her and rearranged them. "I'm used to him," Blanche said as she winked at Elizabeth. "Somethin' would be wrong if he didn't change what I done in this chapel of rest."

"We will remove the flower cards after the funeral and place them in the family's bag. It's important that we read the cards as they come in and place the family pieces closest to the deceased," Uncle Harvey said sagely as if teaching a class.

Elizabeth watched the assembly line comprised of the florist delivering flowers through the back door, Blanche grabbing them, and Uncle Harvey trying to display them before she got her two cents in. "It's as if you are on stage at a theatre. Such precision," she announced trying not to give a round of applause.

Glancing out the window, she saw a car pull to the side of the street. Charlie the morgue rat walked briskly to the driver's side and mouthed, "Are you family?" The driver nodded and was proficiently directed where to park. *Good job, morgue rat*, Elizabeth thought. An attractive young woman emerged from the passenger's side of the vehicle.

"That's the wife," Uncle Harvey smiled.

"But, Uncle Harvey, she looks like she's in her thirties. Mr. Jenkins is seventy-five."

"That's his current wife. Wife Number One will be here too."

"Who's that man with her, a son?"

"No, no, that's Wife Number Two's boyfriend. He's volunteered his services as a pallbearer this afternoon. So thoughtful, bless his heart."

"Uh... Uncle Harvey, who's that other woman with that entourage of people surrounding her?"

"Oh, that's the first wife," Uncle Harvey grinned.

"We have our work cut out for us," Elizabeth whispered.

"Indeed, we do, darlin'," Uncle Harvey nodded in agreement.

The massive door opened; relatives and friends piled into the foyer, each taking selective sides surrounding wives one and two. Elizabeth was reminded of the book she had read recently, *The Hatfields and Mc-Coys*. Glancing at her curb list, she approached the current Mrs. Jenkins.

"Mrs. Jenkins, I'm Elizabeth. I'll be your hostess this afternoon. I'm so sorry for your loss. Are you ready for me to take you in to see your husband?"

"Yes, I am, honey," Mrs. Jenkins said sniffing into her tissue.

Mrs. Jenkins Number One glared at Elizabeth, shooting daggers from her eyes so sharp that she felt the pricks. Hatfields sat on one side of the chapel and McCoys on the other. Caustic remarks were made from both sides of the room during the hour-long, too-long visitation. The corpse was the only one appearing peaceful as if enjoying all the fuss surrounding him. When the visitation was over, the current and legal wife had given orders to Uncle Harvey that she wanted the casket closed for the funeral service. Elizabeth had been instructed that after she heard the final click of the casket closing, she was to escort the minister to the lectern and introduce him.

With a pit in her stomach, Elizabeth stood in the foyer with Rev. Smith of The Church of God as Uncle Harvey and morgue rat Charlie proceeded to the casket for the final ceremonial ritual. As the lid was slowly lowered on the deceased, Wife Number One leapt from her chair and flashed a scowl at Wife Number Two.

"You, bitch. You're not shutting him up now."

A hush silenced the crowd, and without a flinch, Uncle Harvey continued to close the casket with dignity. For even more effect, the current Mrs. Jenkins began to wail at the top of her lungs, dabbing her eyes as black mascara streamed down her cheeks.

Elizabeth began to shake as she attempted to introduce the evangelical preacher with a voice that cracked like a fine bone china cup.

"Amen," Rev. Smith concluded his service. More screaming and cursing was heard on the street as guests left the funeral parlor and scurried to their cars. *The first wife is not about to let it go*, Elizabeth thought.

"I'll see you in court, you whore! He never paid child support for any of his children in the past. The bastard left me in my old age and failin' health to shack up with the likes of you. You ... floozie!"

Elizabeth's jaw dropped as she stood at the open doorway.

"Go to hell, you, old bag. You ain't gettin' nothin' out of me. He didn't love you. We've been lover's since I was fourteen."

Feeling the presence of someone standing behind her, Elizabeth turned around and collided with the preacher. He had witnessed the freak show as well, much to her chagrin. Promptly closing the door as the grieving wives respectively addressed each other as ladies of the night, Elizabeth felt unnerved by the melodramatic display.

Uncle Harvey called his buddy who was the chief of police, who coincidentally was named Buddy, to calm the ladies down. Guests prepared to proceed to the cemetery in great speed so as not to miss out on any of the action that was to arise. Sadie had called the state troopers to meet the riled-up friends and family at the grave site as they began to surround the freshly dug mound of dirt. Six chairs had been placed under the tent for the interment. The boyfriend of Wife Number Two promptly moved three chairs to the other side of the tent so there would be no fisticuff engagement. *So thoughtful, bless his heart,* Elizabeth commended him silently.

When the preacher asked everyone to bow their heads, close their eyes, and raise their hands if they wanted to be saved after the committal, Wife Number One raised her fist in the air and screamed, "I'm gonna kick me some ass." She glared at Wife Number Two as a crowd formed around each widow.

The state troopers intervened, and the mourners were escorted off the grave site. Jumping quickly into the hearse beside Uncle Harvey, Elizabeth sighed. "That seemed like a lot of drama for one afternoon. I was really embarrassed for the poor minister. That family was really rough and all that foul language!"

"You're going to see how the other half lives, darlin'. It will make you feel very grateful. This family is as rough as a corncob, but they have feelings too. We must remember that every deceased body had someone that loved them. Our job is to comfort them no matter what background, social, or financial status they come from."

Early Sunday morning, Harvey rang Margaret. "Tell Elizabeth she shouldn't have worried about the preacher and what he witnessed during yesterday's service. I've had a call from one of his flock. It seems he left a note on his desk and in the night departed with the church's secretary."

Margaret repeated the words to her granddaughter as they stood in the kitchen.

"Tell Uncle Harvey funeral service is the career for me," she giggled.

Years later, *The Jerry Springer Show* would air, reminding Elizabeth of her very first funeral.

That evangelical preacher and church secretary were never heard from again in Sycamore Creek.

PART 2

CHAPTER NINETEEN

Elizabeth's pantyhose were sticking to her legs. *I'll have to have this linen dress dry cleaned again for the third time this summer*, she thought. Standing in the cemetery at the graveside service on a hot July day, she became blurry-eyed from the intense humidity as the sun beat down on the mourners. The minister loved to hear himself talk, and without consideration for his audience, he continued to speak for an hour.

Glancing at Uncle Harvey and his sidekick Mr. Charlie, she noticed their black suit coats clinging to their backs with perspiration. Dabbing at their foreheads with a white handkerchief as drops of missed beads of sweat ran into their eyes, she felt sorry for them—burials should not take place in this type of weather. To make matters worse, Uncle Harvey would not allow his staff to wear sunglasses at a funeral. "It looks too shady, too Hollywood," he had stated more than once.

Elizabeth began to daydream about her future as the Methodist minister babbled on. *There's never a dull moment in that lively funeral parlor ... kind of ironic that it houses the dead*, she thought. *I'll talk to Uncle Harvey as soon as I get in the hearse about college.*

Uncle Harvey and Charlie opened the car doors for the sweaty, limp mourners. With pleasant smiles, they wished them a nice day as they drove away. Slipping in the passenger seat of the hearse, the black leather burned through her linen dress and panties. "Ouch!" she squealed as she lifted up her fanny. Settling slowly back onto the black seat, she glanced at Uncle Harvey to get a feel for the mood he was in.

"You better get used to wearing black on these sultry days, darlin'," he confided. "These black cars really hold the heat."

"Uncle Harvey, I'm at a fork in the road as to which direction I would like to take for my future. I'm considering a Mortuary Science degree or a fine arts degree. However, I think a business degree would be in my best interest. It would enable me to manage the funeral parlor more efficiently and hire embalmers to do the dirty work. I mean I don't mind helping them in the morgue, but the odors make me gag, especially people that have been dead for so long that we can't even embalm them," she said with authority.

"It's time you got the terminology correct. Those cases are called floaters. We are mostly sixty percent water, and after death, our bodies break down to a liquid, gelatinous goo. I use a topical powder that I sprinkle on the cadaver and then pouch them. The body you saw the other day was a real stinker with a repulsive odor that could gag a maggot. Everything you've told me is all well and good, but don't you think you should have some fun this summer and stop worrying about the future so much? You're sixteen, for heaven sakes," Uncle Harvey countered. "You're Margaret's grandchild, no doubt about it."

"Do we have a funeral Sunday?" Elizabeth asked.

"No, not yet, why?"

"Jim Bowen has asked me to go out on his boat for a picnic."

"Oh, he's a nice young man, but remember one thing darlin' ... a girl should be like a butterfly—pretty to see, hard to catch. I remember Jimmy talking to me last year about being an undertaker. I told him I would hire him as soon as he was ready. Lifting bodies all these years has taken a toll on my back, neck, and shoulders. He graduated this year, I believe. There's a community college in Maryland that offers a Mortuary Science degree. I think I'll discuss an apprenticeship with Jimmy. Ole Charlie is beginning to fail, I've noticed. I guess we're all going bad at the same time," Uncle Harvey said.

Sunday afternoon Jim stretched out his arm and offered his hand to help guide Elizabeth onto his boat. He had packed a cooler of sodas and stopped by the local diner for cheeseburgers, which were wrapped in white bags. Leaving the tributary of Sycamore Creek, he would find a more private area for them to feast. Pulling the boat into a gut, he turned off the engine and smiled at Elizabeth as the sun beat down on them.

"I hope you like our picnic. It doesn't look like you eat that much, Elizabeth," he said, taking a long glance at her in the string bikini.

"This is fine. Thanks." She looked up at him shyly. "Uncle Harvey was talking about you working for him just the other day."

"Oh yeah. I've considered being a mortician. I'm in the fire company and have transported bodies to his morgue before. How do you like it? Ever been scared?"

"No, just the opposite. I love helping grieving people get through probably one of the most difficult days of their lives. I get thanked for helping them every time. It's so rewarding."

"Is it because of what happened to your mother?" Jim inquired innocently.

"I suppose." Elizabeth felt uncomfortable with the question and wanted to change the subject. Munching on a French fry, she squinted in the brightness of the sun reflecting off the water and asked Jim to take her for a ride in the big bay. "Go really fast," she begged.

"Sure thing." He started the engine, backed the boat out of the gut and zoomed toward open waters. "Look, look there's a blue heron," he began explaining everything they saw in the bay as if he was the owner of this vast waterscape. The heron on the edge of the marshy grass suddenly flapped it's large wings and lifted gracefully into the air with spindle-like legs dangling from underneath the bird's body. Finding a larger and more private tributary, he lowered the speed until they came to a halt. Turning off the engine, he walked to the anchor and with one quick toss secured the Boston Whaler. He rejoined her, wrapped his arm around her as he brought her closer to his side, and kissed the top of her head. Elizabeth looked up transfixed as his lips slanted and descended on hers. The kissing continued as Elizabeth seemed to melt into Jim's arms.

"You are so beautiful, Elizabeth," Jim whispered, breaking away from their embrace. "Matters could really get out of hand. Maybe we should take a swim and cool off." He opened the hatch and pulled out the ladder hooking it over the stern. "Are you a good swimmer?"

"Nana calls me a fish," she grinned, anxious to lower herself into the cool water. "Oh look, I can touch bottom on my tip toes." With that, she was determined to show Jim her swimming skills as she glided in the water away from the boat.

Jim jumped in the creek, determined to beat her speed towards the open bay. Catching up with her, he hollered, "Race you back!" By the time they reached the Boston Whaler, the wind and tide had shifted causing the boat to rock, making it difficult for Elizabeth to climb aboard. As Jim lifted her up to the ladder, she fell backwards into his embrace. Laughing hysterically, she wrapped both of her arms around his neck. She looked into his eyes as he bent over her and the kissing began again more passionately.

"Let's skinny dip," he suggested breathlessly. Not being able to remove their swimsuits quickly enough he whispered, "Do you want to do it?"

"Yes," she managed to whisper as he picked her up and placed her on him.

"I thought it was amazing ... simply amazing," Jim spoke first after the lovemaking.

Elizabeth nodded. She had lost her virginity in the Chesapeake Bay that hot, sultry, July afternoon. The minute Jim dropped her off at the house, she called her best friend Jacki. "Jacki, I'm a woman now," she exclaimed. The rest of the summer was devoted to skinny dipping for Jim and Elizabeth. They had become inseparable.

Uncle Harvey sent Jimmy to mortuary science school that fall, and Elizabeth braced herself for happy ever after.

CHAPTER TWENTY

With numerous funerals under her belt since the summer, Elizabeth still proclaimed to be a novice. She took great pride in being the girl around town who was born to comfort the grieving. "A natural" was the talk.

Sycamore Creek was in its glory during the autumn season. It had been unusually cold with the temperatures dipping below freezing several nights in a row. Sycamores, maples, and beech trees produced an array of vivid colors as their leaves turned red, gold, and orange, lining the streets in nature's last hoorah. Jack-O-Lanterns decorated porches and Indian corn hung on sheds and outbuildings. Tobacco leaves were hanging in sheaves from rafters in the barns that were designed specifically for drying while bits and pieces of cotton that had refused the pickers clung to their stems.

Every morning Elizabeth woke to black powder gunshots at the crack of dawn. Deer hunters were shooting in the woods and fields just a couple of miles away. Cringing at the boom, she would cover her head with the blanket. She so loved the beautiful creatures. "Do they have to shoot them, Nana?"

"Yes, honey, it's imperative to keep the population down, otherwise Sycamore Creek would become Deer Creek," Nana would counter.

Working evening visitations and funerals on weekends, she lived for Jim to come home from college, so they could be together. When they were separated, she was miserable. The day would come when they would be working together in the funeral parlor. Fantacizing that she would receive her business degree, marry Jim, and live out her days in bliss had become the norm. Jim came from a nice family and Nana adored his manners. *Good stock,* she thought when his name was mentioned.

One night on their numerous dates she had casually mentioned that she didn't want children. The effects of being a motherless child weighed heavily on her mind. There would be no one to care for her children if something should happen to her. Being of stubborn ilk the matter was settled in her head. Jim realized this was a sensitive issue and the topic of children was never discussed again.

On a cold Thursday evening in November, Elizabeth was working a visitation for a gentleman in his late nineties. Standing by the guest book as the viewing was about to wrap up, she heard heavy boots on the front porch and an indescribable ruckus approaching the door.

Ralph, a friend of Uncle Harvey's, barged through the door. His face was flushed, and he was dressed in camouflage. *Not appropriate attire for an evening viewing*, she thought. Nevertheless, she gestured in the direction of the register. "Mr. Ralph, would you please sign our guest book?" Elizabeth smiled ever so sweetly, wondering what that peculiar scent on his garb was.

"No, dumplin', I need to see your Uncle Harvey, I reckon. Tell him it's Ralph Outten."

Elizabeth knew Uncle Harvey was enjoying his Virginia Gentleman in the little parlor and was adamant about not being disturbed. Ralph however seemed a bit distressed, but he was knowledgeable as to the relationship with her uncle, so waited patiently for her to retrieve him.

Softly rapping on the French door and opening it ajar, she announced, "Uncle Harvey, Mr. Ralph Outten is here to see you. He looks a little flustered if you ask me."

"Send him in, darlin'."

Not intending to be a Nosey Rosey, but unable to budge from the closed door, she cupped her ear to listen after showing Ralph in. Curiosity had the better of her, like the dead cat Nana had warned her about: curiosity killed the cat and satisfaction brought it back.

"Hey Ralph," Harvey looked up from his *Wall Street Journal*. He was perplexed by Ralph's appearance.

"You'll never believe this, Harvey. My coon huntin' buddy, Jake, and I were out in the woods on my farm and we had just watched our hounds, bless their hearts, tree a big ole raccoon." Ralph rambled on, leaving Harvey bewildered as to where the story was leading. "He was mean, too, looking at me with wicked eyes as he started to hiss. I shot him down, then I looked over at Jake as he clutched his chest and dropped dead."

"Oh, Lordy Ralph. Are you sure he's dead?"

Ralph gave him a startled look, as if no one had dared question his opinion before. "Deader than a doornail, by God," he insisted.

"Good grief, buddy. I'll get the hearse if you will take me to where he is. I'm sure you've already called his wife, Earlene."

"No ... no, Harvey, I didn't. I just loaded him up, stuck him in the front seat of my pickup and hightailed it over here. He's in your driveway. The hounds are in the back, but dagnabit I forgot with all the commotion to retrieve the raccoon," Ralph said with concern in his voice regarding the dead animal.

"I'll take care of your friend. You have my word." Harvey nodded sagely as if this scenario happened on a daily basis. He stood, patted Ralph on the back, and opened the French door, coming face to face with Elizabeth whose mouth was agape.

"We have a corpse in the driveway. Ralph and I are going to take the body through the back and into the morgue. He sure saved me a lot of work bringing him here," he said. Then, when Ralph was out of ear shot, he said, "I'll call the coroner."

Uncle Harvey tried not to chuckle as he snapped orders at Elizabeth. "Return to your post, remain gracious, and keep the viewing guests occupied."

"But ... Uncle Harvey, the viewing is just about over."

"You'll think of something. By the way, have you seen Charlie?"

"Not all night."

Guests were standing, putting on their coats, and starting to leave.

Elizabeth did as she was ordered. Walking to the front of the chapel, she turned towards the mourners and broke into four verses of "What a Friend We Have in Jesus" and finished with a bravado amen. The crowd, caught up in the excitement, continued with a rendition of "In the Garden." The hymn singing lasted another thirty minutes and Elizabeth assured herself she had saved the day.

Harvey and Ralph had managed to remove Jake from the front seat of the old Chevy truck, taking him into the morgue without any witnesses on the property. The sing-a-long ended and the spirit-filled mourners walked jauntily to their cars, still humming renditions of the old hymns.

Morgue rat Charlie had been acting strange lately due to lack of memory, the results of too much nicotine and formaldehyde. He had opted to spend the evening in the morgue where Miss Alice had been embalmed, cosmeticized, and was ready to be placed in her solid mahogany casket. Being one of the Grand Dames of the Creek, her daughter had brought in a black Chanel suit, three stands of real pearls, white gloves, and barked orders as to how to dress her mother. Blanche had coiffed her blue-gray hair to perfection, spraying the 'do with a can of Aqua Net resulting in barbed wire locks that would remain permanent on her journey to the pearly gates. Harvey had spent the afternoon coloring her cheeks and lips with Revlon's *Love That Pink*. Her daughter insisted that her two-carat diamond ring be removed and given only to her after the ceremony. Feeling gratified that Miss Alice's daughter would be pleased with his artistic ability, Harvey could hardly wait for the private family-only first view.

In order for Harvey to place Jake on the morgue table for embalming, he had to remove Miss Alice and settle her in the casket. Opening the morgue door, he blinked twice not believing what he saw. Charlie and Blanche stood over Miss Alice redoing her cosmetics. Blanche held in her hand Margaret's Estee Lauder's *Youth Dew* powder puff dabbing Miss Alice's face, hair, and hands with pure white powder the color of flour. She was the perfecr example of a corpse as Blanche looked over her shoulder and proclaimed all proud of herself, "She sho is white now, Mista Harvey."

Charlie grinned from ear-to-ear assisting and volunteering with whatever Blanche required of him to make the improvements.

Harvey took a deep breath and bent over double laughing. "I never liked ole baggy drawers either, Blanche. I think that's a real improvement."

Miss Alice's family never used Sycamore Creek Funeral Home again and Harvey never reprimanded his beloved Blanche.

Elizabeth learned that day Southerners are devoted to their people, protecting them like kin. Blanche was just that to the Eyre family.

CHAPTER TWENTY-ONE

Two Years Later

"Jim doesn't seem the same, Nana. I can't put my finger on it, but since he's been away at school and received his funeral director's license, he acts as if he doesn't have time for me. We never go on dates anymore." Elizabeth sighed.

"Well, honey, your Uncle Harvey has him busy at the funeral parlor now that his man Charlie is in and out of the hospital with emphysema."

"I know, I know, and it seems like I'm endlessly on the road to Salisbury since I've started taking business classes. But Jim won't even look at me. He follows Uncle Harvey around like a little puppy dog. Last weekend he had off and his new best friend Brian from mortuary school in Maryland came to visit. I wasn't invited to do a thing with them. I like Brian and all that, but he talks like a girl. I can't quite put my finger on it. It's as if the two of them have a thing going on."

Margaret kept silent. She had noticed a difference in Jim's demeanor as well. Physically, he had lost weight and changed his wardrobe. None of his hobbies included Elizabeth. He seldom called her. More and more, there were handsome young lads hanging around the funeral parlor, proclaiming to be mortuary science students. Harvey seemed rather giddy with all the attention. *I hope he behaves himself*, Margaret thought.

"Elizabeth, you realize that the funeral parlor will be yours someday. Regardless of the relationship with Jim, you're going to have to buckle up and grab the bull by the horns and run the business. The funeral business will make you grow into adulthood rapidly. I'm so proud of you," Margaret said kissing the top of her head.

"Uncle Harvey doesn't seem quite on his game, Nana, and Sadie needs to be informed to clean up her act. That mouth!"

"Well, Elizabeth, Sadie didn't come from very good stock. Her people were never exposed to manners and the finer things in life. She's doing the very best she can. Sadie told your Uncle Harvey that her father abused her both physically and sexually when she was a child while her mother would leave the room. She was refusing to protect her daughter. I don't know how a mother can do that." Nana shook her head.

"Oh, bless her heart," Elizabeth whispered. Her heart softened for Sadie's plight. "Maybe that's why she makes so many mistakes because of all the abuse during her childhood."

"It could be," Nana agreed.

"I don't have classes this week, so I'll be at the funeral parlor. See you tonight," Elizabeth said, giving Margaret a kiss and a wave goodbye.

Elizabeth walked to the funeral parlor slowly. It was unbelievable that the temperature was a balmy seventy degrees on a mid-November morning. There was no escaping her thoughts as far as Jim was concerned. His talents were numerous when it came to the back of the house. They would make a great pair running the business. Embalming came easily to Jim and she had seen his restorative art on accident victims. Jim would work hours on the bodies as his gifted and talented skills shone. However, she loved people and the front of the house was her forté. *It will make a great marriage all the way around*, she told herself, settling her mind.

"Good morning, Sadie." Glancing in her office with a smile, Elizabeth had grown accustomed to her brusque demeanor. Sadie managed a grunt in response. Jim seemed busy himself and avoided her for most of the morning. Elizabeth decided not to acknowledge the knot in her stomach whenever she was in his company. Jim's mission was to impress Uncle Harvey since he was working full-time, never anxious to go home in the evenings. They had not been on a date in weeks. Jim always claimed that Uncle Harvey wanted him to be at the ready, in case a call came in. *He's just overwhelmed ... things will calm down and then he will ask me to marry him*, she thought.

Elizabeth busied herself at the desk Uncle Harvey set up for her in his office. His nerves could not take the bantering back and forth between his niece and Sadie, who lived to argue. Elizabeth had learned to dish it out to Sadie in order to survive the constant teasing.

Writing notes of sympathy to the families they served that month, she glanced at the clock, realizing she had lost track of time. Blanche had brought her a cup of tea at precisely three o'clock. Now the balmy, November afternoon had turned dark and cloudy as raindrops hit the beveled glass panes. She grabbed her purse and headed for the door. "Goodnight, Sadie," she called, opening the door to a brisker, cooler temperature than in the morning.

The Sycamore Creek United Methodist Church choir was going to perform at a revival twenty-five miles away. That evening, the members decided to travel in individual cars, practicing along the way, in hopes of outperforming the competition. Harriet decided to drive, and Virginia opted to be her passenger. The temperature had dropped dramatically, causing patchy fog along the fields and highway. They had taught school together for years and neither had married, counting on each other as they aged. Rain puddles from the late afternoon deluge had turned to ice patches by the time everyone was saved and prayed over. The revival was wrapping up.

Harriet and Virginia were in high gear as they walked to the car arm in arm. Harriet turned on the ignition and cranked the heater up to full blast. Placing the gear in drive, they continued to sing a cappella on their journey home. Hitting an ice patch at fifty-five miles an hour, Harriet lost sense of direction and control of the vehicle. The car ran off the road, slid down an embankment, and sideswiped a walnut tree, pinning the driver's door against the trunk of the massive tree.

The other choir members driving behind them witnessed the accident. One of the fellow choir members named John jumped from his car and ran to the twisted metal that had been an automobile just minutes ago. Other choir members were doing the same.

"Harriet! Harriet!" he yelled trying to open the driver's door that was jammed against the tree, but to no avail. John could hear Virginia moaning as someone told her an ambulance was on the way. As luck would have it a Virginia state policeman traveling in the opposite direction witnessed the fatal accident.

The hospital called Harvey to inform him that Harriet's nephew, the only family she had, requested his services for burial. Harvey and Jim made the removal, but not before Harvey had called Elizabeth to set up the embalming machine and mix the right type of cavity fluid. It seemed he was relying more and more on her to understand just how demanding the business was even in the off hours.

Waiting in the morgue, Elizabeth turned on the fluorescent lights and mixed the fluid in the machine to Uncle Harvey's specifications. Uncle Harvey and Jim walked in with Harriet on a stretcher, zipped up in a green pouch.

"This isn't pretty, darlin'." Uncle Harvey unzipped the canvas cover and opened the rubberized sheet folded around her body. Harriet had died on impact with the left side of her face and entire nose demolished. Elizabeth placed her hand on her third-grade teacher's bruised arm, patting the limb gently. They had always been fond of one another. It gave Elizabeth pause that she had died in such a horrific manner.

"We have no control over how people die, Elizabeth," Uncle Harvey said as though he could read her thoughts.

"I guess not," Elizabeth muttered. She and Jim began to wash the body with a germicidal soap, spraying lukewarm water over the dried blood in Harriet's hair. To set the features on the undamaged right side of the face he closed the eye, inserting an eye cap, and then closed the mouth with a needle injector. She watched him make an incision, finding the carotid artery and lifting it for the purpose of inserting a cannula allowing fluid to enter. He continued searching for the jugular vein in order to remove the blood through the drain tube.

"Turn on the machine, Elizabeth, and begin massaging her limbs upwards toward the heart. We make them pink, so they don't stink."

Doing as she was told, she began massaging the hands, feet, and legs. They slowly began to turn the color of the embalming fluid as it circulated through the body. Harriet was rosy pink after all the trauma she had endured—mission accomplished.

"I'm meeting with Harriet's nephew in the morning. I think he wants to see her if possible. Jimmy, are you up for the task?" Harvey questioned.

"Yes sir," Jim answered.

"Good. My hands shake more than they used to. I'm counting on you to make her appearance naturalistic. You have the whole left side to reconstruct. Put your talent to work. Now, if you will excuse me, I'm going to have a little night cap."

"I have my work cut out for me, Elizabeth. I'll see you tomorrow."

"Goodnight, Jim."

Elizabeth woke early the next day anxious to watch Jim perform his magic. Working with a container of warm mortuary wax he softened it between his hands until he was able to contour the left side to match the right side of Harriet's face. A special cosmetic and brush were used to stipple the flesh. Jim meticulously cut Harriet's hair from the back of her head to form an eyebrow and lashes. One by one he delicately placed the strands in the appropriate spots with tweezers.

Elizabeth sat for hours in awe as Jim created his work of art from the victim's own hair. Sculpting the nose had taken over two hours.

"There you go, my dear," Jim said stepping back from his work to admire the new and improved Harriet.

"This has been totally mesmerizing, Jim. Good job!" Elizabeth exclaimed, feeling her heart swell with pride.

"Thanks. Mr. Harvey said her nephew Joe picked out a silver rose casket. He's coming in this evening to see her. He'll let us know then if he wants to proceed with an open or closed casket before the funeral. "Do you mind meeting with him?"

"Not at all. What time?"

"Six. I'll still be here catching up," Jim assured her.

Five-thirty arrived as Elizabeth waited by the door, listening for Joe's footsteps. Ten of six, she opened the door and politely extended her hand. "I'm so sorry about your Aunt Harriet. She was my third-grade school teacher." She greeted him and ushered him into the chapel.

Joe, Harriet's nephew, looked at his aunt and gently smiled. "This has been quite a shock, Elizabeth. She looks nice considering she was broadsided by a tree. Although, I think she would look more like herself if she had a pair of her glasses on."

"They broke in half and shattered during the accident, Mr. Joe," Elizabeth said in a thoughtful tone. "But, you are right," she concurred.

"Oh, she has a drawer full of them in the house." Joe reassured her.

"If you want to run home and get them I'll wait."

"That would be great. I'll be just a few minutes," he replied.

Joe was only gone ten minutes. "Do you want to see them on your aunt now, Mr. Joe?" Elizabeth asked on his return.

"No, I'll do that when I come tomorrow for the funeral. Thanks, Elizabeth, for everything. She looks so nice."

"You're welcome."

Joe walked back home to Harriet's house. Meanwhile, Elizabeth was on a mission to place Miss Harriet's glasses on her nose, just like she had worn when she was teaching school. With a heavy hand, she slid the glasses on the constructed nose Jim had painstakingly created. Unfortunatley, she managed to remove half of the wax. She looked down at the left lens to see it covered with the substance. Where there had been a nose a few seconds ago was now a hole. *Oh no! All that work! Jim spent over two hours alone on the nose and I've dismantled it in seconds,* her mind raced. Panicking, she closed the doors to the chapel and ran through the funeral parlor to find Uncle Harvey.

"Uncle Harvey! Uncle Harvey!" she yelled.

"Elizabeth, calm down," Blanche said coming around the corner of the kitchen. "I do declare you look like you've seen a ghost."

"I have—one without a nose," Elizabeth cried. "Where's Uncle Harvey?"

"Honey chile, you know he's having his cocktail." Blanche went back into the kitchen, shaking her head from all the commotion.

With the nose tragedy, Elizabeth had lost track of time. *Of course, he's having his bourbon*, she thought. Opening the door to the parlor slowly so as not to startle him, she peeked in the room and ... she blinked hard trying to understand what she was seeing. Jim was sitting on Uncle Harvey's lap with both arms around his neck. They were locked in a passionate kiss and had not heard the door open.

"I hate you both!" Elizabeth screamed.

Harvey stood up with a jolt and Jim slammed onto the floor. Elizabeth ran out the door in tears. Blanche was frying fish in the kitchen singing "How Great Thou Art" at the top of her lungs. Escaping from the shocking display, it never crossed her mind to get her purse and coat. When she reached the house, she took two steps at a time to her room. Tears blurred her vision as she threw herself on the bed.

"Elizabeth, honey, are you all right?" Nana asked.

"Yes," Elizabeth sniffed.

"Have you had anything to eat?"

"I'm not hungry. I'm going to bed."

"I'll be watching TV if you need to talk." Nana frowned, curious to what had happened to make Elizabeth so upset.

In minutes, Harvey walked in with her purse and coat.

"Harvey, have you and Elizabeth had a squabble?" Margaret questioned.

"You could say that, Margaret." Harvey pondered how much information he should make Margaret privy to. "I need to console her, bless her little heart."

"She's in her room," Margaret said not taking her eyes off the screen.

Harvey climbed the stairs, dreading each step leading to his niece's room. He knocked gently on the door, calling her name. "Elizabeth, darlin', we need to talk. May I come in?"

"Yes ... yes sir."

Harvey opened the door and saw her swollen red eyes and runny nose. A look of anguish was on her face, and his guilt became overwhelming. Sitting on the edge of the bed he said, "Sweet pea, now that you're grown, I need to explain to you about my lifestyle. Do you feel like listening?"

Elizabeth nodded yes and waited for the one-way conversation to continue.

"I am a ... homosexual. Even as a young boy I was always attracted to men. But I knew I couldn't own a funeral parlor in a small town with that sort of lifestyle—and be successful. No one knows in Sycamore Creek, but your grandmother and Blanche. I'm so sorry for what you saw. Jimmy doesn't mean a thing to me. I have a partner in Richmond. We've been together for years. His name is Bernard. Please forgive me, Elizabeth."

For just a second, Elizabeth found it hard to breath. She sat up in bed and blew her nose. She had listened to Uncle Harvey's confession. His head was bowed in remorse and empathy welled up in her every being. "How have you lived like this all these years, Uncle Harvey?"

"It hasn't been easy, but I had no choice."

Elizabeth wrapped her arms around him and tried to absorb his pain. "I love you, Uncle Harvey. Your secret is safe with me."

Tears ran down his face as he left her room, causing Elizabeth to realize he had given up a life of happiness to operate a funeral parlor. She wondered if it had all been worth it.

Jim, her first love, quietly left town the next day, never to be seen again.

CHAPTER TWENTY-TWO

It was imperative that Elizabeth enlighten herself on the death business. Uncle Harvey wanted her to know every aspect from the ground up. "You'll make a better owner if you know the ropes," he repeated incessantly.

Their relationship had grown even stronger with Elizabeth's new-found knowledge of her uncle living in the closet—their little secret. However, the subject of what she had witnessed was not a topic of conversation. Life would remain the same at Sycamore Creek.

Morgue rat Charlie could neither read or write, but his abilities as an embalmer's assistant was a pure gift. Since he was unable to decipher a map on road trips to bring bodies back, he would watch for familiar buildings with an ever-constant cigarette dangling from his lips.

Sadie had just gotten off the phone. "Oh hell, we have a dead one, guys." Sadie hollered at her desk. "There goes Thanksgiving! Guess I'll have paperwork to do instead of eating turkey."

Elizabeth rolled her eyes as she rose from her desk to see what all the squabble was about. "Do we have a call?" she inquired.

Sadie grew testy. "What do you think I'm complaining about, missy? Of course, we do. Gunshot wound to the head. He's at the Norfolk City Morgue ready to be picked up. Who do you want to go, Harvey?" Sadie yelled at Harvey's closed door to his office.

"Oh Sadie, we always send Charlie. You know that as well as I do," he yelled back.

"Whatever," she answered brusquely.

"I think I'll ride and keep him company," Elizabeth piped up. It was the afternoon of Thanksgiving Eve and she knew Nana and Blanche would be baking mincemeat and sweet potato pies. *Mr. Charlie could really use some company*, she thought. Adopting the funeral parlor family as his own, the man had no one else to share the holidays with. Chronic coughing spells made her wonder if he would completely loose his breath and keel over. It was just a matter of time before he would be hooked up to oxygen, eliminating time spent in the morgue—his passion.

Sadie made the necessary phone calls while Elizabeth asked Uncle Harvey for petty cash. Charlie loved his black coffee. She was sure a stop would be made on the way down and back from Norfolk for his favorite brew along with a pack of Lucky Strikes. She jumped in the passenger's side of the black station wagon and they began their journey from the Eastern Shore to Norfolk. Charlie drove off like a bat out of hell.

"I hear the man we're going to pick up was shot by his best buddy in a card game," Charlie said with amusement. "Accused him of cheating. Got up, went in the kitchen, opened a drawer, came back, and *pow!* right in the back of the head."

"His friend shot him? It seems so senseless." This was the perfect opportunity to engage Mr. Charlie regarding the secrets surrounding her mother's death. "Did you embalm my mother, Mr. Charlie?"

"Yes, Harvey and me. Suzanne was such a pretty girl, but I just couldn't make her look like herself. Your grandfather took one look at her and collapsed. Miss Margaret was the strongest lady I've ever seen after losing a child, especially under the circumstances. It haunted me for a long time that I couldn't make her as beautiful as she was in life." Charlie grew quiet as if he was reliving a painful memory.

"I wish I could have seen her. I wasn't even allowed to go to the funeral," Elizabeth spoke softly. Crossing the recently constructed bay bridge tunnel, the lights of Virginia Beach could be seen in the clear night sky. Staring at the glow, she wondered if her father ever thought about her and what he looked like today. Her spirits sank with memories of both her parents from so long ago. Bringing her thoughts back to present day, she became more talkative. "How long will it take to load our body?"

"Not long. The crew is waiting for me. You can sit in the office to the left of the door. The guys would appreciate some extra help killing cockroaches. They'll get a kick out of seeing you." Charlie grinned.

"Gross, Mr. Charlie."

They ventured down the ramp to the back entrance of the morgue. Charlie and Elizabeth then went to the rear of the station wagon and rolled out the cot that the gambler would go home on. Entering the building, she saw a large scale on the right to weigh the bodies. In front of the scale, there was a young girl on a cot who had jumped to her death several days ago—off the exact bridge they had just crossed. Elizabeth noticed a Mickey Mouse sheet draped over the body, perfectly folded just above her breasts, revealing her necklace and earrings that had not been disturbed as she plunged to her death in the icy waters. The brunette looked approximately seventeen years old. Elizabeth stared, fixated on her face. The makeup had remained intact, particularly the azure eye shadow covering her closed lids. An FBI agent was standing on top of the scale, snapping Polaroids from every angle. Elizabeth found the office on the right that gave her a perfect view of the scene.

"She jumped Saturday night," one agent said to the other. "A motorist said he saw a girl on the side of the bridge and then she just vanished. It was really raining hard that night."

"I'm glad the Coast Guard found her so quickly. The family should be here at any moment. I have the paperwork all ready to go," the second agent said.

Elizabeth grabbed *The Daily Norfolk* from the desk and pretended to be immersed in the articles as a woman and young boy came through the door.

"Oh God, oh God!" the woman cried hysterically. She ran to the young dead girl on the cot and began stroking the long dark hair. Tears of grief streamed down her face as she began to sing a lullaby in a quivering voice. The little boy stood by his mother nervously prancing from one foot to the other, finally standing on tiptoes to see the image before him. Looking up at the cadaver, he began to whimper quietly. Elizabeth's eyes filled with tears as well. Suddenly, as if someone had turned off a spigot, the crying came to a complete halt. The woman collected herself, glared at the FBI agents, and stated emphatically, "That's not my child."

"Are you absolutely one hundred percent sure?" asked the agent with the necessary paperwork in his hand.

"I said that's not my daughter."

"Are you willing to sign this document stating the fact that she's not?" The agent drilled her as he extended the papers with a thrust.

"Yes," she said softly. The paper was then signed on the same scale where the agent had stood moments before vigorously snapping pictures. Turning back to the girl on the cot, the woman leaned over and whispered under her breath into her ear. Grabbing her son by the hand, they both exited in the darkness.

"I figured that was going to happen. In fact, I would have put money on it."

"So sad ... a mother not claiming her own daughter's body. This pretty little girl will become a ward of the state," the other agent spoke with regret.

"No money for burial. I see it happen all the time." Both agents unfolded the sheet laying across the suicide victim's breast and covered her flawless face.

Elizabeth tried to comprehend not having the means to bury your own flesh and blood. She had grown up privileged and felt very blessed as she became exposed to how the other half lived. The body would be buried in a potter's field and the grave would never be visited. Charlie came through the door with their corpse on the cot, breaking her sorrow.

"Okay kid, let's go," Charlie said as he rolled the body on the stretcher in front of her. "Grab the other end and guide me through the door."

Elizabeth stood and glanced over her shoulder at the draped remains the FBI agents were placing in the cooler. She began to shudder with the thought that this girl, only a few years younger than herself, would remain frozen and isolated on Thanksgiving. Ruminating about her own mother, she silently said a prayer asking her to greet and protect the girl in heaven who was left unclaimed like a piece of luggage at the airport. "She needs you, Mommy," she whispered in the dark as she and Charlie crossed the bridge that would take them back to the Eastern Shore.

Uncle Harvey was waiting in the small parlor with a glass in hand. *This is an evening ritual that he just can't go without,* she told herself. "Uncle Harvey, I just witnessed the strangest thing." She proceeded to describe the events of the evening.

Uncle Harvey gestured to the liquor cabinet. "Go pour yourself a glass of wine. It will take the edge off. I have some bold, divine reds I've been collecting over the years. It's Thanksgiving Eve after all, let's celebrate."

"I might as well join you, Uncle. Experiencing that scene tonight has left me a little melancholy." She retrieved the corkscrew and began to open the bottle with precision until the cork fully emerged with a loud pop. She poured the fragrant rich wine into a Fostoria glass and slowly took a sip. "Oh my, that tastes like velvet," she sighed as the hint of dark red fruit lingered on her tongue. She was grateful to have what was quickly becoming her drinking buddy to confide in.

With a contemplative expression on his face, Harvey looked at Elizabeth and began reminiscing, "You know, Elizabeth, I don't ever remember having a holiday without dealing with a grieving family. I'll be making funeral arrangements tomorrow with the Warren family. It seems the holidays make the heartache worse because they conjure up memories of time shared together with friends and family."

"I think it would be irritating never knowing if you'll be available to celebrate or have dinner with us," Elizabeth thought.

"I always put myself in the family's shoes. They have it far worse than I do. When I put my head on the pillow at night, it's a good feeling that I have helped someone that day. That's what we are here for after all and it's been my calling in life." Uncle Harvey stood up and walked to the cabinet where he poured another bourbon.

The second glass of wine had vanished quickly, and Elizabeth was becoming sentimental. "Uncle Harvey, you are the best undertaker I know. By the way, the man that was killed playing cards, did they arrest his shooter?"

"No, no. They were the best of friends. Sheriff Dalton said charges would not be filed. It's a small town and why put everyone through undue heartache. Both men were in their eighties and pickled. I was thinking this evening about the situation being so similar, when the Collins brothers got into a tiff over darts in their trailer on Sycamore Road years and years ago."

"Tell me, tell me," Elizabeth pleaded, feeling the calming effects of the wine.

Harvey took a sip of his cocktail and began the bedtime story. "Henry and Bobby Collins played darts constantly in their trailer and drank whatever they could get their hands on, like it was Kool-Aid. Bobby took his turn to throw the dart at the board taking a wrongful step closer, releasing the dart in the air. Henry was a hothead and began arguing that his brother was cheating. Walking to a kitchen drawer, he removed a pistol and shot Bobby smack dab in the center of his forehead. He fell backward as whiskey and blood comingled on the floor. Henry stumbled to the phone and dialed the operator asking her to call me. 'Harrr ... vey, I've done shot ... I've shot brother Bobby dead.' There was the longest pause as I tried to put two and two together. 'Where are you?' I asked him, knowing it was one of the Collins boys. 'Sy ... Si ... Syc, oh hell!' He slurred, crying hysterically."

Harvey's eyes twinkled with amusement as he continued the story. "I told him to calm down and take a deep breath. I just couldn't understand him. He told me he would move him to Elm, the next road over.

I heard him drop the receiver and tell his dead brother, as he slung him over his shoulder that he had always been a pain in his ass." Uncle Harvey roared with laughter and said, "I called the sheriff and he met me on Elm Road. Henry was waiting for us on the side of the road, proud as a peacock that he had managed to lay Bobby to rest just miles down the road from the scene of the crime that was unpronounceable in his drunken state."

"What happened then, Uncle Harvey?" Elizabeth inquired.

"Back in the day things were different. Henry never spent a day in jail and died a couple of years later. Such, my dear, is life in a small town," Uncle Harvey said, gulping down the remnants of his libation.

Elizabeth excused herself and stifled a yawn. She walked back to the office and gazed out the window at the full moon, realizing the holidays would always be like this in the years to come. *Every time the phone rings, the caller is a grieving family member, doctor, nurse, or police detective*, she thought.

Collecting her purse and coat, she scooted by the parlor door and looked in to check on her uncle one last time. He was passed out on the Queen Anne sofa and she spotted the empty decanter of bourbon on the floor. Elizabeth became suddenly aware that he was numbing himself for living years as a closeted homosexual, let alone being on call day and night for the small community of Sycamore Creek. "Love you, Uncle Harvey. Goodnight," she whispered as she locked the door behind her.

CHAPTER TWENTY-THREE

"Elizabeth, I've made an appointment with Mr. Baldwin, the president of the First Bank of Sycamore Creek, at two o'clock this afternoon for us," Uncle Harvey said. "Now that you've graduated from business school, it's time to invest half the salary you're making with them. Margaret and I feel it's our duty to see that you will never lose sleep over finances. Therefore, we'll talk to Mr. Baldwin about other options and securities," he spoke with authority.

"But Uncle Harvey, I already have plenty of money." Elizabeth had inherited from two maiden aunts as well as her mother and grandfather.

"You may want to raise a family or retire early someday. I suggest you buy more bank stock. Mr. Baldwin will be more than happy to see us this afternoon. He also mentioned that he would like to introduce his son, Harper, to you. He works in the bank as well. Loan department I think."

"I don't need a loan, Uncle Harvey," Elizabeth said adamantly not wanting to be a victim of an attempted matchmaking.

"Harper senior was an old classmate of mine. Good family. Worth a million."

"Yes sir," she responded, not very enthusiastically.

Later that afternoon, Elizabeth and Harvey sat across from Harper's desk. Mr. Baldwin Sr. had to excuse himself from the appointment to inspect a piece of land for a client of the bank. Upon meeting, Harper Jr. stood and extended his hand to Elizabeth; she grabbed it and blushed crimson from ear to ear. "Nice to meet you," she eked out as she felt the electricity shoot between them.

"Harper, my niece needs some advice on diversifying her investments. Her trust fund principal is large enough that she can live off the interest, if need be. I just want to make sure she's invested in securities that earn the most interest, you understand."

Elizabeth had crossed her legs hoping Harper hadn't noticed her incapability of not being able to keep them still. This man screamed sophistication and class. *What a dresser!* she thought, eyeing his charcoal suit and burgundy tie. Harper's smile spread from ear-to-ear and it was difficult to make direct eye contact without blushing.

Their appointment continued through the late afternoon. Afterwards, Elizabeth rose on wobbly knees and exited with haste—she could not get to the car quickly enough. Harvey had decided to walk home from the meeting as the conversation between the banker and his niece slowly took a turn from finance to social.

"What just happened?" she whispered out loud, turning the key in the ignition. Driving home as if in a trance, she recalled the story her mother told her when she was a little girl. *I fell in love with your father at first sight.* Elizabeth had always thought that emotion was impossible and romantic poppycock, but it had just happened to her. Driving directly to the funeral parlor, she went into the small parlor and found her uncle sipping a little short one. "Uncle Harvey, have you stocked up on my favorite wine lately?"

"Yes, darlin'," he said, delighted to have company making his happy hour even happier.

Blanche had been given the evening off to attend to her church activities. Harvey was prone to sit and drink the evening away, avoiding nutrition except for the fruit garnish in his drink.

"Do you want me to fix you something to eat?" She was concerned he might fall climbing the steps at bedtime.

Avoiding the question, he bluntly asked her, "What did you think of Harper Baldwin?"

"I'm positive he wants me to bear his children," she divulged.

"Whoa, darling! Don't act too smitten or he'll lose interest for sure. It's not proper to bear your soul—always keep them guessing. Fix yourself a glass of wine and let your Uncle Harvey tell you how it's done," he said sagely.

Taking her first sip of wine, Elizabeth settled in the wing chair that held a down cushion, making her sink even lower. The pair had bonded over libations during their five o'clock, happy hour chats. Death, investments, and romance were the topics; after all, he was the expert. By the time Harvey had taught Elizabeth the skills on how to become a player, it was late in the evening and the two had passed out, moving onto dreamland.

Blanche entered the back door calling, "Mista Harvey, what are you doing up this late at night? Every light in the house is on." She rounded the corner and squinted in on the passed-out partiers. "Elizabeth, wake up. I do declare your grandmother will be fit to be tied. I'll walk you home."

Elizabeth stirred and grinned at Blanche. "I'm going to have Harper Baldwin's children." She pantomimed, zipping her lips closed. "Don't tell Nana yet and I want you to be their godmother."

"Look at you, chile. You in trouble now," Blanche flared.

Waking the next morning, Elizabeth sat up and stretched her arms over her head and yawned. "I don't remember last night. I wonder how I got home," she muttered, hoping Nana had not witnessed her intoxicated state.

"Breakfast is ready. Don't forget you have a funeral this morning at the parish," Nana called cheerfully from the bottom of the staircase.

In Elizabeth's cloudy haze, she realized she had escaped the wrath of Nana, having cultivated a healthy fear of her as a child. *I guess she was already asleep when I got home*, she surmised. She would ask Uncle Harvey what happened when they got to the church. Showering and putting on her makeup, she quickly dressed in a black suit and pearls. *Thank goodness I don't have to think about what I'm going to wear every day,* she concluded. Nana gave her a good morning kiss, never questioning her whereabouts the night before. Elizabeth practically ran to the Episcopal church to save time.

"How are we feeling, darlin'?" Uncle Harvey inquired with a slight smile that played across his lips.

"Not so good," Elizabeth said, rubbing the top of her forehead.
"You'll learn." He never brought up the incident again.

The peninsula of Virginia was filled with the have and have-nots, the likes of which Elizabeth had never known or seen. Uncle Harvey buried everyone regardless and she soon realized his Robin Hood theory: steal from the rich and give to the poor. The wealthy only wanted to be laid out in mahogany or copper caskets at the front of the church. Even in death, one-upmanship prevailed. The poor settled for cardboard boxes decorated with a gray flocked material fabric, which the funeral industry dubbed "cloth covered wood." The design resembled the 1930s wallpaper in the Mom-and-Pop Italian restaurant around the corner from the funeral parlor.

This would be the first funeral she and Uncle Harvey would work with the new Episcopal priest sent from the Tidewater Diocese.

Earlier that morning, over a bowl of steaming oatmeal, Nana told Elizabeth, "He's a flower child of the sixties. He drinks a lot of communion wine in the evenings and pours the chalice full on Sundays, even if there's hardly anyone there to receive—he practically gulps it down. The altar guild makes numerous trips to the liquor store on any given morning for Mogen David. Pearl says that he's constantly humming 'Norwegian Wood' in his office. The girls have nicknamed him Father Donovan Peace-Love."

Uncle Harvey took her aside when Elizabeth entered the parish. "This new priest is really different. He's on a mission to preach the ashes to ashes, dust to dust mantra. When Mrs. Singleton came in to make funeral arrangements for her husband, Father Peace-Love was in tow, insisting that he assist her with the choosing of the casket. I ended up stuffing her two hundred and seventy-five-pound deceased husband in the new box du jour—tighter than a can of sardines. I did everything but stand on my head to talk her out of the choice, but she turned the decision-making over to the good Father. This is the first time a cloth covered wood has entered St. Paul's. Mr. O'Bannon from O'Bannon Funeral Home in Norfolk worked with him for the past two years. I understand he never misses the cocktail reception after the funerals, even doing shots with his flock. Mr. O'Bannon said it really hurt his sales the past twenty-four months. This could really hurt my business as well—the Episcopalians are the wealthiest clientele that I have, the bulwarks to Sycamore Creek Funeral Home. I'll get Margaret to talk to the Bishop of the Diocese and find out what's going on, since she's a big contributor. In the meantime, let's hope Mr. Singleton doesn't fall through his box. Thank goodness we have a pall to place over the casket." Elizabeth saw a sign of relief cross Uncle Harvey's face.

At the conclusion of the Burial of the Dead: Rite One, Harvey and Charlie began to roll the casket from the front of the parish towards the back following Father Peace-Love. Elizabeth swore his chanting sounded like the tune "With A Little Help from My Friends." Elizabeth processed behind the casket with the widow's hand wrapped tightly around her arm. This practice was methodical—Uncle Harvey style, organization personified. The aging pallbearers were instructed to stop in the narthex, lift the cloth covered wood receptacle off the church truck, remove the pall, and continue to the grave site. Obeying orders, the six men lifted with all their might, and with a big heave-ho, raised the casket. A thud echoed as Mr. Singleton, just like Humpty Dumpty coming off the wall, fell through the box and hit the floor. Women screamed, children cried, and all the king's men could not put him back in the box again. The staff and anyone who kindly volunteered carried the body into the awaiting hearse and it sped towards the funeral parlor across the street. Mrs. Singleton went home, took a Valium, drank a vodka, and gradually calmed her nerves. The new solid bronze casket that Uncle Harvey replaced her husband in, was of course, on the house.

Uncle Harvey hung his head that evening as he downed more bourbon than normal. "Tongues are going to wag and it's all going to be all my fault that I sold this widow a cheap casket. Everything has its day and I've probably seen the last of mine. I guess I'll stick it out a few more years. I am beginning to lean on you more and more as time goes by."

Elizabeth stood to refresh his drink, keeping her back to the liquor cabinet, so he wouldn't see the tear trickle down her cheek. She loved Nana, Uncle Harvey, and Blanche in this Southern quaint town. As far as the misfit Sadie, she would continue to be a pain in her posterior.

"Harvey, I contacted the Bishop immediately after yesterday's debacle. Father Donovan Peace-Love was moved from the rectory in the night to a monastery in the Virginia mountains—to harvest grapes for wine," Margaret relayed over dinner the next evening.

Harvey chewed and swallowed the last spoonful of Brunswick stew and raised his Cabernet Sauvignon glass. "Cheers," he bellowed.

CHAPTER TWENTY-FOUR

"Elizabeth, Harper Baldwin's on the phone!" Nana called, covering the receiver with the palm of her opposite hand.

"I'll pick up in my room. Thanks, Nana." Trying to contain her excitement, she answered as matter-of-factly as she could, "Hello?"

"Elizabeth, I've been thinking about you and couldn't wait a day longer to ask you to dinner Friday night. I'm a member of the country club. Have you been?"

"Yes, it's beautiful." Elizabeth remembered Uncle Harvey advising her to play hard to get as excuses flashed through her mind. "I have to check my itinerary to see if there are any viewings that evening."

"I'll wait."

Harper sure is persistent, Elizabeth thought. Taking her time looking through her appointment book, she hesitated before picking up the receiver, not wanting to appear overtly eager. He needed to realize just how important she was.

"I'm free on Friday night."

"Great, I'll pick you up at six o'clock sharp. See you then."

"See you then," she whispered her mouth so dry due to nerves. "I really like this guy," she said to Lambchop, her marmalade cat curled up on the canopy bed.

Blanche had gifted the kitten to Elizabeth when she found it in the smokehouse. It had been abandoned by its mother and barely had its eyes open. Blanche had shown her how to feed the little fur ball with an eyedropper and warm milk. The little kitten soon learned how to suck the cream.

Lambchop was Elizabeth's confidant and she continued her conversation with him. "Now what to wear?" she questioned seeking, the cat's approval. Opening the closet, she gazed upon black dresses, black suits, navy dresses, and navy suits. "I'll accessorize with something of color, and of course, pearls." Lambchop yawned and never offered his opinion as she rummaged through the jewelry box that contained pearls, pearls, and more pearls. "Hmm... the only thing I have with color is my signature red lipstick," she explained to the bored feline.

Elizabeth and Jacki, her best friend since the first day of equestrian school, journeyed frequently to Norfolk to buy the Chanel red lipstick and nail polish. Shopping had become a hobby, an escape from the telephone that rang constantly in the funeral parlor. Unfortunately, Uncle Harvey had also implemented an open-door policy to the entire community. Jacki and Elizabeth formulated excuses to ride the roads on Saturdays. They would meet at the funeral parlor antagonizing Sadie with their freedom.

"You have roller skates on your ass, Miss Fancy Panties," Sadie would snarl at Elizabeth who would simply blow her a kiss, agitating her ever the more, as she skipped out the door, not to return home until midnight.

Friday afternoon, Elizabeth did her nails, spent time in front of the mirror primping and practicing facial expressions, and looked up words in the dictionary. It was important to impress Harper with not only her beauty, but intellect as well.

The doorbell rang at five forty-five and Elizabeth heard Blanche greet her date. "Come on in, Mr. Harper, we've been expectin' you."

"Thank you. I brought Miss Margaret some flowers, but they need a vase."

Margaret walked into the foyer. "Oh Harper, you shouldn't have. Use the tall vase under the sink, Blanche," she instructed. "Do come in and have a seat. May I offer you a drink?"

"No, ma'am. I have reservations at six o'clock, but it is so kind of you."

Elizabeth listened to the conversation, trying to ignore the butterflies in her stomach. She was determined not to make a grand entrance on the stairway until she was summoned—she wanted to have Harper witness the most breathtaking moment of his life.

"Mr. Harper doesn't have all night, chile. Now git yourself down here," Blanche barked.

Just like that, her movie entrance was thwarted; Elizabeth obeyed Blanche's command. Spotting Harper in the foyer, she felt breathless. He appeared as if he just walked out of the pages of *Gentleman's Quarterly* magazine. Grabbing the banister tightly with one hand, she took the steps gingerly in her higher-than-normal heels.

"You should see what he drove tonight. Lord a mercy." Blanche could not contain herself, placing the vase of flowers on the round foyer table. She was as excited as if Harper was her date for the evening.

Elizabeth spoke politely to Harper as he leaned over and gave her a peck on the cheek. "I suggest we go," she said, cutting her eyes at Blanche to remain quiet. From that point on she relaxed because Harper immediately began a social dialogue that continued through the evening.

"How do you like my vintage Jaguar?"

"I really don't know one car from another, but it rides divine," she concluded.

"It's a 1967 E-type, British racing green with a six cylinder, three two-barrel engine that I have had up to 175 miles an hour in the country. The exhaust manifold glowed red because of the heat and I could see it through the bonnet."

"Cool," Elizabeth replied. He might as well had been speaking Latin, but she continued to show interest so as not to be rude.

His deep blue eyes grew more intense as he spoke. "The original E-Type has a clean aerodynamic shape. The E-Type is arguably the most famous car of all time." With that said, Harper shifted gears to start an increasing rate of speed on the way to the country club.

She quickly realized she shouldn't have worried over the past couple of days about conversation with her date because he had been jabbering non-stop since opening the car door. Every subject Elizabeth mentioned he was an authority on—a walking encyclopedia.

Arriving at the front door of the club, Harper was ebullient, jumping out of the Jaguar and handing the keys of his pride and joy to the valet in a white dinner jacket.

"Good evening, Mr. Baldwin," he said as his eyes danced with excitement to park the Jaguar. "She sure is a beauty."

It's obvious they are not discussing me, she thought, but rather the Q.E. Elizabeth had decided to nickname Harper's precious automobile after the English Queen herself.

After being seated, Harper told the server, "The lady will have a glass of champagne and I'll have the usual."

The staff was eager to appease him, and their drinks arrived in minutes. *Harper is part of the highbrow country-club set*, Elizabeth determined noticing his usual was a Pimm's on the rocks with an orange slice. She sucked down the glass of champagne that was served in a French bird bath glass. Being in the company of such a cultured man filled her with anticipation. He began reading the menu and speaking French fluently. *His manners are impeccable*, she thought, staring at him mesmerized.

"Do you like champagne, Elizabeth?"

Before she could answer, he summoned the server and asked for a bottle of Cuvee Dom Perignon. Elizabeth knew it was expensive as she had an innate sense of all things costly since arriving from the womb into the hands of her mother's doctor, according to Nana. Quicker than a greyhound sprint, the champagne bottle arrived and was poured while Harper ordered shrimp cocktail for two.

"The lady and I will follow the first course with filet mignon, temperature medium, scalloped potatoes, and asparagus tips. Ask the chef to pair our entrée with a bottle of your finest Bordeaux. Also, tell him at the end of the meal we'll be having the chocolate soufflé with your vintage cognac," he instructed the waiter who memorized the order.

"Yes sir, Mr. Baldwin," he politely said.

Elizabeth wondered to herself if Harper thought the lady accompanying him for the evening was incapable of ordering her meal, but realized all Southern gentleman did this as it was instilled in them by their fathers.

"Thank you, Harper," Elizabeth said as he lifted the bottle of champagne out of the ice bucket beside their table. She raised the glass to her lips and sipped the fizzy liquid as it tickled her tongue. Feeling relaxed, she surprised herself by becoming more chatty than usual.

"Elizabeth, I am so impressed with your portfolio. I have diversified your assets into different investments. Did you know you are one of our wealthiest stockholders?" he concluded with a grin.

"Ah ... thanks," she replied.

Harper decided to educate her on finances for the rest of the evening, often questioning about her other holdings. He assured her his inquiries were in her best interest.

"You seem to know all about me, Harper, more than I know myself, as far as what I have."

"You'll never have to worry a day in your life with me at the helm. The principal grows more and more each day, especially with the higher interest rates this year. I noticed you never withdraw. You're beautiful and rich—what a great combination!"

Feeling giddy with all the compliments in one evening, Elizabeth pardoned herself to powder her nose. Noticing her legs growing wobbly, she tried to regain balance before walking across the floor of the club as if in a dream. Entering the ladies powder room, she spotted a silver tray holding mouthwash in a crystal decanter, crystal cordial glasses, and lotions. On the other side of the sink was a tray holding hand towels to use after washing. A white wicker basket was under the sink to hold the damp towels after use. "I'm going to do this at the funeral parlor," she spoke aloud to no one.

Exiting from the powder room, she walked across the floor smiling at Harper. Her guard was up as every head turned to watch her prance across the room. Harper rose and pushed back her chair seating her expertly.

A nice lady walked by and whispered in her ear, "Honey, the back of your dress is tucked up in your pantyhose, exposing your fanny."

Elizabeth thanked her and squirmed in the chair until she released the bundle that had her entangled. Moving from side to side of the chair, she felt her face burn with embarrassment causing her to drink more than intended. A trio playing old jazz tunes reminded her of both parents in their happy days. *I'm in love*, she thought ... blinded by Harper's good looks, intelligence, and his interest in her overall well-being.

"Let's dance," Harper was saying after the entrée and before the soufflé. Grabbing Elizabeth's hand, he glided her around the floor—everything was becoming a blur. They made it back to the table. He dropped her in the chair as he continued to talk about money, and how lovely she was. "I guess it's time we call it an evening, unfortunately. I think we better skip the soufflé."

Elizabeth stifling hiccups, could only nod as the entire date was surreal.

Harper handed the valet his ticket; when the car arrived, the second valet opened the Jaguar's passenger door and Elizabeth slid onto the saddle-colored leather seat. Harper drove her home and parked in the oyster shell driveway.

"Elizabeth," he said, holding her hands between his, "I want you to be my wife. Will you marry me?"

Gazing at Harper, she attempted to speak, but a wave of nausea caused her to projectile vomit onto the beautiful leather seats and gear shift. "I'm so sorry. I have the flu," she cried just before she passed out.

"There, there, I'll get you inside and clean the car later," he said as he rang the doorbell. Then he explained to Blanche and Margaret that Elizabeth was not feeling too well. "Something didn't agree with her this evening. It must have been the shrimp." Harper carried her up the stairs to her room and Blanche promptly began wiping her face with a damp washcloth. He excused himself and said to Elizabeth, "I'll call you tomorrow."

Dressing Elizabeth in a fresh nightgown, Nana and Blanche tucked her in bed and placed a glass of ice water on her night table. She woke up mortified and thought life was over as she had known it. *Nana is going to disown me, and Harper will never call me again.*

A little tap sounded on the door and Blanche entered with toast and tea. "I'm sorry you're feelin' poorly, Miss 'Lizabeth," she said so loudly it hurt her ears. Everything was hurting, but mostly her pride.

"I'll be in my room today," she mumbled as she sat up and started to wretch, making it down the hall to the toilet just in time.

"God doesn't like ugly, chile," Elizabeth heard Blanche say in between dry heaves.

"Help me, Jesus ..." is all Elizabeth could utter in reply.

Harper Baldwin called at noon to inquire about her flu and never mentioned the embarrassing way Elizabeth had christened his vintage Jaguar. "You made me the happiest man last night," Harper said excitedly.

The silence stretched between them and Elizabeth did not know how to fill it. Finally, she said, "I don't know what you mean."

"My darling Elizabeth, you agreed to marry me."

CHAPTER TWENTY-FIVE

"After only one date?!" Margaret arched her brows, not happy with news of the engagement her granddaughter sprang upon her.

"He's a nice man, Nana," Elizabeth said softly, trying not to second-guess her decision. "Uncle Harvey thinks it's great. He's delighted we've made the decision to get married six months from now. A New Year's Eve candlelight wedding will be so romantic, especially if it snows."

"This New Year's Eve? You hardly know each other? Where will you live?"

Elizabeth sucked in her breath. "Harper knows how close we are, Nana and he's suggested we move in with you. Of course with your approval," she jabbered nervously.

"Nice of him." Margaret didn't crack a smile. Things were moving at way too fast a pace, and there was something she just couldn't put her finger on...

"I love this house, Nana. I never want to move."

"Your name is on this house as well as all the other rental properties. I insist you keep it that way. The Eyre family takes care of their own. I know Harper's family, but not him very well. As long as you are both comfortable living with me, I guess it will work."

"What could possibly go wrong?" Elizabeth had to admit she was confused by all the events that had taken place so rapidly. "I'm needed at the funeral parlor," she said excusing herself from the tension between them.

Walking outside in the June heat of Virginia, she noticed how green the leaves on the Sycamore trees and antique boxwoods contrasted with the clear blue cloudless sky. A sailboat glided through the water at a fast clip on the creek heading towards the bay. The sunlight twinkled on the water appearing like handheld sparklers on the Fourth of July. Summer, particularly days like this, conjured up memories of happy times with

Jim that one special day...

Walking into the rear of the funeral parlor Elizabeth's nostrils identified the odor of a decomposed body. *Uh oh*, she thought, *we have a floater*.

Uncle Harvey walked out of the morgue, closing the door behind him. "We have the sixteen-year-old girl that vanished in Virginia Beach during June week," he said, shaking his head. "It's been in *The Daily Norfolk* and on the radio the last several days."

"Oh right, I heard about that on the Norfolk station. She went missing after a night out at a boardwalk dance club. Wasn't she sharing a hotel suite with six other high school students from Silver Spring, Maryland?"

"Yes, that's right. They found her strangled on a rural road about seven miles from here. The son of a bitch really knew where he was dumping her body too—it's so desolate on Sheep House Road. I must warn you, Elizabeth, this situation is bad. He strangled her with a wire coat hanger that he had straightened and placed around her neck, tying the wire around her wrists behind her back, yanking it until she suffocated. The hanger became embedded in her neck and because of the natural process of body gases, it eventually ripped through the hypodermis, the final layer of skin. I hate for you to see this, but you need to be exposed to all facets of this business, even the backroom a little more often. At your age I had seen it all."

"But... Uncle Harvey, odors really bother me, and I can smell her... the body already."

"I have a mask for you, darlin.' Inhale a deep breath. Let's go." He opened the door and Elizabeth saw Charlie leaning over the corpse pouring cavity embalming fluid into a black pouch. He didn't wear a mask and his ever-present cigarette barely hung from his lips, dropping ashes into the body bag.

"You're going to blow up some day, Charlie. Fire and chemicals are a bad combination." Harvey seemed miffed. "When I unzipped the pouch after the fire company boys brought her in, I exposed a black mass that represented what skin there was left." Educating his niece, Harvey explained: "This body has been in the woods approximately a week in the hot sun. The natural gases inside the body have expanded and distended, attracting flies. The flies laid their eggs in all the orifices. The maggots have consequently eaten the first layer of skin called the epidermis that protects the body, as well as part of the second layer—the dermis. Charlie just poured cavity fluid on the remains and then he'll sprinkle a topical powder, both will kill the smell and preserve at the same time. The medical examiner went to the location where she was dumped and came here as well. We'll transport the body to Maryland as soon as ole Charlie here cleans up."

The embalming seminar being over, Elizabeth stared at what once was a young girl. The skin had slipped or been eaten away, and hair was dislodged from her head. Remnants of fingernails were discolored as well. "This is unreal, Uncle Harvey. It sickens me. Was she molested too?" Elizabeth had donned the mask that Charlie had handed her, but it could not dissipate the odor that seeped from the pouch. She began to gag, unable to view the details and stages of decomposition any longer. What a contrast from the beautiful summer day she had just experienced on Market Street.

"No doubt she was sexually molested. They'll find him ... Bastard," Uncle Harvey replied.

"I won't be traveling to Maryland with you on this one, Mr. Charlie," she said.

"I'll be driving with the air-conditioner full blast and the windows down," Charlie said.

By the end of the week, Elizabeth read in the local paper that on Monday, Carolyn Riggs was found strangled on a dirt road outside of Sycamore Creek. An Accomac, Virginia man, who police say Riggs met at a teenage nightclub, was arrested Wednesday and charged with first-degree murder. He was being held without bond in the county jail.

The article continued: Riggs was a cheerleader and aspiring model and had just finished her junior year at a Silver Spring area high school. On June eleventh, she went to Virginia Beach with six other teenage girls to spend a week in the resort. The girls spent the days on the beach and their nights roaming the boardwalk and going out to clubs, according to Rigg's friend, Melissa Kane. On June fifteenth, Riggs went to an alcohol-free dance club with Kane. Kane stated Riggs spent four or five hours dancing with a young man she met there. About three o'clock in the morning, the man drove Riggs and Kane back to their hotel. When Kane exited the car, Riggs told her she would come up to the room in fifteen minutes. By the next morning, Riggs had not returned. That afternoon, Kane called police and reported her friend missing. Police told her not to worry, that her friend, like most other young people who are briefly reported missing at the beach, would eventually turn up.

Elizabeth closed her eyes and took a deep breath before finishing the article. The Accomac man, Mark Brittingham, was convicted of perverted sexual practice previously in November. Then in March, he was accused of grabbing a female acquaintance by the throat, choking her and demanding sex at her home in Sycamore Creek.

The remains of Carolyn Riggs body left a horrific impression on Elizabeth. Just viewing the aftermath of such a violent crime made her ache for the parents who would never be able to touch or kiss their daughter again. Nana had shared with her that she had kissed her daughter the last day of her life ... comforting to a degree. *I guess there's a reason to be grateful in everything,* she considered.

That night, after reading the newspaper article and saying prayers for the family of Carolyln Riggs, Elizabeth fell asleep holding a small silver-framed picture of her mother. It had a way of soothing her. It was a habit she had started when she was young. She gripped the black and white photograph until morning ... until she opened her eyes.

CHAPTER TWENTY-SIX

Harper had a secret: it wasn't money—it was the love of money. He knew it was an unethical reason to get married, but his goal was to be the richest man in Sycamore Creek and that dream would come to fruition by making Elizabeth his bride. The future looked bright having her by his side; she was beautiful, classy, and wealthy. She didn't know what she was worth. *Yes, she's always had a silver spoon up her rear end*, he concluded. He was eager to get his name on all her holdings. Harvey Eyre was going to leave her the funeral home, the only one in town. She had real estate in Virginia as well as a farm in West Virginia. Royalty checks for drilling natural gas were deposited in her account every month. The lease was written and signed in 1901 by one of her ancestors. He had done his research. *My lord, I could live on that check alone*, Harper thought, self-assured he would stand to gain a fortune.

The dividend check from the bank stock could buy that expensive pair of golf clubs he had his eye on and enable a complete overhaul of his vintage Jaguar. Cuban cigars, aged cognacs, and tailored-made suits were in his future—he could just taste it. He watched over all of Elizabeth Barclay's financial transactions like a hawk.

For her own welfare, he reasoned.

"Oops, I have to cancel my date," he said to the old Chesapeake Bay Retriever that his father bought and trained for hunting years ago.

Picking up the receiver, he called Elizabeth hoping the news would not distress her. He was pushing his luck knowing how women could be.

"Good morning," Elizabeth answered, sounding perky.

"Good morning, my wife to be. I'm afraid I'm going to have to cancel our trip to Williamsburg today."

"But ... we've had this planned all week. The weather is absolutely gorgeous." She sounded flummoxed.

"I know, darling, but my golf team wants to play. Seldom do we have a summer day without high humidity. I'll make it up to you I promise."

"What about tonight? You said we were going to dinner at the Regency Room in the Inn."

"Yes, well, we have a poker game at the clubhouse scheduled after the game over a couple of beers. I don't know what time I'll be home after that. We'll get together tomorrow. Maybe go sailing."

"Harper, I took today off. I was supposed to help Uncle Harvey with a fireman's funeral. He was upset with me for bowing out without much notice. Firemen from all around the state will be in attendance. I really feel awful leaving him in a pinch, but I wanted to be with you. I don't have the nerve to show up at the funeral parlor now. I ... guess we can do something tomorrow." Elizabeth closed her eyes and groaned. This engagement was getting off on the wrong foot. *Nothing worthwhile ever comes easy*, she told herself. Harper was constantly cancelling dates because of his social schedule. The boys and their outings took precedence over her. Without fail, flowers and jewelry would follow the next day after a disagreement.

"I'm so sorry," Harper said. Elizabeth thought he sounded sincere ... yet again.

"Me too," she sighed.

"See you tomorrow," he said quickly disconnecting.

Elizabeth walked into the kitchen to retrieve another cup of coffee. Nana glanced up from kneading her yeast rolls. It was a Saturday morning tradition to bake, one started long ago by her mother. "What time are you going to Williamsburg?"

"I'm not." Elizabeth tried not to let her bad mood come across.

"What happened? You were so looking forward to it."

"Harper said something came up." Elizabeth didn't want to divulge the reason—she had to think about her fiancé's behavior. Her grandmother was so wise and had the uncanny ability to see right through people, enabling her to judge their character. *I'll worry about that tomorrow*, she lamented, not coming to terms with what Nana's expression indicated.

"Honey, are you positively sure you love him?"

Elizabeth was uncomfortable with the question and only nodded her head *yes*. "A man's got to do what a man's got to do, I suppose."

"Remember what I've told you. Don't rely on a man; learn to be independent. I'm giving you good advice. You don't need a man for money."

Elizabeth had memorized these words of Nana's long ago. It had been instilled in her brain. She loved Harper ... or was it infatuation? After all, his knowledge of the finer things in life intrigued her. Their future shone bright with all the luxuries and comfort life had to offer. She would never be in want.

The phone by her bed jarred her awake. *Why doesn't Nana answer the phone?* Elizabeth thought in her haze as she awoke from a sound sleep. Stirring, she realized it was Sunday and Nana was probably at service. She usually went to Rite One which was at 8:30 a.m.

"Hello," she mumbled, rising stiffly and propping herself up on one side with her elbow.

"Elizabeth, Uncle Harvey here. I know it's Sunday morning, but I have Charlie picking up a middle age couple from the hospital this morning. Can you give us a hand? Apparently, they were hit by a bolt of lightning that just came out of nowhere."

"Sure, let me make a call. I'll be right there."

"I'll give you all the information when you get here. Thanks, darlin'."

What's good for the gander is good for the goose, Elizabeth thought. Before falling asleep last night, she made up her mind that she did not intend to spend another Saturday evening alone. The guilty feelings she experienced yesterday for not working the firemen's funeral with Uncle Harvey had left her melancholy. Harper's inconsideration for her feelings would have to come to an end. She wouldn't stand for it and would express her concern in person as the opportunity arose. Picking up the phone, she dialed his number.

"Hello," Harper answered with a groggy hungover voice.

"Good morning. I have to work today," she began to explain, cutting right to the quick.

"Do you have the couple killed by lightning?" Harper interrupted.

"Yes, have you heard?"

"It's on the news. Last night, at the stock car races seven people were leaving early and witnessed a streak of lightning hit a couple holding hands on the way to their car in front of them. They were killed instantly and three of the other seven were injured by the force of the bolt. They are still unconscious, according to the hospital. It happened in a field outside of the track."

"Uncle Harvey seemed a little shaken. I won't be able to go sailing today, let alone a trip to Williamsburg," Elizabeth huffed. She couldn't help but feel a little smug. "Harper, the next time we're together I need to discuss something with you."

"Fine." With that, he hung up.

During the summer months, people would flock to the stock car races outside of town. The track was fairly large for the Eastern Shore. A big Saturday night consisted of drinking beer and watching cars drive around the track.

Jerry and Martha decided they had had enough of revving engines and drunken crowds for one evening and opted to leave the races early. They exited the stadium and they walked hand in hand to their car. Their plan was to stop by the VFW and have a drink before going home. This night was special—it was their twenty-first wedding anniversary.

Jerry had earphones on his head and a Walkman in his jeans pocket. A belt with a large Texas-style, metal buckle held up his new denim trousers. Martha was dressed in jeans, t-shirt with a picture of a can of Budweiser on the back, and a new gold chain around her neck that Jerry had just given her as an anniversary gift before leaving their rancher. She held her husband's hand tightly. They had been high school sweethearts, marrying the same June they graduated.

Jerry was relaying to Martha the events of the race heard on his Walkman when a streak of lightning bolted down from the sky and hit the metal band in the center of his head connecting the ear phones. The lightning strike traveled down his body, through his hand and into the hand of his wife. Moving upward to her neck and back down her body, exiting through her vagina. Fans leaving the race screamed in horror as the couple dropped to the ground in unison.

Elizabeth entered the morgue at the funeral parlor as Charlie was preparing Martha and Jerry for embalming. Having only one morgue table, he left Jerry on the stretcher, opting to embalm Martha first.

"Look at this, Elizabeth," Charlie walked over to the stretcher, pointing his boney finger for emphasis at the burns on Jerry's body. "Lightning entered the metal band across his head. See where he's burned? All on their anniversary night too. Such a shame."

Elizabeth nodded, staring at the perfectly marked black line charred on his bald head.

Charlie continued, "Look where his zipper melted into his groin and the belt buckle looks as if it was branded into his flesh. I've never seen anything like this."

Assessing Jerry's branding from metal burns, Elizabeth walked to the morgue table where his wife of twenty-one years laid in repose. "Oh my God, Mr. Charlie, look where her necklace singed her throat. Look, look the wedding ring is embedded in her finger." Glancing back at Jerry's left hand she noticed the streak of gold embedded into his as well. "Until death do us part." she exhaled.

"I know it's horrible. Lightning has a place it enters and exits. It entered him and exited out her. Get ready. This will be a doozy, a double funeral for sure," Charlie said with his Lucky Strike dangling from his lips.

"Mr. Charlie, your ashes are falling on Martha."

"Not going to hurt her now. She's already been burned," he chuckled, amusing himself with a little morgue sense of humor.

I guess that's his way of coping after all that he's seen, Elizabeth surmised.

The afternoon of their funeral, two caskets were positioned side by side at the grave. The children of Jerry and Martha saw their parents laid to rest—simultaneously.

CHAPTER TWENTY-SEVEN

New Year's Eve

"Uncle Harvey, it's beginning to snow," Elizabeth exclaimed, as she took her uncle's arm and prepared to enter the narthex of the parish. As they walked down the aisle, she saw the church glowing in candlelight. Magnolia leaves and white roses added to the dreamy setting. The pews were filled with happy guests, an air of excitement for the coming year, and joy for two of Sycamore Creek's own tying the knot. Harvey had arranged for a flutist and violinist from the Norfolk Symphony to accompany the organist with classical selections, setting the tone making the evening enchanting.

Harper never took eyes off his bride as his dream was about to come true. He would be worth a fortune in less than thirty minutes, if the priest cooperated with his timetable.

"You may kiss the bride," Father announced.

The music rose to a high pitch and Harper extended his arm to the wealth management of his dreams.

The usher opened the door as the bell pealed merrily. Harper and Elizabeth stepped outside into a cold torrential rain.

The second night of their honeymoon, Harper gazed into Elizabeth's eyes as they sat in the Regency Room of the Williamsburg Inn. After they ordered cocktails, Harper took his wife's hand and raised it to his lips, kissing the back side. "When we get home to Sycamore Creek let's call my attorney and revise our wills. Have you thought about adding my name to all your holdings? I am your husband now, and what's mine is yours, and yours is mine."

Elizabeth swallowed hard. She had informed Harper months ago everything she owned was in her name and her grandmother's. *Nana would veto Harper's suggestion*, she thought.

"Harper, Nana has business set up with her attorney and I'd feel uncomfortable asking to put your name on her assets. I've told you before what's mine is mine. Why are you so fixated on this?"

"But I'm putting your name on everything I have."

"What? The Jaguar?"

"Well, yes."

"Are you planning to pay rent for living with Nana and what about utilities? We can't just sponge off of her."

Harper grew silent as the cocktails arrived.

"Harper, answer me," Elizabeth clenched her jaw.

"We'll talk later," Harper said.

"In other words, you have a problem with that?" Elizabeth eyed the man who was now her husband. "It was doomed before we ever took the vow," she whispered as her nostrils flaired with anger.

Just then, the waiter placed an appetizer of Oysters Rockefeller on the table in front of Harper.

"May I have one?

"Get your own," he hissed.

Elizabeth held the police report in her hand and read it carefully. "This is hard to believe, Uncle Harvey," she murmured. "Listen to this, Sadie."

"A grain elevator superintendent, Hubert P. Evans and a truck driver, Calvin Adkins, both employees of a grain elevator company, were loading a truck with soybeans from a steel bin that was eighteen meters high and twenty-three meters in diameter. The superintendent ascended the outside ladder and descended the inside ladder of the bin. He then stood on the beans, trying to unclog the open front floor hole with a garden hoe. The truck driver, who was in radio contact with the superintendent, stayed outside the bin. The truck driver told the worker in the bin they needed to stop the loading

operation and take care of another customer at another building for ten to fifteen minutes. The driver shut off the unload conveyor. When he returned to the bin, he told the superintendent that they needed to run the unload conveyor for about three more minutes to fill the truck. When the truck was filled, the driver turned off the unload conveyor and told the superintendent to exit the bin. The superintendent said it would be easier to exit the bottom side door of the bin, but the driver advised the superintendent that there was too much product in front of the door to exit there. Because he did not want to climb the ladders and despite a second warning, the superintendent insisted on leaving by the side door. As the truck driver started to leave to deliver his load, he heard the superintendent call for help on his radio. The driver summoned emergency medical services and found the superintendent totally engulfed by soybeans. The coroner pronounced the superintendent dead of asphyxia at the scene. There was an estimated twelve hundred kiloliters of soybeans in the bin at the time of the accident. The employer's written safety and health program prohibited entry into bins from above the level of the grain without a body harness, with lifeline or boatswain's chair, an attendant and suitable rescue equipment. It was company policy never to enter a grain bin from the top. The superintendent had thirty years of experience in the grain handling industry."

Elizabeth laid the report down on Sadie's desk and sighed, "What a horrible way to die."

"Well, Hubert should have known better. He always was a know-it-all. I did him once in his family's barn ... or was it the school bus?" she pondered. "He wasn't all that—"

Harvery interrupted with a sigh, "That will be enough of that, Sadie." He never knew what was going to come out of Sadie's mouth next. *She claims to have had sex with every male in town,* his thoughts wandered, *but it's probably all bogus ... she has a real abhorrence for men.*

"I still think it's heartbreaking," Elizabeth reiterated her feelings. She had grown accustomed to Sadie's vulgarity. Sharing Sadie's stories with Nana in the evenings she could count on Nana's comment: "not very refined."

Hubert Evans's funeral was the next afternoon and Charlie had worked his magic once again. The casket would be open to the public for the services in the chapel.

Elizabeth walked to the front of the alcove after the service ended and stood behind the lectern as Uncle Harvey and Charlie closed the curtains for privacy and for sealing the casket. Smiling at the mourners she announced, "Pallbearers, we will not need your services at the funeral home this afternoon. Please, however, meet us at the back of the hearse when we arrive at the cemetery." With her spiel finished, she began handing arrangements of flowers to Charlie to put in the station wagon.

Elizabeth recalled looking at her curb list before the service and found it uncanny but amusing that all of Hubert's brothers names ended in Bert: Albert, Gilbert, Dilbert, and of course, the deceased Hubert. They were huge men with bulging muscles, sporting beards, and wearing leather motorcycle jackets with their names labeled on the side.

Albert approached Elizabeth with tears in his swollen eyes, likely due to all the Jack Daniels from the night before as well as nips of the strong whiskey swallowed in the parking lot as the viewing was underway. "Let's crack the Jack," one brother announced to the other swaying around the foyer.

"I wanna tote the sumabitch Goddammit," Albert jumbled with a thick tongue standing in front of Elizabeth.

"I beg your pardon?" Elizabeth glanced at Albert's name on his jacket with empathy.

"I wanna tote the sumabitch Goddammit," he repeated. Tears had spilled over his eyes and began to stream down his cheeks.

"I'm truly sorry. I can't understand you. Please speak a little slower."

"I WANNA TOTE THE SUMABITCH GODDAMMIT." Albert thought by raising his voice Elizabeth would surely be able to grasp his words.

Elizabeth had heard this garbled accent before, from the descendants who lived on the islands in the bay of the Chesapeake. Words ran together, and the old folks said it was a Cockney accent from old England coupled with a lazy, slurring tongue heard regularly on the Shore. She began to pat Albert's arm and made the announcement that Hubert's brothers were indeed needed as pallbearers at the funeral parlor that afternoon.

Albert smiled as all the Bert boys began to tote the sumabitch brother Hubert Goddammit to the awaiting hearse.

CHAPTER TWENTY-EIGHT

Ten Years Later

Jacki had become Elizabeth's dearest and closest friend throughout the years, a friend she could share secrets with and confide her innermost feelings. Elizabeth remembered the day Jacki told her she was going to marry Sean, the man she had been waiting for all her life. A year later she became pregnant with a son. They were the ideal family.

Returning home Saturday evening after yet another shopping excursion to Norfolk, Elizabeth broke her silence. Emotions erupted within her and she could not hold back any longer. "I am so overwhelmed at the funeral home, Jacki. I just feel exhausted all the time. With Uncle Harvey slowing down, he insists I help him meet with the families. I assist Sadie writing the obituaries, printing the memorial cards, clean behind Blanche, and weed the flower beds behind Roger as well. I've been known to wash the hearse too. I go home, fall into bed, and start all over the next day. It seems the staff is going bad all at once.

"What does Harper say?" Jacki inquired.

"We don't spend a lot of time together, actually. He's always at the hunting lodge this time of year when he's not at the bank. Nana said just the other night she seldom sees him. He's so caustic and condescending towards me that I don't even have any desire for relations. He criticizes everything I wear, say, and do. If I didn't know better, I'd think he was having an affair. You have such a good marriage with Sean, and Adam is so adorable. How old is he now?"

"Twelve. Can you believe it?" Jacki's eyes brightened when she spoke of her son. "Sean and Adam are taking their 4-wheelers and riding around the farm this afternoon. It's a father and son tradition they started a few years ago when the crops are out. Adam used to ride with his daddy until he got big enough for his own ATV. You should see the mud on them when they return. Mud's caked on those two from head to toe. I told them this morning to be careful and wear their helmets," Jacki laughed and rambled on and on, not wanting to address the rumors she had heard about Harper. She was protecting her friend from gossip at all costs.

"They'll be fine. Sean knows that farm like the back of his hand," Elizabeth said, reassuring her. "Thanks for being such a good friend to me, Jacki." She squeezed her hand as they came off the Chesapeake Bay Bridge Tunnel and back onto the Eastern Shore.

"It will all work out, Elizabeth. You're just tired; I mean, my God, you see death every day! I don't know how you do it. I couldn't. I don't go to funerals unless I have too."

"It's my passion." Elizabeth signaled her blinker, turning onto the long dirt road surrounded by empty fields on each side. Jacki lived in an old farmhouse that was in Sean's family and the old home place had been given to them by his parents when they moved to Florida. She had decorated the one-hundred-year old house with a Currier and Ives theme straight out of New England. Elizabeth had enjoyed their jaunts antiquing for Windsor chairs and Blue Willow china.

"What are all these cars doing in my driveway?" Jacki questioned as Elizabeth's headlights passed and shone on all the vehicles. "This can't be a surprise party. It's not my birthday or anniversary," she said. She sounded perplexed.

"Something's going on. Oh look, there's Sean on the porch," Elizabeth said.

Sean ran to Elizabeth's car as soon as he realized it was them, grabbing at the passenger's side door to open it before Elizabeth could come to a complete stop. *He looks like a deer in headlights*, Elizabeth thought, not wanting to alarm Jacki.

"What's wrong, honey?" Jacki asked as she got out of the car. Sean's body language made her freeze with concern.

"Oh God, Jacki, it's Adam. He's ... he's dead." Sean grabbed his wife as Jacki screamed and fell to her knees.

Relatives and close friends poured out of the house onto the porch. Hovered together, the crowd stood in disbelief not knowing what they could do to ease the pain for a woman who was just told her only child was dead.

"Call an ambulance," Sean hollered.

He accompanied Jacki in the back of the ambulance while Elizabeth followed in her car. The attendants rushed her to the emergency room where she was given a sedative. "Elizabeth, I can't believe this is happening. It has to be a bad dream," Sean spoke with shock, as the doctor and nurses attended to his wife.

Elizabeth held tightly to Sean's hand, praying he wouldn't crumble in front of her eyes. "Do you feel like telling me what happened?" she asked, not knowing what an emotional minefield Sean had gone through during the afternoon.

"I told Adam today would be a good day to ride the farm. We just got the crops out before Thanksgiving and there was a cold freeze last night. I watched him shoot past me ... he loved to race. The ATV he was on looked like a bucking bronco as we went over mounds of dirt. I thought he was well-skilled on the damn thing. He hit a patch of ice beside the ditch, and he was thrown off and crushed by his own ATV. Jacki will never forgive me ... Adam didn't have a helmet on. The doctor said he suffered from a concussion, broken bones, and spinal cord injuries resulting in a broken neck. He didn't have the strength to control the 4-wheeler. I swear it looked like his leg got caught in the moving rear wheel, yanking him off his seat and pinning him under the machine. It weighs five hundred pounds or more and rides so fast. I feel responsible for my son's death, Elizabeth," Sean grabbed his wife's best friend and sobbed in her arms. "Tell Mr. Harvey to take good care of my boy."

Elizabeth walked out of the hospital and drove back to the funeral parlor in a trance. Opening the door to the morgue, she saw Uncle Harvey and Charlie bathing the battered, black-and-blue child on the morgue table.

"I don't know if we can make him viewable, Elizabeth," Uncle Harvey whispered. "His skull is crushed."

"Please, please for Jacki. Please. I beg you."

"You've been through four days of hell, Elizabeth. I'll make reservations at the Williamsburg Inn and we can spend the weekend so you can get your mind on something else ... maybe get some much-deserved rest. You haven't slept at all this week," Harper, said genuinely concerned. "You've constantly been by Jacki's side during this dreadful ordeal."

Elizabeth nodded and smiled at a side of Harper she rarely saw. "That would be nice. I'll get Blanche to pack a suitcase for me. At this point, I don't have the strength to even think about what I'd need."

The days were sunny and mild, enabling Elizabeth to visit the antique gardens in the Historic Colonial Foundation. She loved Virginia history, and Williamsburg was a familiar and comfortable destination for her. Before leaving for Sycamore Creek to return home, they stood in line outside Raleigh Tavern for gingerbread cakes to take to Nana. Turning to Harper, she said, "I need to sit down on that bench over there. I feel as if I'm going to faint." Harper walked her to the bench and sat beside her, putting his arm around her for support. Leaning her head on his chest she asked, "Do you have the luggage in the trunk?"

"Yes, honey. We're checked out of the Inn."

"Please help me to the car then. I want to go home."

Harper drove back to Sycamore Creek as his wife laid against him in silence.

"She's had a breakdown due to exhaustion," Dr. Lewis told Margaret and Harvey. "She needs plenty of water and I'll prescribe a sedative, so she can sleep. Bedrest only, for a week."

"She's been under so much pressure with the death of Jacki's son," Margaret lamented.

"Unplug the phone," Dr. Lewis advised.

Elizabeth awoke several hours later sensing she wasn't alone. Blinking hard in the soft glow of the lamp on the night table, she saw her uncle sitting in the chaise facing her bed.

"How are you feeling, darlin'?"

"Tired ... so tired," she managed to whisper.

"We have to make some changes and soon," he said with concern.

"Where is my husband?"

"He's at the hunting lodge," he stated. But he thought to himself, *he's more interested in boy's night out than his wife.*

CHAPTER TWENTY-NINE

"Hello, Bernard. We need to talk," Harvey said, not his usual chipper self.

"What's wrong, my love?" Bernard questioned.

"My niece has had a breakdown. It's stress and exhaustion due to this damn business. She's been diagnosed with suffering from a low-grade depression. I guess I've put too much responsibility on her. Charlie resembles a corpse and Sadie can't remember what happened yesterday. I shouldn't find fault; my mind isn't what it used to be either."

"Well, my God, Harvey! Every night we talk you're drunk as a skunk! Your brain is pickled. You need to drink more water; the membrane is totally dried out."

"You never have been one to mince words. Please consider moving in with me and assisting Elizabeth with the funeral parlor. I do delcare I'm at my wit's end."

"Are you kidding me? Sycamore Creek is so hillbilly," Bernard replied as if he had been highly insulted. "I have an excellent position here in Richmond. There's a rumor I may be manager soon. They love, love, love me here. Besides, people will talk about us at your beloved hoedown swamp ... or creek, whatever."

Harvey countered, "Think about it. I'll be retiring soon due to my health."

"Well! Look who just walked through the door. If it isn't Miss Fancy Panties herself. Welcome back." Sadie smiled briefly. "You seem a little too young to have had a nervous breakdown."

"I didn't have a nervous breakdown. I collapsed from fatigue, Sadie."

"What, too much shopping?" Sadie asked with a flippant attitude.

Elizabeth knew it was futile to argue. She walked past her desk and entered the office shared with her uncle.

Uncle Harvey rose and hobbled around his desk, giving Elizabeth a bear hug. "I'm so glad you're back."

Still weak, she quickly pulled out her chair from the desk and eased into the familiar distressed leather. "I'm glad to be back. I even missed Sadie, if that's possible. Uncle Harvey, you look so pale this morning. Are you feeling poorly?"

"No different from any other day, I suppose. We have a visitation tonight that I may have you work, if you're up to it. The ole Gray boy that lived in his car down by the docks froze to death the other night. Sheriff Dalton said he'd been homeless for several years. Watermen found him as they were preparing to go oystering on the bay this morning. Poor man spent his days at Kelly's Pub until he staggered to his car every night around one o'clock in the morning. I hope and pray that he's now finally warm." Harvey shook his head with sadness.

"Who will be viewing him tonight?" Elizabeth questioned.

"Just his daughter, Nancy. They were estranged. She made his funeral arrangements and paid for everything. It was good of her to let bygones be bygones."

"I'll be glad to console her tonight, Uncle Harvey." Elizabeth lamented that she and this woman shared a bond—estranged fathers. Thoughts of Edward came frequently since she had been bedridden. *Things fade with time*, she recalled Nana saying more than once.

"Thanks, darlin'. I'll be upstairs in bed if you need me. I have that ringing in my inner ear today. Again."

"Just look at my desk. I'll be here for the remainder of the day. Please ask Blanche to fix me a bite to eat, before the daughter comes in. I don't know how long she'll end up staying and I don't want to rush her."

"Sure thing," Harvey said, walking into the kitchen.

Elizabeth spent the rest of the day catching up on paperwork that

Sadie did not have the presence of mind to tackle. Perhaps she was just too lazy.

"I have your Brunswick stew ready, chile. I put extra okra in it too, just the way you like it. You want to eat in the kitchen with me?" Blanche asked.

"You know I do, Blanche, just like we've always done." Elizabeth glanced at the clock on the wall and was surprised to see it was five-thirty.

"What time's your viewin'?"

"Uncle Harvey said Nancy is coming in at six-thirty. We better eat now."

Before Elizabeth was through eating her stew and hushpuppy biscuit, the doorbell chimed. Wiping her mouth on the linen napkin, she hurried to the door and opened it. Standing in front of her was Nancy Gray. They had graduated together from private school. Nancy never wanted for anything in school; she was tall, blonde, and rich. She wondered how she could have been so clueless to not associate Nancy's first and last name.

"Oh Elizabeth, can you believe what's happened to my father since we graduated from school?"

"Please come in, Nancy. I'm here to help you." Elizabeth extended her hand to an old schoolmate who looked completely lost.

Together they walked to the casket holding hands. Elizabeth freed her hand from Nancy's when she bent over her father and kissed his forehead.

"Daddy, Daddy... I'm so sorry I turned my back on you when mother left. She turned me against you, saying it was all your fault. Oh, Elizabeth! My mother fell in love with another man seven years ago and Daddy was never the same. He began drinking heavily and eventually lost his insurance agency. All day, every day, he hung around the bars at the docks. It was so embarrassing to me that I didn't want any association with him. Now I can never get those years back. Please forgive me Daddy!" Nancy wailed as she lay her head on her father's chest.

Elizabeth bit her bottom lip as her eyes welled up with tears. She could not allow herself to sink into further depression. She needed to be strong so she could help those who needed her. "Someone's coming in the door. Did you invite anyone else to stop by?"

Nancy nodded yes, "Two of his buddies begged me to let them come say their goodbyes. I hope that's all right?"

Elizabeth greeted the two men who staggered into the chapel. They could barely stand, still swaying from left to right as they finally reached their destination. Arriving in front of the casket, they bent over their friend and seemed determined to sit him upright.

"Come on, old buddy, let's have one more swig before you reach the pearly gates. Get up," they both said as they grabbed his jacket. Lifting the corpse in the air, they dropped the body back into the casket, then stumbled to the floor on top of each other.

"I'm afraid, gentlemen, that will be impossible," Elizabeth said, trying to protect Nancy from the uncomfortable scene. After a fair amount of coaxing, the cohorts agreed to go and she showed them to the door.

"I'm so sorry about the intrusion, Elizabeth. You see the low-lifes my father got himself hung up with." Nancy hung her head, not being able to make eye contact as she spoke. She kissed Elizabeth on the cheek and thanked her for everything, leaving in shame.

Walking back to the chapel, Elizabeth checked the thermostat and began turning off the torchier lights around the casket. Stopping long enough to straighten Mr. Gray's jacket from all the mercilessly tugging, she heard the front door open.

"Who's there?" She bolted out of the chapel, coming face to face with the two drunks. *Damn, I didn't lock the door when Nancy left,* she thought.

"We stopped back by to take you out for a drink," one slurred. "We won't take no for an answer." They fell lazily over, one at a time, in slow motion—knocking into each other like pins in a bowling alley.

She started to panic as she ran to her office and picked up the phone. Shaking, she began to tell the police dispatcher she was in need of help.

"It's Elizabeth Barclay! Please help! There are two drunks in the funeral parlor trying to kidnap me—it's an emergency!"

"I'm sending Sheriff Dalton right away, Elizabeth," the dispatcher said.

Worried about the deceased, she ventured out of the office and caught the pair at the casket once again. "Let him rest in peace," she screamed. Her Irish had gotten the better of her as her cheeks reddened; she was determined not to tolerate their drunken behavior any longer.

One drunk grinned at the other. "Look, Freddy, the little lady is ready to go have that drink." They staggered towards Elizabeth who was now standing in front of the staircase banister. They attempted to pull her out the front door. Holding on for dear life, she gripped the newel post with one arm, as the inebriated pair pulled her suit jacket off the other shoulder. The tug of war lasted only a few minutes—which seemed like hours—before Sheriff Dalton burst through the door.

"Come on, boys, you've caused enough commotion for one night. Let's go to the station. Are you all right, Elizabeth?"

Catching her breath, Elizabeth composed herself. "Yes sir, I think so. Thanks for coming. It's been quite a night."

Saying their goodbyes, Sheriff Dalton along with Frick and Frack left the building. Elizabeth collapsed in the nearest wing chair and then heard Uncle Harvey's weak voice.

"Elizabeth, what's all that noise? Is everything okay down there?"

"Yes, Uncle Harvey, the police have left now."

All he could manage to say was, "That's nice."

Elizabeth softly closed the door behind her and wrapped the wool scarf around her neck. Walking home as a cold wind blew in from the creek, she said a prayer for her father, hoping she would never be in Nancy's shoes. When she felt emotionally stronger, she would plan her course of action.

CHAPTER THIRTY

Five Years Later

"You have not touched your dinner this evening," Margaret said, eyeing her granddaughter. "Are things good with you and Harper? He never eats dinner with us."

"Tonight's Rotary; tomorrow night's Lion's Club; poker night with the boys Friday; and we go to the country club every Saturday with that same boring set," Elizabeth sighed, rolling her eyes.

Margaret sat silently, not wanting to voice her opinion for fear of upsetting her granddaughter. *They have a most unusual marriage*, she thought. Their social life together revolved around the country club, otherwise, they went their separate ways.

"Nana, did you see where they finally captured Ronald Essex?" Elizabeth asked, eager to change the subject. "He's the creep that went on that three-day killing spree."

"No, honey. I've not read the newspaper or watched any news today. I don't remember any killing spree."

"You remember, he was the guy that kidnapped and robbed a cab driver in Norfolk and stuffed him in the trunk, then drove around the city, leaving him to die. He abandoned the cab on a side street. He then hitch-hiked to the Eastern Shore of Virginia, where he was picked up by that sailor who lived here. You know, the one we buried."

"Oh yes, the Armstrong boy, but I never heard what happened."

"This guy Essex pulled a gun on Mr. Armstrong and ordered him to drive to the same road where we picked up that girl who was killed in June. I mean, it was almost the same exact spot in the woods. He shot the sailor several times before taking his car and money. According to Sadie, he pleaded for his life. How in the world she knows is beyond me? The woman thrives on gossip, especially if it's gory or sexually-oriented."

"That's *that* class," Margaret said disgustedly.

"So, the next day, this Essex guy—still driving the sailor's car—walked into a convenience store in Exmore and shot the clerk in the head at close range. We didn't bury him, though."

"Oh Elizabeth, I don't know how you remember all this dreadful stuff."

"Let me finish. It's so weird Nana, that he was in this area and nobody knew it. After murdering the man in Exmore, he returned to Norfolk and killed a teenage couple at a gas station—shooting them in the head at close range as well. The Norfolk police saw a car matching the description of his vehicle leaving the convenience store in Exmore. They chased him on Shore Drive, where he abandoned the car and ran on foot through the woods at that pretty little park."

"Which one?"

"You know Nana, the one with Spanish Moss hanging from the trees in the swamp."

"I think that park is so charming. Virginia is as far north as Spanish Moss has ever been spotted."

"Right, right, anyway the police surrounded him and they had an old-fashioned shoot out until he ran out of ammunition. That's how they got him."

"Take a breath, Elizabeth, for heaven sakes."

"His mother was interviewed, and you know what she said?"

"I'm sure you're going to tell me."

"Well, following his arrest, she said her son wanted to die and be killed in a gunfight with police. He didn't have the guts to kill himself."

"That's such a shame." Margaret shook her head, filled with cynicism. "It's all about the murderer. Why do they even quote his family?"

"I agree, Nana. This jerk showed no remorse. He claims he's Satan and was laughing during his capture."

Margaret's mind flashed back to the dark days of being in court and watching another killer grin as he sat pompously on the stand with her daughter's blood on his hands. "The courts won't do anything to him—it's all a farce. There is no justice for the victims and their families."

The phone rang and broke the tension at the dining room table. "I'll get it, Nana." Elizabeth jumped up and grabbed the phone in the kitchen.

"Good evening."

"Hello. I'm calling for an Elizabeth Barclay."

"I'm Elizabeth Barclay. What can I do for you?"

"Elizabeth, I'm Shirley Hamilton. I'm your father's bookkeeper and caregiver."

Elizabeth wasn't sure what to say next—she had gone completely numb. "Is he alive?" She managed to whisper, as she composed herself.

"Oh yes, but I need to warn you he's not in very good health. I'm concerned with a situation that has arisen. Supposedly an attorney friend—a younger man—has talked your father into completely cutting you out of the will and substituting his name instead. He's bringing the revised will over tomorrow morning, along with his secretary who is going to sign as a witness. I just had to inform you. Edward talks about you all the time. He says he loves his daughter."

Elizabeth listened intently trying to absorb all the information Mrs. Hamilton was relaying. "What time tomorrow?"

"Nine o'clock."

"I'll be there."

"Elizabeth, brace yourself, your father doesn't look the way you saw him last. He's very thin and has a gray beard. He sits at his bar all day in a bathrobe. The alcohol has played havoc with his brain, but he'll recognize you. I won't mention that you're coming. Have a safe trip."

Early the next morning, Elizabeth drove at a high rate of speed across the Chesapeake Bay Bridge Tunnel to her father's duplex. "I have to get there before Daddy signs that revised will," she said out loud. She began practicing her dialogue for the encounter that was about to take place with the unethical lawyer. *He'll wish he never coerced my father on such a ploy*, she thought.

She knocked on her father's front door. A smiling lady appeared and greeted her.

"Hi, Elizabeth. I'm Shirley. It's so nice to finally meet you. Look, Edward, it's your daughter."

Edward's eyes became round as saucers as he blinked hard, focusing on the woman that stood on the other side of the bar. "I can't believe you're here. Oh my God, it must be a dream," he said with moist eyes.

"Daddy." Elizabeth walked around the corner of the bar and embraced her father.

"What... what takes you here? I thought you had long forgotten me."

Shirley spoke up, "I called her, Edward. It's about the will. Elizabeth needs to talk to Mr. Marks this morning." Shirley spoke in a reassuring manner with a soft voice.

Elizabeth cast her eyes upon the shell of a man who once was her father. His eyes were clouded with cataracts, making her wonder if he could even see her at all. A gray beard sprouted from his chin. He puffed on a long, thin brown cigarette brought to his lips by a scrawny skeletal hand. Wrapped only in a white terry cloth bathrobe, she worried if he was cold. The January day was dark and damp and snowflakes had just started to fall from an ominous sky.

"That's great. He'll be happy to meet my daughter," Edward said, not realizing the consequences. He sat with a perplexed expression due to all the confusion of the morning.

The doorbell rang, and Elizabeth answered the chime promptly, opening the door and extending her hand. "Hello, Mr. Marks. I'm Elizabeth Barclay, Edward's daughter."

Mr. Marks and his secretary's eyes grew large; they were stunned into silence.

I'm just in the nick of time, she thought.

"Uh ... uh, your father asked me to execute a new will. I brought it over for him to sign. We've become very close since he informed me that the two of you are estranged. He doesn't know why you've disowned him."

When Elizabeth spoke, her voice shook with fury. "I'm a Barclay, and you will not inherit anything that belongs to me. My father built this duplex with my mother's life insurance money, and I'll see to it that you don't receive a dime."

"Mr. Barclay, may I see you in your bedroom?" Mr. Marks asked nervously.

"Sure. Isn't my daughter a real beauty? Just like her mother. She loves her daddy. That's why she's here today." Edward grabbed his cane and hobbled behind his superficial friend—the attorney.

Elizabeth's tirade had just begun. She stood in front of Mr. Marks secretary with both hands knotted into fists at her sides. "I'm going to call the bar association and report what this jerk is trying to accomplish. It's unethical and illegal. My father is clearly suffering from alcohol dementia."

The secretary's eyes were wide with fright. Zipping up her jacket, she hurriedly made an exit out the door, then jumped into Mr. Marks car and sped off.

"I'm so glad you're here," Shirley said with relief. She sat at the bar, pleased that Mr. Marks had been caught off guard with his devious plan.

"I'm so sorry you had to witness my temper, Shirley. I cannot thank you enough for calling me."

Mr. Marks filed out of the bedroom with Edward behind him. "I told him I wasn't signing anything unless it was approved by my daughter," Edward said smugly. He was enjoying all the attention after spending day after day alone.

Elizabeth's eyes shot daggers at Mr. Marks. "Go now." She motioned towards the front door. "Before I call the police and charge you with trespassing and embezzlement."

Mr. Marks gasped, then after donning his trench coat and grabbing his brief case, he walked briskly down the street in the rapidly falling snow—out of Edward Barclay's life forever.

"I love you, my daughter," Edward said, grinning ear to ear.

"Me too, Daddy," Elizabeth said as peace filled her heart, something that had been missing for years.

CHAPTER THIRTY-ONE

"Miss Margaret, now that Elizabeth is spending the majority of her time taking care of her father, I think we need to talk about the future," Harper said, sipping from the mug of his morning coffee. "She's not here to help you handle your business affairs."

"I can manage," Margaret frowned suspiciously. "What exactly are you alluding to, Harper?"

"Only in regards to the properties. I could be a great deal of help with maintenance. Elizabeth's concerns are with her father and as you know, she suffers from depression. She's constantly popping Xanax and there's always a wine glass in her hand. If my name's on the real estate, I'll be able to protect her interests."

"Protect her interests from what, Harper?"

"From losing them."

"What a thoughtful idea. I'll go over all the deeds. Let's plan to have lunch Thursday here in the dining room. I don't like to discuss my personal business at a restaurant in public." Margaret gave Harper a tentative smile.

Harper smiled back. His plan was easier than he thought.

Leaving the bank at noon on Thursday, Harper stopped by Blossom's. Margaret's favorite flowers were irises and he had spotted a vase as he passed by the window. Ann Marie, the local florist, greeted him and said she knew Margaret's taste. With flowers in tow, he whistled on his way to Margaret's and Elizabeth's large Victorian home, soon to be his as well. His earlier plans of abundance were finally coming to fruition.

"Anybody home?"

"I'm in the dining room, Harper," Margaret called out.

As Harper strutted in, he stopped abruptly. He could feel his face heating up as his gaze met with Margaret's attorney, Mr. Price.

"I believe you know my attorney." Margaret smiled triumphantly.

"Uh ... yes, I do. Good afternoon, sir," Harper replied extending his hand.

Mr. Price rose from the dining room chair and grasped it. "Nice to see you, Harper. How's your father?"

"Fine, thanks for asking." Charm oozed from his lips.

"Harper, as you know, I've been the Eyre family attorney for years. My father was before that. The Eyres are one of the biggest land owners on the Eastern Shore of Virginia. I cannot advise Margaret, in all good faith, to put an in-law's name on what will be Elizabeth's. I'm here to protect my client's best interest." Mr. Price, not mincing words, had immediately gotten down to business.

Harper scowled at Mr. Price. "Fine." He raised his hands in a gesture of defeat. "Have it your way, Miss Margaret," he said as his scowl grew even darker. Realizing he had been set up and that they were on to his manipulating tactics, he gruffly said, "If you will excuse me, I'm going back to the bank. I've lost my appetite."

"Will you be joining me for dinner?" Margaret asked with concern in her voice.

"No ... no, I'm going to the hunting lodge until Elizabeth returns from her father's."

He was outraged and walked at a fast clip back to his office. He sat and planned a way to smooth over the most recent conflict with Margaret. Coming this far, giving up was not an option; he would proceed to execute his goal.

"Well, Margaret, your woman's intuition was right in regards to having an insecure feeling about Harper's intentions. Just for good measure, I suggest you investigate further by checking the contents of the safe deposit box at the bank that's in your name and Elizabeth's." Mr. Price squeezed Margaret's hand, hoping his advice had eased her mind. He'd always admired her tenacity.

"Funny, great minds think alike. Harper said he's taking a few days off for a vacation. I had planned to check the safe deposit box tomorrow while he's gone. Thank you for your help. I'll be in touch." Margaret sighed with relief.

The following afternoon, Margaret handed the safe deposit box key to the teller and then followed her to the bank vault.

The teller inquired, "Miss Margaret, would you like some privacy in the small office across the hall?"

"Yes, honey. Thank you very much." Margaret settled in the leather office chair and began to open the box she and her granddaughter shared. Taking a deep breath, she had promised herself she would not let her imagination run away with her, like it had during the night—causing her a terrible bout of insomnia.

Emptying the contents of the metal box placed in front of her, she sorted through the certificates of deposit, deeds to all the properties, Last Will and Testament, and various other items she had deemed important. She asked herself out loud, "Where's the bank stock certificates?" Christmases, birthdays, graduations, and all special occasions were celebrated with shares of bank stock gifted to Elizabeth. With quivering hands, she began to slowly go through the papers sprawled across the desk. After a meticulous search, she discovered there were no bank stock certificates to be found. Collecting the contents and neatly placing them in order, she summoned the teller and handed her the key. With the box safely secured in the vault, Margaret asked her if the Mr. Baldwin, Sr. was in his office.

"Yes, ma'am, he is."

"I would like to see him immediately," Margaret spoke with urgency.

The teller noted that she was visibly upset. "Please follow me," she said.

Harper Sr. rose from his desk as Margaret entered his office. "Margaret, it's so good to see you."

"Harper, we have a problem."

"Oh dear, what is it?"

"I've just gone through my safe deposit box and Elizabeth's bank stock certificates are missing. They were in her name only and the two of us share the same key. Does this warrant a call to my attorney?"

"That won't be necessary. We'll find them; I promise you. Please don't get yourself upset, Margaret. You look a little flushed." He poured her a glass of ice water from the pitcher that sat on his desk.

Sipping the cold water Margaret began to settle her nerves. "You know this preempts your son trying to get his name on all the real estate holdings that's in Elizabeth's name. Lord knows what else he's forged." Margaret's mind kept darting off in different directions fearing the worse. "I think it is absolutely essential that a background check is done on your son," she spoke with authority, finding the strength to protect Elizabeth. "I don't want a thief in my home."

"Margaret, the certificates of bank stock will be reissued immediately. There's no need to notify the board—I'll handle this on your behalf ... and privately. Trust me, we don't want this out in the public. It could lead to Harper's ruin."

"I promised my daughter Suzanne that I would look after her child in the event something should happen to her and I always keep my promises."

Harper, Sr. thought of the rush of excuses on the tip of his tongue to explain his son's behavior. He just didn't have the energy to clarify them. "Harper, Jr. was not brought up this way. I pray their marriage does not end in divorce," he sighed.

After a pause Margaret responded, "I don't intend to mention this to Elizabeth. She has enough on her plate, being the only caregiver for her father. Thankfully, they have renewed their relationship and I haven't seen her happier in years." She smiled to herself.

Standing, Margaret thanked Harper, Sr. for locating the problem, then walked down Market Street to the Eyre homestead.

Finding herself at the foot of her daughter's grave, she knelt and prayed that God would give her the fortitude to conquer each new day, and the courage to tackle the impending burdens that Elizabeth's kindness, beauty, and wealth would bestow upon her now and in the near future.

CHAPTER THIRTY-TWO

"I really appreciate you driving down here to take care of your Daddy," Edward said, filling his tumbler with ice cubes before adding vodka and orange juice. "When am I ever going to meet your husband?"

Elizabeth thanked him with a smile. "I don't know when Harper will be able to get away from the bank." In retrospect, she looked forward to jumping in the car and being free of the responsibilities pertaining to life at Sycamore Creek. The marriage with her husband had grown distant—time spent together felt awkward and strained. Ironically, the gloom of depression had lifted since her father had come back into her life. He spent hours talking about her mother, sharing stories that Elizabeth was completely unaware of. Nana found it difficult to speak of Suzanne, claiming she just couldn't remember incidences—a matter of constant denial. Since visiting her father, she had gotten more acquainted with both parents. When she was home at Sycamore Creek, tension filled the air between Nana and Harper. They avoided each other at all costs, making her curious as to what had changed the relationship.

Bringing her mind back to the present, she watched her father take the first sip of alcohol for the day—it was only nine o'clock in the morning. "Daddy, I have to pick up your prescriptions this afternoon, and you are in desperate need of a haircut."

"You can take me to my Greek barber and then we'll go to the Jewish Mother Jazz Club for a little short one."

"I really like the Jewish Mother. The food is so good. That'll work out fine. I'll run your errands after I drop you off at the barber shop."

"You know your mother left me for a goddamn Greek."

"Daddy, please don't use the Lord's name in vain."

"Oh, sorry, darlin'. I am very sorry." Edward sat shaking his head. "Goddamn Greek ... your mother ... God bless her," He was fixated on the memory.

Elizabeth spent the morning washing Edward's hair in the sink and helping him dress for the afternoon. Opening the closet in his master bedroom, she noticed the Brooks Brother suits, starched shirts, ties, and dress shoes had all but disappeared. It alarmed her the first day she visited the duplex two years ago that the oil paintings of marine art, particularly the Chinese junk painted with moody greens and blues she so loved had vanished. The rooms were sparse with only a few pieces of furniture left. *So-called friends have taken advantage of him or he's gambled everything away,* she surmised. On the days that Elizabeth wasn't there, he could be found at his bar, bathrobe wrapped tightly around his tiny waist. Calling his daughter seventeen to twenty times a day, he was consumed in righting the wrong that had plagued their estrangement.

Because of chain-smoking and deterioration of the brain due to chronic alcoholism, Edward maneuvered his way down the duplex staircase slowly, stopping for breath every other step. Elizabeth had ordered him a new cane with a pewter horse head to grab. Between the cane and his daughter, he managed to finally drop himself in the passenger's seat of her car.

When they arrived at the barber's parking lot, Elizabeth jumped out of the car and walked around to the passenger's side to help her father maneuver into the shop.

"Johnny, I would like you to meet my daughter. She looks just like her mother," Edward said grinning from ear to ear.

"Her mother must have been gorgeous," the older Greek man said, glancing from father to daughter.

"Thank you," Elizabeth giggled. "Would you please cut my father's hair and shave him too. I'll be back to get him after I run his errands. See you in about an hour, Daddy."

"No problem. Take your time. We have a lot of catching up to do. Right, Johnny?"

Feeling at ease that the old Greek was going to babysit her father, she took her time grocery shopping. With essentials purchased, Elizabeth drove back to the barber shop. Turning onto the road, she spotted a man with a cane standing in the middle of the four-lane highway. Drivers slowed down and came to a complete halt, allowing the man to cross the busy intersection. The closer she got to the pedestrian, she came to the realization that the man holding up traffic was her legally blind father, on a mission to find the Jewish Mother in the next block. "Oh my God, that's Daddy," she exclaimed.

With trembling hands, she circled the block in rush hour traffic, spotting him trying to open the door to the restaurant, so he could hobble in. By then her blood pressure had peaked, leaving her dizzy. Frantic, she found a parking spot on the side of the building. Collecting herself, she entered the restaurant and walked swiftly towards the dark bar in the back. Spotting her father on his favorite bar stool, Elizabeth saw the bartender meticulously pouring Edward's martini in front of him. Tapping him on the shoulder, he turned and sheepishly grinned like a Cheshire cat.

"Have a seat, daughter. I've been thinking about your mother, and when we'd go dancing, I'd ask the orchestra at the Cavalier Club to play her song, "Someone to Watch Over Me," written by Gershwin. Now that was quality music, not like the stuff they play today. Good God," he said, shaking his head.

"I didn't know that was her favorite song. I love that song," Elizabeth responded. "Please tell me more about her."

They talked until dark, and then she drove him home and tucked his frail body into bed. She had become the parent.

The next morning while sipping their coffee, Edward asked her what her favorite car was. Hesitating she thought about Harper's vintage Jaguar that he so loved, which had finally bitten the dust. Refusing to pay for his expensive hobbies, the British beauty ended up on the auction block. "You know, Daddy, I love the lines of a Jaguar. You just can't find a car that's more classic. It just screams good taste."

That year on her fortieth birthday, a brand new, white Jaguar was delivered to her home at Sycamore Creek from Checkered Flag Jaguar in Virginia Beach. A large pink bow adorned the roof with a card that read: *For all the birthdays I missed. Love, Daddy*.

Running to the phone, Elizabeth called her father, choking the tears away. "I can't believe it. Thank you," she said breathlessly. She would deal with Harper's envy later—and with delight.

"Elizabeth, I've called my bookie and placed a bet on the Washington Redskins for you," Edward said with great pride.

It was late September and Monday Night Football was about to be televised. "Thanks, Daddy. Now don't forget, I'll be there early in the morning. I have to make an appearance in court regarding another speeding ticket. I've gotten a plethora of them lately."

Edward chuckled. "It's that Jaguar engine. I'll have the coffee made for you. Love you. See you in the morning. Night now."

"Goodnight, Daddy," she whispered.

Crossing the Chesapeake Bay Bridge Tunnel, Elizabeth was grateful she wasn't fined in the Exmore, Virginia court room. *I really must watch my heavy foot now*, she told herself. Turning on the radio, she searched for her father's smooth jazz station out of Norfolk. The sun was so bright, shining on the bay, it sparkled like crystals. The atmosphere was visibly clear enough to see Virginia Beach from the winding bridge. The radio blared, and Elizabeth swallowed the lump in her throat as "Someone To Watch Over Me," unexpectedly played. *Ah, Mommy's song*, she remembered her father confiding in her.

Turning the Jaguar into the parking section of the duplex, she glanced up at the second floor. *That's odd*, she thought, *it looks so dark*. Entering the apartment, her eyes glanced towards the coffee maker which had never been touched. "Wake up, sleepy head," she called out walking towards the bedroom. "Daddy, wake up," Elizabeth swallowed her gasp of shock as her eyes stared at the ashen gray corpse. He was lying peacefully in the fetal position.

Remaining calm, Elizabeth sat down on the side of the bed and touched the side of his face. "Now you can find peace and be with your true love—forever," Elizabeth whispered.

After sitting and talking to her father for a few last moments, she collected her emotions and called Sycamore Creek Funeral Home. Before Sadie identified herself, Elizabeth interrupted, "Sadie, is Uncle Harvey there?"

"Of course, he lives here. Sometimes I don't think you ..."

"Sadie, I discovered my father dead this morning. I need him to make the removal and cremate. I'll take care of the death certificate; his doctor is right down the street," Elizabeth barked at Sadie.

Sadie's mouth fell open. "I'm so sorry," she said anxiously. "I'll get him on the road ASAP."

Waiting for her Uncle Harvey, Elizabeth organized the memorial service and determined how she would handle all the business affairs. *Nana's input will be tremendous*, she thought.

Following the hearse that carried her father back to the Eastern Shore, she recalled the day he told her, "Just throw my ashes in the Atlantic."

"No, I'm going to bury your ashes next to my mother," she had told him, looking into his clouded eyes that filled with tears.

It suddenly dawned on her that her mother's favorite song "Someone To Watch Over Me," she had heard just hours ago journeying across the bridge was a sign that her parents were now together—forever.

CHAPTER THIRTY-THREE

Elizabeth weighed the words before she began the conversation with her aging grandmother. "Nana, I'm just not that happy with Harper. Jacki told me when I was in Virginia Beach taking care of my father, he began seeing his best friend Patrick's wife."

"You mean Sharon?" Nana eyed her granddaughter, hesitating about whether to elaborate with her knowledge on Harper's affair or not. It had been the talk of the Creek.

Elizabeth slowly nodded. "Since my father's death I have contemplated divorcing Harper. Life is just too short not to be happy. He constantly finds fault with everything I do to the point of embarrassing me in public. I just can't tolerate living this way any longer. We have absolutely nothing in common and started living separate lives years ago, even though we're in the same house. I just don't need a man to feel whole. Please don't be upset with me," Elizabeth pleaded.

"I have detected the strain in your marriage for years. I totally agree with you that it's not a good match. Harper has one love—the love of money. He has the attitude that life is all about him. Sharon calls here constantly inquiring about his whereabouts. When you were in Virginia Beach, he was never home in the evenings. According to my friend Pearl, the gossip is all around the Creek. Sharon is blatant about the affair, hoping to climb the social ladder. They were spotted coming out of a motel in Exmore."

Margaret had opened a can of worms and it was impossible for her to stop until she finished speaking her mind. "Your grandfather was a ladie's man and I chose to look the other way—not addressing the facts. That's what women did back in those days. Hardly any girl went to college after high school in this town. So, with no education they were stuck in unhappy marriages due to lack of finances. You, however, are independent. Sweetheart, it would be in your best interest to move on. You deserve a man that truly loves you—for you."

"Nana, you never told me about Poppy's infidelities," Elizabeth said, still stunned by her grandmother's confession.

"Oh, my goodness, yes. He spent weeks before and after the closing of the hotel for the season. Supposedly alone." Taking the kettle off the stove, Margaret poured two cups of Earl Grey Irish Breakfast tea in china cups and saucers, placing a shortbread cookie on the side. "The gals in Virginia Beach loved your grandfather's sense of humor and twinkling blue eyes. I threatened to leave him once, but he begged me to stay. Each time he would sob and promise to never be unfaithful again—that would last until the following spring." Nana rolled her eyes. "I know he loved me and did not want a divorce. Some men just cannot help themselves—they are weak," Margaret added softly, as if confiding a secret.

"You know, Nana, all those women at the country club act as if I'm their best friend, but I can tell they're jealous of me. They all have green eyes—eyes green with envy, so superficial. So, it's true, Harper is seeing Sharon of all people? I wonder if her husband knows? It could get very ugly. Actually, I don't want to go through the emotional pain and loss of Harper's dirty laundry. I want to call Mr. Price immediately and set the divorce in motion—today." Elizabeth's eyes filled with tears, regret for all the years that she had wasted.

"There's a reason for everything, dear. This too shall pass," Margaret said sagely.

Elizabeth stood and patted her grandmother's shoulder. "This is nothing compared to what we've been through in the past. I have watched you for years deal with adversity, always with dignity and refinement. I can cope with this. I'm not delaying divorce any longer."

Elizabeth climbed the staircase slowly, to collect herself. She needed to organize her thoughts before she started the procedure of ending close to three decades with a man that had become a total, self-absorbed stranger.

Elizabeth knocked on Harper's office door at the bank. "Do you have a minute?"

"Sure, I'm surprised to see you in the middle of the afternoon. I thought you were going to start back at the funeral parlor today."

"I have other business to finalize before going back. I had an appointment with Mr. Price this morning."

"Oh, about your father's estate? Good idea to get that in the works. I take it you inherit everything?" Harper's questions were coming at her rapidly before she had time to answer them.

Elizabeth searched his eyes before she said hesitantly, "Harper, I am filing for divorce."

Harper glared at her as he raised his voice, "Divorce?! There's never been a divorce in the Baldwin family! I've been a good husband to you. I don't know where this is coming from!" He was in attack mode.

"Harper, you've not been faithful. You're screwing your best friend's wife," Elizabeth said in a heated whisper.

"Prove it, prove it. My word against yours. Good luck." Harper's voice was still boisterous causing her to squirm. "After work, I'll be at the house to collect my things."

"I told Mr. Price this would be a friendly divorce. He said there was no such thing. We need it to be civilized. We loved each other at one time, didn't we?"

Harper narrowed his eyes. "Get out," he said with gritted teeth.

Elizabeth sat at the kitchen table and watched Margaret peel pota-toes for dinner as Harper packed his clothes upstairs. The Grandfather clock on the staircase landing ticked away the seconds. *Funny*, Elizabeth thought, *the years passed us by. We had plans and dreams to travel abroad that we never got around to*. She had cut out pictures of coastal cottages from design magazines, intended to be their future retirement home. *Never got around to that as well*. Staring down at the table for what seemed like an eternity, she heard Harper descend the stairs. When he loaded his last suitcase, he slammed the front door for dramatic effect.

Margaret flinched as she stood at the sink with her back to Eliza-beth. Watching Harper pull out of the driveway, her mind raced back to him carrying Elizabeth up the stairs on their first date, so many years ago. He was so attentive, and she was so young. "He's gone," she said, realizing another chapter of their lives had closed.

One year later

Elizabeth, Jacki, Nana and Uncle Harvey sat around the dining room table sipping their after-dinner coffee.

"Would any one like another cup?" Blanche asked, walking through the kitchen door to the dining room.

"No thanks," they all said in unison.

"New beginnings as of this day forward," Margaret said squeezing her granddaughter's hand.

"I still feel overwhelmed with the pain Harper put me through. He's been so vindictive. I never dreamed he had such a mean-spirited person-ality. Not one girl from the country club set will return my calls or go out to lunch with me. They all dropped me like a hot potato."

"Elizabeth, I've told you they were not your friends to begin with.

Women are not going to want you around their husbands, which means there's a trust issue in their marriage. The same thing happened to me when I became a widow," Margaret advised.

"You have to let it all go and rise above it. You are not doing yourself any good dwelling on friendships that were so phony," Jacki said. She had stood by Elizabeth this past year, witnessing the familar grieving process to the one she had experienced when her son died.

"Who has a divorce party for heaven's sake? I've never even heard of such a tacky thing," Elizabeth said as she began to weep again.

"Someone in the worst of taste when it comes to social graces," Uncle Harvey barked. "I think society has lost its mind. Divorce is not something to celebrate. It's hurtful and a loss to the opposer as well as the seeker. Reveling in public at the expense of another person's mental health is bad manners and down-right vulgar. Harper was not raised to be so callous. He's been a major disappointment this past year," he said swallowing the remnants of the expensive port he brought over for the occasion from his collection.

"I was good to that man," Margaret said. "I should have pressed charges when he stole Elizabeth's bank stock certificates. Where would this family be without the counsel and direction of Mr. Price? He has been invaluable to the Eyres throughout the years. Come join us, Blanche, for a cup of coffee."

"Don't mind if I do." Blanche entered the room and pulled up a chair. She had seen this family through trials, tribulations, laughter, and tears. Her loyalty was unwavering. "I'll fix you a pecan pie with lots of extra whippin' cream, just like the time ole Peanut throwed you off," Blanche chuckled, slapping her knee.

Everyone remembered how stubborn the horse had been and they joined in the laughter. The tension around the table began to dissipate.

"Harper lived for money. It was his God. Let me tell you what money can't buy," Nana said thoughtfully. "Money can't buy kindness, manners, respect for others, taste, class, and most importantly sincere friendships.

Friends and family that you see sitting around this table will sustain you for life, and when Uncle Harvey and I are gone, you will have your memories of us to hold on to, Elizabeth."

"You are right, Nana, from this day forward new beginnings are coming my way," she replied.

CHAPTER THIRTY-FOUR

Sadie's eyes rolled as Elizabeth walked into the funeral parlor. Meeting her gaze, she asked, "Who's in there with Uncle Harvey?"

"You're about to find out," Sadie said with a disgruntled frown.

"Come on in my office, Elizabeth. I have someone I would like you to meet." Harvey spoke with a frail voice.

Elizabeth had noticed her uncle's health was deteriorating by the day. Even though it was a mild winter, he sat behind his desk dressed in a wool turtleneck and large bulky sweater—daily. Gone were the starched shirts and suits he meticulously wore in the past. Often taking naps in the afternoon, he still complained of being exhausted. Blanche tried to make his bed in the mornings with his monogram sheet folded over the duvet, but the linens were so damp from night sweats that she had resigned herself to stripping the bed and washing the queen size sheets on a daily basis. Never griping, she made frequent trips to the drugstore for sore throat syrup or salve for mouth ulcers that appeared weekly. The Virginia Gentleman bourbon bottle sat in the liquor cabinet—untouched. The daily cocktail hour she had once so enjoyed with him was now non-existent. Harvey, a once younger, boisterous, heavyset man was now only half his normal size. He fought giving up the ship. After all, he had devoted his professional and personal life to serving the community for several generations when they needed him most. Now Elizabeth was following suit even though she knew, first hand, the havoc this business could create on one's well-being.

"Elizabeth, I would like you to meet Bernard Pyle."

Bernard stood and extended his hand. It was so thin she hesitated to squeeze it for fear she would cause damage. The man standing in front of her was pale and gaunt. His orange red hair and scruffy beard of the same color made her visualize a fire siren. Continuing to check his disheveled appearance, she could not help but stare at his white shirt with numerous wrinkles, as if he had just crawled out of bed. His trousers were held up by a belt looped around his waist, indicating a significant amount of weight loss.

"It's good to finally meet you. I've heard about you for years. Your uncle adores his niece," Bernard sniffed, clinging to her hand as his eyes bore into hers. He made her feel uncomfortable.

"Nice to meet you too." She smiled cordially, but not overly so. *I think I see a hint of contempt*, Elizabeth speculated.

Harvey, witnessing the tension between his life partner and niece, struck up more conversation as it took a lull. "Bernard is here at my request to assist us with the funeral parlor. It seems everyone wants to retire on the Eastern Shore of Virginia, and I know, darlin', you are fully aware that we just can't keep up with the volume. Bernard will do all the embalming like Charlie and I used to. Charlie, God bless his soul, may he rest in peace. I miss that old guy, so devoted. He never turned me down when I called, no matter what time it was, day or night."

Elizabeth began to tear remembering Mr. Charlie. He loved what he did and died the same day he entered the nursing home, as if he willed his own fate. *That was then, and this is now*, she thought, *no need to dwell*. "Would you care for a cup of tea? I heard Blanche rummaging around in the kitchen," she asked her new colleague.

"No ... no, too much to do. I'll be in the morgue reorganizing the bottles of cavity fluid and sterilizing the instruments. There's dried blood on everything. I abhor a dirty morgue. Nasty."

"We have a trade embalmer that comes when we need him from across the bridge. I'm afraid he's not very tidy," Elizabeth countered. "I guess beggars can't be choosers."

"Not on my watch. I've gone over the contracts also, and I need to have a conference with Harvey. These prices are just way too low. I don't know how you've ever kept in business! I brought a contract from Richmond that I can use to get this firm on board."

"Bernard, if you will excuse me, but with all due respect, this is not Richmond. The majority of our people here are blue collar or low income. Although we are not setting the world on fire, we have always made a decent living." Elizabeth smiled sweetly.

"She's right, Bernard. I never gouge my families," Harvey eked out.

Bernard ignored them and with fingers clicking in the air over his head, he said, "Chop, chop, everyone! We have work to do." Hurrying by Elizabeth he stopped abruptly, turning around and barked, "I think we need to retire Blanche. The sooner the better, that old gal has seen better days. I saw dust on all the furniture when I came in last night." Not waiting for a reply, he swiftly swished towards the morgue, swiping his index finger across the mahogany library table.

Speechless, Elizabeth was caught totally off guard. "Uncle Harvey, I never envisioned Bernard so bossy. Is he here for long?"

"Oh darlin', he'll get over himself eventually," Harvey chuckled. "He's hiding behind his nervousness, but as far as your question goes, he's here for the duration."

Sadie spoke up, "That little twerp has been barking orders at me all morning. Do it this way, do it that way. He can just kiss my—"

"Calm yourself, Sadie," Harvey said.

Blanche came in from the kitchen bringing Elizabeth's tea. "You know what he reminds me of?" she asked. Before anyone had a chance to answer, Blanche continued, "A damn Yankee. Good Lord a mercy if I do say so myself."

Throughout the entire day, Bernard was seen practically running throughout the funeral parlor, Pledge and feather duster in hand. At one point he stopped and asked Sadie, "Who takes care of the rolling stock?"

"What the hell is that?" Sadie was dumbfounded.

"The fleet, you know, first removal car, hearse, and limo." Bernard rolled his eyes. *I am truly in Mayberry, Aunt Bea and Opie will arrive in any minute*, he thought.

"That would be Blanche's brother, Roger. He washes all the vehicles before every funeral. Does a good job too, I might add."

"I always had my maintenance man clean the top of my hearse with a toothbrush. Those little crevices can be a real nightmare." With that, he exited again, swishing at a swift pace.

"Kind of reminds me of the Road Runner, don't you think?" Sadie huffed.

"He'll fire Blanche over my dead body." Elizabeth felt her anger rise at the mere thought of him hurting Blanche. "What's he doing now?" Elizabeth asked, as she saw his head bob up and down, peeking through the window in front of the large boxwood.

"He's spying on us. That dude has a screw loose." Sadie frowned. "Where's Harvey?"

"He's taking a nap. Have you noticed how frail he's gotten? Let's not worry him with Bernard's actions," Elizabeth sighed, trying to protect Uncle Harvey from the hornet's nest that had just, in one night, encapsulated the funeral parlor.

"We'll just all band together," Sadie said with conviction. "That little twit has another thing coming if he thinks he's coming between you, me, and Blanche."

Smiling to herself, Elizabeth never recalled Sadie being so devoted to the staff. *Odd. Bernard has performed a miracle in just one day*, she thought.

That evening at the dinner table, Elizabeth relayed to her grandmother the events of the day. "I just don't see what Uncle Harvey sees in him. He looks dreadful and has the personality of a wet eggplant. Funeral directors are usually personable. Nana, you should have seen how he was dressed. Uncle Harvey is always so meticulous. Bernard's appearance is so slovenly. It's been at least a week since he's shaved. Not to mention *that breath*, a definite lack of oral hygiene—how uncouth! Bernard's not staying in Uncle Harvey's room. I noticed when I took him his tea this afternoon. He's in the room at the far end of the hall. How's he supposed to hear him at night in case of an emergency?"

"Your Uncle Harvey feels vulnerable and lonely. He wants somebody around to keep him company. It's Bernard's turn to reciprocate. Harvey's been generous to him."

"I know Bernard doesn't like me; I can just feel it Nana."

"Well, sometimes we have to learn to compromise. You and Bernard may be business partners someday, after all."

"Oh Nana, bite your tongue. He's despicable."

Six Months Later

"Elizabeth, while you were at Arlington Cemetery yesterday burying that World War II veteran, I witnessed Bernard breaking the law." Sadie confided the news that was about to make Elizabeth explode.

"Oh Sadie, no. Uncle Harvey is so out of it, all he does is stay in his room. No one is keeping an eye on Bernard and he's running around here all willy-nilly. What did you see?"

"Well, before he went to the cemetery for the graveside service we had arranged for two o'clock, he removed all the diamonds off of Mrs. Bunting's fingers. The family had already been in to say their goodbyes."

"He gave them back to the family at the grave, didn't he?"

"No ... no he took them upstairs and put them in his room."

"How do you know, Sadie?"

"After he left, Blanche and I made it our business to find them. Sure enough, you know that little black leather box that sits on his dresser?"

"I think so."

"Low and behold there they were—Mrs. Bunting's diamonds. Plus, women's broaches, pearl earrings, and even a small antique diamond watch. He has been stealing off the corpses all along without us seeing him. That little bastard's sneaky. I knew he had an evil look the first time I saw him, those beady eyes and all," Sadie said, happy with her analysis.

Elizabeth was ready to scream with frustration. "This could ruin our business, Sadie. If the people of Sycamore Creek find out we have a jewel thief in our funeral parlor, we are toast! All that Uncle Harvey has worked so hard for will be lost. The Virginia Board of Morticians will suspend our license and shut us down faster than Grant took Richmond."

Blanche came in from the kitchen, "Miss 'Lizabeth," she called. "We've got a problem. Come quick."

Elizabeth and Sadie jumped from their desk chairs and followed Blanche to the kitchen window overlooking the driveway and garage.

"Who's that?" Elizabeth asked.

"That's Hector," Blanche said with a huff. "He's telling Roger what to do. I ain't never in my life seen nothin' like it. Roger's been here since Moby Dick was a minnow. Hmph!"

"Who in the world is this Hector guy?" Elizabeth stood transfixed on the scene she had witnessed from the window.

"This is just beyond belief," Sadie grimaced.

"I'll go see what's going on," Elizabeth said slipping on her coat and exiting the back door.

"Everything all right, Roger?" she asked.

"Miss 'Lizabeth this is Hector. Mr. Bernard said I was to train him for the future. Mr. Harvey is supposedly retiring me."

"Oh, hell no, Roger. You're not going anywhere, and you don't have to call him mister. He should be calling you mister—you're older than he is. Where is Bernard?" She was quickly becoming a hothead these days. *Or is it lack of tolerance*, she pondered.

Sensing Elizabeth's distress, Hector stood frozen with eyes as round as saucers. "Bernard hired me ma'am."

Elizabeth ran her hand through her hair. She seldom lashed out in front of the employees, but she felt off-kilter. Evil had come to Sycamore Creek in the way of a demon from Richmond.

CHAPTER THIRTY-FIVE

Sleep didn't come easily to Elizabeth even though she fell into bed exhausted. The turmoil at the funeral home was never-ending and she didn't have her mentor to fall back on.

Uncle Harvey had "taken to his bed" as the old folks around the Creek use to say. Suffering from extreme and unexplained tiredness, he had all but given up on the day-to-day operations that he was once so fond of. He looked emaciated with his dark sunken eyes and there appeared to be a tumor on the side of his neck. He didn't want anyone to see him because of the purplish blotches on his skin, nose, and eyelids. Elizabeth tried not to stare when she visited him several times a day in his bedroom. He made journeys from bed to bathroom suffering from chronic diarrhea as well. Her heart ached when she would ask his advice concerning the business, often times he just stared into space. Memory loss seemed to prevail. There was no way she could discuss this villain had who entered into her life—his lover.

One afternoon, she sat in the wing chair opposite his bed sipping a cup of Earl Grey tea. Uncle Harvey drifted off to sleep as she watched his labored breathing, his chest rising and falling with difficulty. Catching her off guard, he suddenly awoke and with a rational voice stated, "Elizabeth, promise me you will retire after I'm gone. I've been tied down to this business all my life—its servant. I always wanted to travel and visit art museums around the world. Don't die with regrets, darlin'. Sell it ... sell it all. You've never seen a hearse with a luggage rack, right?" Uncle Harvey gave a faint chuckle.

"Uncle Harvey, I just couldn't imagine selling Sycamore Creek Funeral Home. It's been my life—the child I never had. I thought you wanted me to continue on with the business.

"Elizabeth, it's not that life is short, it's just that you're dead for so long. Take your Uncle Harvey's advice," he eked out and promptly dozed off asleep.

Bernard entered the room without the courtesy of knocking. "We need to ship him off to a nursing home. I can't manage this business, and be a nursemaid at the same time," he spoke with desperation showing in his eyes.

Doing her best to remain calm, she took another sip of her tea before answering. "Nana and Uncle Harvey raised me in their middle years when I was only a child. Now it is my turn to take care of them. I will not discard them like a day-old newspaper."

"I'm just saying, I think he needs to go to a medical facility. He has a very serious disease, Elizabeth. Actually, it's life threatening."

"What do you mean 'disease?' Enlighten me as to what's going on, Bernard. I have a right to know." Elizabeth felt the knot in her stomach developing into sharp cramps.

"I was hoping he would tell you, saving me the trouble. Your Uncle Harvey has AIDS."

"AIDS!" Elizabeth gasped, bringing her hand to cover her mouth in shock. "How did he contract AIDS? He's in his eighties. We've only had one or two AIDS cases in the funeral parlor during the last decade. Our trade embalmer always took the necessary precautions to wear a mask and double glove, along with garb that made him look as if he was ready to walk on the moon. Uncle Harvey wasn't even in the morgue at that time." Stiffening her spine she glared at Bernard, knowing the answer was trouble.

He refused to respond.

That's answer enough, she thought.

Harvey opened his eyes and shocked them both with a strong voice. "Tell her the truth, Bernard, tell her," he continued until his voice became a faint whisper.

Bernard swallowed hard and looked at Elizabeth with remorse. "Elizabeth, your uncle and I have been secret partners for years; however, because of not wanting to leave his hometown, he chose to stay where he grew up as a boy. He would visit me in Richmond when he could. The consequences of being gay in this hillbilly town would have been devastating to his career."

"I know all that, Bernard," she interrupted. "How?"

"Well, we had an open relationship. After all, I'm twenty-five years younger and I couldn't see him all that often. I was infected with HIV, but no symptoms showed up for ten years or longer. I unfortunately passed it on to Harvey. Because he's so much older, his immune system gradually weakened, and AIDS developed. He's known his plight since he went to the doctor with shingles."

Burying her face in her hands, Elizabeth closed her eyes. "Let me think this through." After a few minutes, she went to the side of her uncle's bed and stroked his bald head. "Do you want to go the hospital, Uncle Harvey?"

He exhaled and raised his head slightly off the pillow. "I think it's time, darlin'," he said with staggered breaths.

Elizabeth kissed the top of his head and excused herself to call the ambulance. Feeling as if she had been kicked in the teeth, she walked downstairs and asked Sadie if she would make the call.

"What's wrong with Mr. Harvey?" Sadie asked.

"The aging process," Elizabeth said. She would protect her uncle's reputation until the day she died.

At one-thirty that following morning Nana, Bernard, and Elizabeth watched Harvey die peacefully due to the high dosages of morphine that had been administered. The death certificate listed the cause of death as pneumonia. AIDS was never established on the form because the doctor signing the document was an old, hometown Sycamore Creek boy.

"What kind of service did he want?" Margaret asked, dabbing her eyes with a Kleenex.

"You know, Nana, I think a year ago he knew. He just knew he was going to die soon. He made me promise that there would be no hoopla. Just a simple graveside service. I told him the whole community loved him and it would be huge. I couldn't talk him into a church funeral. He shook his head no and said the subject was closed."

"I think Harvey was always ill at ease about his lifestyle. Times were different back then. He use to share his secrets with me as if I was his sister and not his sister-in-law. Actually, I want the same thing as far as burial goes, except I want a private service."

"Nana, I'm surprised. Why is that?"

"I've been through enough after all the heartache I've personally witnessed, besides all my close friends are gone. The one thing I look forward to is seeing your mother."

Elizabeth slipped her hand in her grandmother's and prayed she would have a few more years to spend with her heroine—her Steel Magnolia.

The will was read the next afternoon in the attorney's office. All Harvey Eyre's holdings had been left to Elizabeth with final instructions to always keep Sadie, Blanche, and Roger employed. Walking out of Price & Price Law Firm, a feeling of loneliness engulfed her. The people she loved most were dying one by one. *Oh, the life cycle*, she thought. She had to admit to herself she was frightened by the fact that she now owned a funeral parlor and had to depend on a licensed funeral director to operate the facility. "I guess I'm stuck with Bernard," she said out loud to the wind blowing off the Creek. She tried to remain optimistic, despite doubts about owning and operating a funeral parlor that would curtail her freedom entirely. Nana's right as usual, money doesn't buy happiness, she contemplated.

Ducking into the Episcopal parish to say a prayer for Uncle Harvey's soul, she knelt and thanked all her ancestors for all the generosities they had bestowed upon her in the past. Leaning back in the oak pew, she realized an angel had always been watching over her since she was five.

Offering another prayer, a peace enveloped her being. It was her angel, Suzanne.

"Elizabeth, can I see you in your office?" Sadie asked with a bewildered expression.

"What now, Sadie?" Elizabeth had thrown herself into the daily operations of a business that consumed her and left her depleted. Lack of patience was beginning to show with the staff. Uncle Harvey's death and Nana's failing health made days frequently unbearable—she was pushed to the limit.

Closing the door behind her, Sadie sat down opposite the desk. "I want you to be aware of something that really concerns me. I'm very suspicious of Bernard's bookkeeping skills since you gave him free rein of the ledgers." Sadie was doing the upmost to disguise her reservations and fears, not wanting to upset Elizabeth further.

"What exactly do you mean, Sadie?"

"Well, when he sells a wooden casket for a memorial service and burial, the body is taken out and then placed in a cardboard box. The wooden casket is put back on the floor in the exact same place. The family thinks their loved one is being cremated in the casket they selected and purchased. He's raised the prices of all the merchandise, you know."

Elizabeth blinked hard, trying to grasp what was spewing out of Sadie's mouth. "Are you positively sure?"

"Yes. I have not ordered a wooden casket purchased for cremation in months, ever since Mr. Harvey died, bless his heart. I snuck into the selection room the other day and sure enough, there's not one casket missing. Also, Hector does exactly what Bernard tells him. I think they're lovers. I see them out in the garden—slapping, tickling, wiggling, and giggling as cars drive by."

Elizabeth listened intently to Sadie. They had formed a trust her uncle would have been proud of. "Sadie once again, if this gets out in the public Sycamore Creek Funeral Home will be no more and the good name Uncle Harvey worked so hard for will vanish like the wind."

"What are we going to do?" Sadie asked.

"I'll talk to Bernard. Enough is enough."

Bernard eyed Sadie suspiciously as she walked out of Elizabeth's office. *I wonder what that dyke's up to now?* he thought.

"Bernard, can I see you in my office?" Elizabeth stood in the doorway catching his look of disdain. "It's been brought to my attention that the wooden caskets you're selling for cremation are being placed back on the floor of the selection room. This situation is illegal and reeks law suit."

"Of course, they are. I'm trying to help you make money since you refuse to allow me to raise the casket prices. Nobody in the public will ever know. Just relax. You make a big deal out of everything."

"Big deal? This is a big deal! It's fraudulent. We're talking felony. My lord, you act as if you're above the law!" she exclaimed. "And what about all the jewelry that seems to go missing form the deceased?" she asked.

"Well, I do have a very dear friend that's on the Virginia State Board of Morticians." Bernard winked as if he were sharing a secret.

"The Board is appointed by the Governor and is honorable. Oh, and another thing, leave Hector alone. He's married with three little children. Do you have no shame? You're HIV positive, for God's sake. You're on a path to self-destruction. Stop sleeping with every young guy you can get your hands on. Uncle Harvey was gay, but he carried himself with dignity. I don't know how he ended up with you." The harsh words spewed from her lips and she immediately realized the hurt they had caused glancing at Bernard. His bravado and self-righteous attitude had all but disappeared.

"I miss Harvey too, you know; you're not the only one. We were together for years. My life has been a mess because our love couldn't be open. It's debilitating when you cannot live in your truth. Life just becomes one big lie. Mine has been hell because of it—I've been into drugs, alcohol, and bad boys."

Elizabeth sat shocked that Bernard opened up to her, never expecting to hear his confession. Having a soft spot in her heart, she looked at the broken man—with pity. He was following in Uncle Harvey's footsteps with the exact same symptoms, she had noticed.

Bernard continued, "Harvey was my best friend, and helped wean me off the drugs and male prostitutes. Look where it got him." Bernard began to sob uncontrollably. "He was an answer to all my prayers. By the way, I've infected Hector too."

Elizabeth's mouth dropped. There were no words.

CHAPTER THIRTY-SIX

"Stephen Dennis has an upcoming parole interview next month. I usually write a letter to the Virginia Parole Board, Victim Input Program, but lately I just don't feel like dealing with it. Do you mind taking the task over?" Margaret asked her granddaughter at the breakfast table.

"Nana, I could have been doing that all along. Why didn't you say something?" Elizabeth swallowed the last spoonful of her oatmeal and sipped what was left of the orange juice in the crystal tumbler. *No matter how old I am, Nana will always treat me like I'm a child*, she thought.

"I didn't want to worry you. Dennis doesn't want to be paroled anyway. He's been incarcerated for years and would not know how to adapt into society if released. His mother passed away years ago. I remember one day she saw me in the post office and as Lillian's eyes met mine she began to weep hysterically, running out the door. I heard her nerves went bad and progressively worsened through the years to the point she was unable to visit her son. If he was released from prison, he has no living relatives that would take him in. So, promise me you'll keep up with it after I'm gone. We want the Parole Board to realize there are still family members living, and it's imperative that we have input."

Elizabeth grew quiet before speaking, "Of course, Nana. Nana, can I ask you a question?"

"Sure, honey."

"I will never be able to forgive Stephen Dennis. What he did to my mother just can't be forgiven. Have you been able to?"

"Well, Elizabeth, it's been very difficult, but there is one thing I know. Time helps heartache and pain fade. It doesn't go away entirely, but you learn to block unbearable things out of your mind. In other words, time does heal all wounds. It's not been easy, but I decided to live a peaceful life, and in order to do that I had to forgive—for myself. I will never forget; how could I? Dennis will never know the pain he caused this family. We all suffered in our own private way. His gruesome crime cannot be undone by a mere apology. We, however, do it for ourselves not just the offender. You had grown quiet and withdrawn when you were a child. I was bound and determined to raise you to become a happy, healthy, young woman, so I had to let go of my bitterness. What good would it have been to go through life embittered. We are survivors you and I. Strong southern women."

Elizabeth looked at her grandmother with a thoughtful expression. "You are one of the most remarkable ladies I have ever known. Hopefully, I'll be able to forgive someday not just Stephen Dennis, but Harper Baldwin, my so-called superficial girlfriends, and Bernard. The way I see it, Bernard killed Uncle Harvey and if that's not bad enough he's infected Hector too."

"Oh, Elizabeth, no! He has three small children. What's wrong with this world? I'm glad I'm the age I am. I don't want to be around to see what's going to happen next. Your Uncle Harvey adored Bernard. They were together for years. He would be livid with Bernard for having an affair with Hector under his own roof. May he rest in peace, God bless his heart. I've noticed lately you look so fatigued. That funeral parlor is going to be the end of you. I think now is the time to get out completely. I'm sure some firm would grab at the chance to purchase it, after all life is short. Have you thought about selling the business?"

"As a matter of fact, I received a letter just the other day from a corporation in Georgia that's interested. They buy small Mom-and-Pop operations. They expressed interest in making an appointment with me regarding purchasing the parlor. I've been seriously thinking about it. I guess what I'm trying to say is that I'm dying to live. I would make sure the contract stated that Sadie would remain employed for as long as her health held out. The poor woman is almost seventy-five with limited hearing and eyesight. Do you have any objections if Blanche and Bernard live here? Blanche has practically lived in this house most of her life, and Bernard has no one. He'll depend on me to be his caregiver. I'll have to swallow the impatience and frustration I feel towards him, to help him cope with the dying process. I don't know how I inherited such a corrupt man! Thanks, Uncle Harvey." Elizabeth rolled her eyes looking up at the ceiling.

"We can't turn our back on these people. God has blessed us financially and it is up to us to share the wealth. Blanche and Suzanne played together with their dolls for hours when they were little girls right here under this dining room table." Margaret picked up the antique lace tablecloth as if she could still see them. "As far as Bernard goes we can't let him die alone and afraid. No human being deserves that. God will be the judge as to his fate," Margaret said, with the wisdom that comes from heartache.

Elizabeth then rose from the breakfast table and put her coffee mug in the dishwasher. "I have a funeral service at noon, then how about I come home, pick you up, and we go for a drive to see the Assateague ponies?"

"That would be delightful. I'll be waiting." Margaret said as she blew an air kiss to her granddaughter.

Fun has long gone out of the word funeral, thought Elizabeth as she walked towards the funeral parlor with dread. It wasn't the same without Uncle Harvey and his death had taken its toll on her. Like everything else, the industry had changed. It had become more and more corporate. Government intervention had brought copious amounts of unnecessary paper work and lawyers circling like vultures. Nothing was simple due to one regulation after another. Not to mention the potential employees that crossed the threshold of the funeral parlor's doorway inquiring about a job. Nose rings, multiple piercings on their faces, and tattoos of zombies marked their arms and legs. The young women she had interviewed sat across from her desk with plunging neckline dresses and red stilettos—nightclub attire. The Gothic trend had opened the door to a new generation of mortuary science students that she was unwilling to adjust to. Suddenly she was sixty and considered old school. *Yes, it's time. Nana says everything has it's day*, she thought.

Bernard approached her before she could unbutton and hang up her coat. "Do you want Hector to put the funeral home parking signs out? Do I need to call a police escort to help us get to the grave? What time is the funeral?"

Elizabeth bit her lip trying to steady her nerves before answering. Every funeral was like the first one he had ever worked. The HIV infection was slowly decreasing healthy brain function, and she had managed to cultivate patience with him. "I have everything under control, Bernard."

Bernard shrugged and went about his business unaware of all the questions he had asked, just moments ago.

"He just doesn't act right, more and more forgetful all the time," Sadie said. "Just how old is Bernard anyway?"

"He's a few years older than I am, I think."

"The other day I heard him ask a widower how long he was married to his wife? The gentleman answered sixty-three years and Bernard replied, 'You've been with her long enough,' instead of saying 'You've been with her for a long time.' Good grief. It's a wonder we do any business at all. It's a far cry from when Mr. Harvey was here," Sadie concluded.

"Oh Lord, Sadie, it just never ends. Nana and I were in the dining room the other night having dinner and I saw our hearse go by. Thirty minutes later it came back. Hector was driving and I figured he was filling it up with gas, getting it ready for the next day's funeral. A couple night's later I saw the same thing happen again. So, I asked Hector about it the next morning, and come to find out his truck had been repossessed by the bank. He was going to the grocery store for his wife in our hearse with the name plate in the window—Sycamore Creek Funeral Home. I just give up."

"Mr. Harvey wouldn't put up with the likes of all this," Sadie barked.

"Let's get this funeral on the road," Elizabeth said, ignoring Sadie's comment.

The funeral and graveside service wrapped up in two hours. Elizabeth was parking the hearse in the garage when Blanche scurried out of the funeral parlor towards her.

"Miss 'Lizabeth, we have to go to the hospital right now. Miss Margaret fell in the grocery store's parkin' lot and broke her hip. They took her in the ambulance," Blanche exhaled and trotted towards the van.

Parking the hearse, Elizabeth scurried and jumped into the van speeding to the hospital. Upon entering the emergency room, Elizabeth told the lady behind the desk that she was Margaret Eyre's granddaughter. Following directions, Blanche and Elizabeth briskly walked to the section in the emergency room that was sanctioned off by a curtain on a rod. Pushing the curtain to one side, she saw her grandmother on the bed with an intravenous drip of morphine in her arm as well as a doctor by her side, asking questions.

"It really hurts," Margaret whimpered. Elizabeth had never seen her wince with so much pain. The vibrant woman that she ate breakfast with that morning was vulnerable and fragile by afternoon.

"Elizabeth Barclay? I'm Dr. Drew Benson. Your grandmother has a fractured hip and we need to take her into surgery immediately. She'll be prepped for the operation in a matter of minutes."

"Dr. Benson, will she be okay?" Elizabeth asked, examining his face.

"Yes, she'll be in the hospital for a few days, and then we'll move her to a facility where she'll receive therapy. She has relayed to me all the medications she takes on a daily basis. What a remarkable lady for her age. Her vital signs are so strong. After the surgery I'll inform you how everything went. The waiting room is on the second floor. Now, if you will excuse me."

"Thank you, Dr. Benson," Elizabeth said. Turning towards her grandmother she placed a kiss on her forehead. "I love you, Nana."

"I love you with all my heart. Remember what I told you this morning."

Elizabeth began to tear. "I will. I promise."

"Move chile' so I can give Miss Margaret a kiss too. I loves you too, you know."

"Blanche, the three of us women have had quite a journey together. Keep the faith. I love you, too," Margaret slurred before drifting asleep.

"Let me buy you a cup of coffee, Blanche," Elizabeth said, blowing her nose.

"Thank you, Miss 'Lizabeth. I need to settle my nerves."

They sat down at a small table in the cafeteria. Elizabeth blew into the cup of freshly brewed hot coffee before speaking. "Blanche, my grandmother and I had a heart-to-heart this morning about life and forgiveness. It was as if she was giving me a gift on how to be truly happy."

Blanche sighed, "She's quite a feisty lady. I ain't never seen anythin' like that woman in all my years. When bad things come her way, she seems to take it in stride. God don't put any more on us than we can bear, the Bible say. What did she say this mornin'?"

"To be happy as hard as it is, you have to forgive people that have wronged you. Forgive your enemies so you don't grow embittered. A happy heart is one of peace."

"That's what the good Lord say, chile'. Jesus know it hard, but it was what he do on the cross. He do it, why cain't we?"

"Blanche, have you truly forgiven your enemies?

"Yes, every mornin' when I's gits up. First thing I say is my prayers. He know, he know," Blanche said, pointing upward towards the ceiling with her index finger.

Elizabeth swallowed hard and said, "You've been so good to our family all these years. I don't know what we would have done without you. It's hard to believe you are in your early eighties. It's time to enjoy life and not work so hard. I would like you to come live with us full-time.

"Oh Lordy. You mean retire? Hard work is all I ever know. I'll come live with you and take care of Miss Margaret. How 'bout that?"

Elizabeth smiled. "That will be just fine. I'll pay all your living expenses and whatever else you'll need. You'll always have a roof over your head, after all, you helped raise me, Blanche."

"I couldn't love you no moe if you was my own chile," Blanche said quietly.

Elizabeth grabbed Blanche's hand and held it tightly in hers while they finished their coffee. She couldn't explain the emotional feeling of peace and sadness that swept over her simultaneously. They both rose and took the elevator to the second floor.

"It seems we be sittin' in here an awfully long spell," Blanche said glancing at the clock on the wall.

"I agree," Elizabeth said, weary from the wait. The words had barely left her mouth when Dr. Benson appeared from the other side of the door.

"Let's go in the chapel across the hall," Dr. Benson uttered without making eye contact. Once inside, he gestured for them to take a seat. Sitting across from the women he began, "I am afraid we lost your grandmother on the operating table, Miss Barclay. The procedure was going well, and we were moving right along like clockwork when her blood pressure peaked, and she suffered a massive stroke. My team worked frantically to revive her, but to no avail. I'm terribly sorry. Is there anyone we can call for you?"

"Thank you, Dr. Benson, but no. I own a funeral home. I'll call my man to make the removal. When will she be released?"

"About an hour." Dr. Benson stood, patted Elizabeth on the shoulder, and whispered, "You have my condolences."

Elizabeth and Blanche watched him walk away as they sat in stunned silence. Blanche reached for Elizabeth's hand this time as they found strength in one another yet again. "You been knowin' this was gonna happen all day long, haven't you, chile?" Blanche said dabbing her tears as they streamed down her face.

"Yes, Blanche, I did. Ironic—Nana did too. Let's go home."

Turning off Highway 13 onto Market Street, Elizabeth glanced at the Sycamore trees lining the main drag. The late December afternoon had grown cloudy, as it did every day before early dusk this time of year. The creamy-whites of the tops of the giant sycamore trees made a striking contrast to the dismal, moody sky.

Elizabeth had developed an affection for the sycamores since early childhood. They signaled the change of every season, especially the massive one outside her turret window. It seemed it had been only yesterday that the dark green leaves changed color into bright yellow at the beginning of autumn, not lasting but a couple of weeks before falling and decaying on the brick walk. The ancient sycamore was rounded with a dome-shaped crown. She was captivated by the twisted branches that provided shelter for the squirrels and a cacophony of birds during the nesting season. Summer brought an abundance of bees as the drooping clusters of yellowish-green flowers produced nectar.

"You know, Blanche, Poppy told me when I was a little girl that an old sycamore tree provided protection for General Washington's troops during the battle on the Brandywine Battlefield in Pennsylvania in the eighteenth century. He said it was a symbol of hope and protection for this country," Elizabeth rambled, breaking the silence in the van.

"Always been my favorite tree," Blanche added contemplatively. "I heard in town just the other day the Creek's oldest sycamore, I think they say it be one hundred, is dying. The town men are choppin' it down after Christmas. Pity, I hate to see the ole girl pass."

"Me too, Blanche. It will create a bareness after bringing such majestic beauty to our Creek. The ancient tree is our namesake, but then again—everything has it's day," she whispered, not being able to hold back the flow of tears.

EPILOGUE

Three Years Later

Elizabeth sat at her great-grandfather's Georgian desk, contemplating the letter she was about to write as memories flooded her mind. Her parents, grandparents, Uncle Harvey, and Bernard were all now deceased. After Elizabeth sold the Sycamore Creek Funeral Home, Sadie had retired, and within the year, she was living in a senior care facility due to failing eyesight. Elizabeth visited her once a week bringing her a bag of her favorite snacks. Sadie had softened with the aging process and they enjoyed reliving old times.

Elizabeth continued to live in the old home place as the town of Sycamore Creek became more progressive. Cafés, art studios, bed and breakfasts, and dog-friendly patios lined the streets. Washingtonians made the Creek a favorite sailing destination. "Come Heres" remodeled the run-down Victorians and painted the old ladies with colors approved by the newly formed historic commission.

"We're upscale now, Blanche." Elizabeth teased.

"I never in my life seen nothin' like it," Blanche said, adding her two cents worth. Elizabeth had moved her into Margaret's bedroom. She enjoyed walking to town, church on Sunday's, and kept herself and her brother Roger occupied planting a perennial garden in the backyard. Foxgloves, black-eyed Susans, and bachelor buttons were purchased from the local nursery.

David walked in the library and saw his wife deep in thought. They had met and married last year after he had sailed up Sycamore Creek stopping for lunch at the marina. There was a historic building at the end of the wharf that had been turned into an upscale seafood restaurant and tiki bar. The Blue Heron came highly recommended by friends that had a retirement home in the area. David often reminisced about that sunny June day, seeing Elizabeth and her friend Jacki sitting on the outside deck of the restaurant at a café table sipping chardonnay. Both were accompanied by their furry babies who were sleeping under the table. Elizabeth had a brindled grey-hound at her feet and Jacki's companion was a black, curly cocker spaniel. The pups raised their heads simultaneously, pleading for another morsel of food. The order was promptly obeyed as the women ate their shrimp salad sandwiches and organic potato chips. David had docked his sailboat and walked towards the women smiling at them on the way. "Good afternoon, ladies." His heart skipped a beat as he asked Elizabeth, "May I pet your grey-hound? My late wife and I had greyhounds. When she died I retired, bought a sailboat and began living on it. It was on my bucket list. The hounds had all passed away by that time. We enjoyed rescuing them off the track—such a despicable industry."

The rest was history as they say—Elizabeth became his wife several months later, still keeping her maiden name. *Why change it now,* she thought, *I'll always be Elizabeth Eyre Barclay at the Creek.*

"Why such an intent look Elizabeth?" David asked with concern, standing in front of the solid mahogany desk.

"I've just received a letter from the Department of Corrections Victims Services Unit. Apparently, Stephen Dennis, you know my mother's killer, has been taken to a medical facility. They can't tell me what his condition is because of the privacy act, but alluded he is gravely ill. It's all brought back a flood of toxicity. It's imperative that I write this letter."

"Don't look backwards, Elizabeth, it will only bring unnecessary heartache."

"I have to look back so that I can move forward. All my life I have strug-gled with low-grade depression. Feelings of not being good enough in any of my endeavors have often haunted me. I was always different—not the norm. I was the kid in school whose mother was murdered by a stalker. For years my long-range goal was to find happiness or at least inner peace. I know now happiness is an inside job. I'm doing this in memory of my grandmother."

Elizabeth picked up the pen and started to write.

Dear Stephen Dennis...